Screams From The Dark Ages

Foreword by
Christina Henry

Edited by
Heather Ann Larson

BROKEN BRAIN BOOKS

Table of Tales

001. Foreword – Christina Henry

005. Sister. Maiden. Witch – Savannah R. Fischer

021. The Bishop – Jeani Rector

037. Forged in Blood – Elizabeth J. Brown

057. Saxon Fodder – Kimberly Nicole

067. The Riddle of the Bone Witch – Christy Aldridge

091. If I Could Just Speak – MJ Mars

105. Black Death – Ali Jane Sweet

Chronicles of the Court

117. Web of Truths - Elizabeth Devecchi

139. The Witch and the Serpent - Lisa Vasquez

161. The Little Old Woman - Asia Brito Guerrero

175. The Shoemaker - Laura Bilodeau

187. Marrowland - K.K. Monroe

211. Screams from the Dark Ages - Heather Ann Larson

235. There's a Rumor of Witches Here - Jae Mazer

Screams From The Dark Ages: A Medieval Horror Anthology
Copyright © 2025 by Broken Brain Books
Print ISBN-979-8-9866751-7-6
Edited by Heather Ann Larson
Cover design by Christy Aldridge / Grim Poppy Designs
Print and eBook layout by LM Kaplin

Foreword Copyright © 2025 by Christina Henry
"The Shoemaker" Copyright © 2025 by Laura Bilodeau
"Forged in Blood" Copyright © 2025 by Elizabeth J. Brown
"Web of Truths" Copyright © 2025 by Elizabeth Devecchi
"Sister. Maiden. Witch." Copyright © 2025 by Savannah R. Fischer
"The Little Old Woman" Copyright © 2025 by Asia Brito Guerrero
"Saxon Fodder" Copyright © 2025 by Kimberly Nicole
"Screams from the Dark Ages" Copyright © 2025 by Heather Ann Larson
"If I Could Just Speak" Copyright © 2025 by MJ Mars
"There's a Rumor of Witches Here" Copyright © 2025 by Jae Mazer
"Marrowland" Copyright © 2025 by KK Monroe
"The Bishop" Copyright © 2025 by Jeani Rector
"The Witch and the Serpent" Copyright © 2025 by Lisa Vasquez
"The Riddle of the Bone Witch" Copyright © 2025 by Christy Aldridge
"Black Death" Copyright © 2025 by Ali Jane Sweet

All rights reserved.

No portion of this book may be reproduced in any form without written permission from the publisher or author, except as permitted by U.S. copyright law.

FOREWORD

Christina Henry

They're called the Dark Ages, that period in Western Europe from roughly the fifth century to the tenth century (and sometimes up to the fifteenth century, depending on the scholar and their personal opinions). The deposition of the last emperor of Rome – one Romulus Augustulus, a poor kid who was placed on the throne at the age of ten and forced out by an invading general – is seen as the inciting incident for this period of darkness. This era, it was claimed, was primarily defined by ignorance and violence, because these people had lost the light that was the Roman Empire.

It was Petrarch, the great fourteenth century scholar and poet, who first looked out on the vast landscape of time between the end of the Roman empire and his own, who decided that very little of cultural import had happened and labeled it "dark." It is probably to be expected that a Tuscan scholar wouldn't think much of the world after the empire from his peninsula had faltered.

Western Europe wasn't quite the cesspit Petrarch imagined, but it wasn't a spectacular place for women. As with every period in history, money and status made some difference in how women were treated. Some educated or upper-class women were able to exert power and influence as abbesses of churches or members of the nobility. However, the vast majority of women were defined solely by their relationship to a man – her father, brother, husband, or the lord who owned the land she lived on.

Women could not possess their own property (that belonged to the closest man in the vicinity, with very few exceptions), assuming there was any property to be had. Peasant women, of course, had nothing except their labor, and their labor was often given in service of someone else with little or no compensation. They could not learn an occupation or hold any kind of elected office and thus had no voice in how they were treated nor any means to improve their status.

Poor diet and maternal mortality rates during this period meant that a lot of women didn't live very long. Though the short, average lifespans of the medieval period are often skewed by high infant mortality rates, some scholars believe the average life of a Dark Ages peasant woman was roughly twenty-five years. That's a very short and very hard life, one in which she spent most of her time laboring at home or assisting her male relatives with the processing of crops for their landlord.

These are, of course, broad strokes, and in some regions of Western Europe, women had more power – to own property, to take part in business transactions, and so on. But the lives of women during this period were largely dictated by men and by the Christian Church, which was run by men.

Literacy rates during the early medieval period are generally thought to be no higher than 10 or 20%, and the literacy rates of women were much, much lower – possibly as low as 1.5% in some areas. This means that there are very few records of the lives of women simply because they didn't read or write. Even noblewomen weren't widely literate in the Dark Ages, and the inability of most women to take part in any kind of financial transaction means that records of women's lives are particularly sparse compared to men's.

Now, what about all those witches – who were, nearly without fail, women - that were supposed to have proliferated in this time? There had been laws against harmful magic since Roman times, and a common belief in witches is documented as far back as ancient Greece. However, many people also believed in the power of healers who practiced "good" magic and relied on folk remedies and charms to protect them from malevolent spells.

That did not stop many early medieval governments from passing laws against harmful witchcraft, with penalties for the practice ranging from slavery to execution. As always, it was dangerous to be a woman, and much more dangerous to be a woman who had power or knowledge.

The Dark Ages have undergone a major reassessment in the last several years, with scholars redefining the era as early medieval and moving away from the notion that millions of people in Western Europe were just laboring in mud, watching the Black Death loom on the horizon. Yes, there were arts and culture and (some) advancements, in the way that things do seem to keep grinding forward despite the best efforts of many to stop them.

The lives of women, though - particularly poor

women - were perilous in more ways than one. Any woman who didn't have a man to control her was suspect, and those women who managed to grab and hold on to power of any kind were exceptional. Maybe the screams from the Dark Ages that we hear are the howls of women - women screaming their pain, their fury, their promises of revenge.

-Christina Henry

SISTER. MAIDEN. WITCH.

Savannah R. Fischer

The cauldron bubbled over the hearth, the fire stoking my concoction toward the perfect temperature. The aroma of simmering meat, root vegetables, and bone broth filter through my abode as I sweep away the day's filth.

I gaze out the window, watching for Richard and his steed on the horizon. Nothing yet. Truthfully, I'll probably hear that damned beast before I see him.

Finished sweeping, I tread carefully into Richard's forge. Even though he would never let a man know he dared let a woman touch his precious tools, it is my duty to maintain this space as well as our home. Daily, I fetch the coals, stoke the fire, ensure the quality of the billows. It is I who polish each finished piece to an eye-catching sheen. Without my help, Richard's work wouldn't have caught Sir Lionel's attention. *I hope the knight finds his new sword becoming of his station.*

A multitude of hoof beats assaults my ears, the cacophony catching me off guard. *Has something happened to Richard?* I clasp the rough fabric of my dress in my fists as I dash back into my home. I chance a glance out the window only to see a flurry of horses, with Richard and the sheriff leading the pack. *Pray tell—what is happening?*

The stampeding cavalcade approaches at alarming speed.

My heart threatens to hammer out of my chest. I feel it in my marrow; something is horribly wrong. I cough, my throat dry as sun-dried bone, my tongue a thick slab of useless meat in my mouth.

A pounding on my door shakes me to the core. Whatever evil is about to descend upon my life has arrived.

"Goodwife James," booms the sheriff, his deep voice resonating through my flesh like a wardrum.

My blood sings to me, beckoning me to run. *But run where?*

"Goodwife James," the sheriff roars again, "open this door immediately, you insolent woman."

My fingers fumble against the wooden board keeping our front door closed. I open the door, finding the sheriff, red faced and fist raised, at my threshold.

Without preamble, he grasps me roughly by my wrists and heaves me from my home. "Is this the accused, Goodsir James?"

The accused? I try to meet Richard's eye, but he keeps his gaze firmly upon the sheriff, refusing to meet my wondering stare.

His shoulders are steeled, his jaw set—I know that

look well. Whatever he has started, he intends to see it through to the bitter end. His voice rings out, cold as the iron sword he rode off to deliver yesterday morn. "Yes, sheriff. That is indeed the harlot."

Harlot?

Richard gives me no time to think as he continues with his answer. "She bewitched me last year, keeping me under her thumb with manifold charms. I am ashamed to admit I only just broke free of her spell."

The sheriff's grip is crushing, the bones in my wrist screaming from the pressure. He turns his stark glare to me, his beady eyes devoid of any semblance of remorse or pity.

"You hear it straight from her husband! Amidst the host assembled before us, Goodsir Richard James accuses his wife, Goodwife James, of witchcraft. Her wiles resulted in a marriage that I now decree annulled before God and these witnesses."

I gasp, the shock like a slap of frigid water to the face. *Me? A witch?* Richard still won't meet my eyes. *How could he do this to me?*

Sobs shake my frame as the sheriff ties me to his horse, proclaiming something or other about the dungeons. It falls on deaf ears as I watch Richard help a blonde waif descend from his horse.

Oh, now I see. I have been replaced. My homely nature is no match for this flaxen beauty.

Without further ado, the sheriff and his entourage wish Richard well.

The horse jerks my wrists, rope burning into my tender flesh, as I'm forced to leave my home. I cast a forlorn glance over my shoulder.

Richard's new woman tends the fire, while he gazes at her appreciatively.

May all your food burn forevermore, you bastard.

I awake to darkness, my eyes ill-adjusted to the dirty cell I find myself in. My body aches, muscles rigid and sore from the untold distance we traveled. My raw wrists are circled with heavy chains, trapping my arms above my head so it feels as if my shoulders shall rend themselves from their sockets.

My feet throb at the memory of yesterday's journey. I walked behind the sheriff's horse until my bare feet bled, leaving a trail of crimson in my wake. Finally, a knight took pity and threw me over his horse before making haste for the local lord's duchy.

Shadows obscure my surroundings as I await whatever cruel twist of fate lurks beyond the wooden door.

From beyond, high-octave screams laced with pain pierce my consciousness. Moans and wails fill the air, lamentations for mercy that will go unanswered by man and God alike.

Hidden away in the far reaches of the darkness, I weep.

A key rattles in my cell door. A servant boy enters first, followed by the largest man I've ever seen. He's a hulking brute, his clothes stained with blood, his face covered with a hood that only shows his soulless eyes.

Fear coils deep in my gut. Involuntarily, I piss myself. *A torture master?*

"Bring the witch to me," he growls.

The servant boy scuttles to me. He rushes to undo my chains. The sudden freedom of my suspended limbs causes renewed pain to course through my extremities. The boy struggles to lift me, but my legs are liquid like the piss flowing down between them. He gives up.

I drop to the dirt floor, face first in a puddle of my own filth. I don't have time to feel humiliated.

The torturer is upon me, grabbing me roughly by the hair. My scalp screams in agony as he pulls me by my tresses. Strands snap under his forceful grasp, some ripped out in bloody chunks.

Tears stream down my face. *Blessed redeemer, what sin have I committed to deserve this?*

God remains silent as the man drags me into a large circular chamber. Torches flicker around me, painting the room in reds, yellows, and oranges. My captor removes his hood, revealing a face caked with gore. He is one of Lucifer's own, a demon on earth. I see the room for what it is: a portal straight to hell.

"Wench, you stand accused of witchcraft. Beezlebulb himself shan't save you from my clutches. Only a confession can save you now." He forces me upright, my legs trembling but refusing to fold again.

Without warning, I feel the tip of his blade at my throat.

"Mark my words, witch. You will die. It is up to ye if it will be at my hands or at the stake." Without warning, he slashes down, cleaving my shift from my body. He laughs as I scramble to cover my nakedness.

Of all the indignities so far, this is the worst. *To be naked in front of a man that is not mine husband is a sin in and of itself. Am I truly abandoned?*

Before I can string together another thought, the torturer yanks me onto a wooden device from my nightmares. He presses my back against the cool wood. He pinches my exposed nipple with one hand as he fastens my wrists above me with the other. His touch is rough, seeking only to cause pain and misery. Without warning, he bites my nipple, twisting the tender flesh between his rotten teeth.

A scream tears from my mouth.

He releases me, blood dripping off his lips in the torchlight. His wicked grin curdles my insides as he fastens my ankles to the bottom roller of the contraption. Suddenly, he's back. His lips are harsh upon me, his sulfur breath forcing its way down my throat along with his tongue. His hand twists my maimed nipple until I fear it might separate from my breast. He bites my tongue. I taste blood as he pulls away.

"I see what Sir Richard means. You are indeed bewitching." He eyes my most sacred part, and I remember there are more types of torture than just the rack.

He wouldn't dare—would he?

The flickering flames reflect in his eyes as he moves to the wheel. He cranks, the wood clanking as my already tired muscles scream at the forced stretch. I'm standing on my tip toes. He pauses, leaving me suspended in agony.

Like a glutton at a feast, he returns to my breasts. He pinches, twists, and bites, leaving me writhing under his touch. Each involuntary squirm shoots pain from my fingers to my toes. He relents.

I try and fail to suck in a deep breath. Stretched to my limits on the rack, I can only sip short, shallow gasps of air. My lungs burn with the inability to fully expand. I blanche when I see the hooded man return, a hot poker in his hand. *God has abandoned me after all.*

My torturer brings the hot iron to my wounded chest, burning my already damaged nipples.

My shrieks echo off the stone walls, creating a symphony of suffering. The smell of my burnt flesh assaults my nostrils as my torturer turns to my inner thigh.

My voice crescendos to a fever pitch as the poker mutilates my body further. The sounds coming from me are no longer human. The poker finds a new home on my stomach. I can't breathe. I can't think. All I know is hellish torment from which there is no earthly escape.

My torturer removes the poker. A thickly gloved hand slaps me across the face.

"Harlot, you ain't felt pain yet."

I piss myself again, the liquid stinging my fresh burns as it cascades down my ruined legs. The man returns with pincers. I'm too weak to struggle. All the fight has left me. I just want to die.

He grins wolfishly as he clamps the tool on my smallest toe. Without warning, he slices through flesh and bone, brutally ripping a part of my soul along with the appendage. There's a sickening squelch as my toe hits the floor. He grabs it, holding my gaze as he chomps it between his rotten teeth.

Bile rises in my throat, but my position doesn't allow for me to retch. I swallow my vomit as he lines the tool up on the next toe.

"Have mercy," I plead.

He has none.

Pain greets me when I awake. I passed out somewhere between the removal of my third and fourth toes. I sob, unable to move as the torment from the rack, coupled with my amputated appendages, leaves me weak beyond measure.

Beside me, I hear a low voice chanting. *Is that you, Lucifer? Or Lilith?*

The voice is feminine, gentle but also angry. It grows closer, until the owner whispers against my ear. "Do you live, child?"

All I can muster is a low moan, but it suffices.

A comforting hand wipes the sweat from my brow. The chanting continues in a language I don't understand.

Slowly, the pain subsides, replaced first by a dull ache, then the miraculous bliss as my nerve endings stop responding.

"Be at ease, child."

The woman snaps her fingers. A purple flame dances in the palm of her hand, beckoned forth from some otherworldly plane. *A real witch!* The light shows me a stooped crone with matted hair and only one good eye. She too is missing her toes, as well as the fingers of the hand not holding the flame.

"I see the cruel work has begun on you. They swear a confession will set you free, but they lie. Lie! I have never, will never, hide what I am. Yet still I am tortured, a mere plaything to that hooded brute. Once he tires of us, he will send our maimed bodies to the stake for one last indignity."

"I'm not a witch," I whisper, shocked at my companion's brazen admittance of her crimes.

"Would you like to be?"

"I—"

"It just might save your life."

My thoughts swirl like the cosmos I once gazed upon in the fields with Richard. Fury flows through my veins. I was once just a girl. A daughter, sister, a maiden, a wife; why not add witch to my list of titles. If I'm going to stand accused of something, I might as well become the very thing these fragile men fear.

Before I can change my mind, I grab my companion's hand.

Power courses between us like the land's mightiest rivers. She pulls me to her, holding tight. The flame in her hand grows to engulf us, bathing us in ethereal radiance. All around us dance wall-high flames of purple and white, but I am not afraid. In the blink of an eye, the all-consuming fire gives way to darkness. This time, the gloom holds no air of mystery, no apprehension or dread.

Whatever fate holds for me, I am at peace. This power, it is mine. No man can take it from me.

"Welcome to the sisterhood. My name is Elisaria. We must make haste; we don't have much time."

"I'm—" I freeze, my name foreign on my tongue. The screams of my former self have left my mouth dry. It's time to reclaim myself. I am Sara no longer. No more Goodwife James. "My name is Sabine," I say with a newfound confidence resonating deep in my chest.

"Good. Whoever you were entering this place, she has died. You must reclaim yourself. Make yourself untouchable. They may cause you pain, but you will give them no reaction. Nothing frustrates a man more than not getting his way."

I smirk at the truth of her words. Men truly do throw worse tantrums than mere babes when they are told no. I witnessed it when my father beat my sister, when Richard beat me. But worst of all, I felt it in my soul when my sister's husband beat her to death only for the law to look upon him as a hero for ridding the world of evil. My heart hardens against mankind with their senseless entitlement and self-important attitudes. This world runs on the labor of women, but men claim all the glory. No more.

"What must I do, Elisaria?"

She leans in, whispering in my ear once again.

"Repeat after me, sister. *Purpureus deae sanguis per me fluit. Custodi me a dolore.*"

I taste the power of the words on my tongue. My body is abuzz, immune to the injuries of my former self. She is truly dead, my body and soul reborn in the sacred flames.

"Say this spell, and our goddess shields you. Come what may, you shall withstand," Elisaria says.

"What if they remove my tongue?"

"Pray it as fervently as we used to worship at the altar of the dead saints. Our goddess will hear your plea and meet your need."

Over the next several days, Elisaria teaches me a litany of spells. My favorite is the healing spell, *sana contritum corpus*, which she used on me when I awoke. We run through several more spells, including conjuring water, which I greedily lap from my hands as fresh rain pours from above. It beats the watery gruel and stale bread the guards occasionally throw our way. They can't have us starving or they can't witness our continued torture.

The last spell Elisaria says is most important, a hex for death and disease. "Don't utter this until you absolutely mean it," she says, whispering the sacred phrase and striking a spider dead in its web. "The intensity of your rage determines how well the spell works. The goddess gives it to us as a last resort. Only use it if you must."

"Elisaria, why have you not escaped?"

Her eyes shimmer as her mouth pulls into a smile that warms my soul. "Oh, sweet child, it's simple. My goddess told me you were coming. I had to keep the faith so I could save you."

Booming footsteps approach our cell, silencing our

conversation. Elisaria mouths "be brave" as the key slides into the lock. The door slams into the wall, revealing our torturer in the torch light.

"Ahhh, my little witches have been talking. Let's see what my newest pet has for me."

He snarls as he grabs me again by the hair.

This time, I don't go without a fight. I reach up my fingers, raking at his hand, drawing blood.

He hisses at the unexpected assault.

I bet everyone down here is so broken they just don't fight.

"You bitch!" he roars.

Oh, the insults of men. When they can't break you, they simply resort to name calling, as if their opinion of us means more than anything else.

My lips curl into a snarl as I stare him down. He slaps me across the face, but I stay on my feet, unflinching in the face of adversity. *Sister. Maiden. Witch.* He shall not have me.

"I'm not afraid of you," I growl as he advances.

"You will be." He grabs me by the waist, throwing me over his shoulder like a sack of animal feed.

I kick, punch, and scream the whole way to the torture chamber. My blood roars in my ears, an all-consuming fury at the mistreatment of countless men and women at this brute's hand fueling me. I plead to my goddess for strength, reciting the spell for shielding.

The man throws me against the wall, my head cracking dangerously against the stone. I feel warm blood trickle against my forehead, but I am immune to the pain.

I force myself to my feet, ready to fight. I run, headbutting my attacker in the gut. He crashes into the rack, knocking over the machine in a clatter of wood and metal. I'm on him in an instant, pelting him with repeated punches to the head. He bucks under me, a primal roar escaping his throat.

Try as I might, I am simply too small to take him down for good. The brute succeeds in bucking me off, murder dancing in his eyes as he sets his gaze upon me.

"You will pay, insolent whelp." He throws me into the wall again, breaking my nose.

I hear the shattering bone. Blood coats my face, entering my mouth in a torrent.

He grabs my hair again, yanking out clumps from my scalp. He has come undone, mentally unprepared for the challenge of an obstinate woman.

Sister. Maiden. Witch.

He grabs me roughly as he ties a rope around my hands, then my waist.

The cords are so tight it's hard to breathe. I struggle to remember the spell Elisara taught me. I know what's coming next—the witch's bath.

He forces me to walk to a barrel, his grip tightening on my throat as he shoves me under the stale water.

I thrash, fighting for air. I scream, bubbles flying into the water as I choke. I can't remember the spell. This is it. All of this, just to drown face-down in a barrel. *No. Think Sabine. Think!*

The spell comes to me with a whisper from the goddess herself. *Respirare aquae*. I pray the words like the most holy chants from my childhood, willing myself to hold on. My lungs scream. My chest seizes, begging for precious air to flow into my body. But still, I persist.

The goddess whispers to me, *Be still my child.* I comply, letting my body go limp in my attacker's grasp.

He keeps me under longer, ensuring what he believes is my demise. He hauls me backward, throwing me prone upon the floor.

I gasp, granting my lungs the precious air they so

desperately need. The goddess preserved me this far, but this fight is far from over.

The torturer stands above me, stunned. "But you, you—you were dead!" His eyes bulge in disbelief and, dare I say, fear, "You really are a witch."

Yes, I am. I stand, water dripping from my naked form, gooseflesh breaking out across my skin. Power courses through me, fueled by my righteous anger. How many innocent men and women has this man tortured, maimed, and killed in some sick display of cruelty and power? No more.

I speak the sacred phrase, black fog issuing forth from my lips like a plague. I continue to chant, staring down my oppressor as the fog inches closer to his face.

It envelops him, erasing his gore-covered face into darkness. He screams, the sound echoing off the stones much like mine did the last time we were in this room.

I stop chanting, the black smoke having completely hidden the man in its midst. I snap my fingers, and the vapor dissipates, leaving a bloody, mangled mess in its wake..

The man's eyes and tongue are gone, flesh hanging off his face in bloody strips. His outside matches the horror that lies within, raw brutality merged with disdain for human life. He is revolting.

I step back, shocked at the carnage my magic wrought.

He's lucky I only maimed him. The sounds that come from him are no longer human.

I smile.

He hasn't felt pain yet. None of them have.

Pounding footsteps echo toward me. The ruckus alerted the sentries. Two guards grab me, thrusting my arms behind me as they force me down the hallway. We're met in the middle by two more guards holding

Elisara.

Her eyes say it all—it is time.

We are whisked up the stairs, naked as the days our mothers birthed us but twice as filthy. The sun hurts our eyes, causing us to squint against the assault. Before us towers a wooden platform with the bane of all our fallen sisters, a large pole carved into a stake.

A crowd is assembled, jeering at us, calling us consorts of Satan, harlots, succubi.

Sister. Maiden. Witch. That's what I am, you impudent swine.

The guards rush Elisaria up the platform, affixing her waist with thick corded rope, her hands behind her back. Once she is situated, it's my turn.

The men push me forward, taking no care not to cause additional injury.

With my maimed feet, it's all I can muster not to give them the satisfaction of falling on my face. The wood is rough and splintery as I, too, am affixed to the stake. My hands find my sister's, our grip steadfast.

As the guards throw tinder around us, setting the stage for the burning fire, I stare out into the crowd. My eyes fall upon my betrayer, my husband, Richard.

I knew he would come, not out of guilt but out of duty. It is expected that the accuser attend the execution of the accused, and even among spouses there is no exception.

I fix my unwavering gaze upon him, watching him squirm under my scrutiny. *Vile worm, you are unworthy of the dust which lies upon your boots. I will lay you low for all to see.*

The wood pile assembled, the executioner rises to the platform. He unrolls a scroll, loudly declaring our crimes to the crowd. "These women stand accused of witchcraft, of cavorting with the devil to curse their husbands and our land. For their crimes, there is only one punishment."

"Burn them! Burn the witches!" chants the crowd in a frenzy.

I feel Elisaria squeeze my hand, the warning clear in my mind. *Not yet. Let them think they've won.*

I mutter the spell for protection as the executioner sets fire to the bundles around our legs. Flames lick my skin, desperate for a taste of my flesh. My magic holds, protecting me. I stare at Richard, whispering to myself.

The crowd pays him no heed as he falls to his knees, his eyes bulging as if an invisible hand holds his throat in an iron grip. He paws at his throat, gasping for a breath that will never come. The crowd continues chanting for my death, immune to the death occurring in their midst.

I keep my stoic vigil, glaring at Richard until his heart takes its final beat and he falls to the ground, head lolling to the side with his tongue bulging from his mouth.

I give Elisaria's hand three squeezes. The time is nigh for our revenge, for all the sisters who have gone before us and for all those who will suffer after we leave this mortal plane.

Our voices raise as one. I hear not just Elisaria and myself but the voices of our sisters from beyond the grave joining in to rain down destruction upon these people so obsessed with purity and piety, what a woman should and shouldn't do, that they miss the brutality happening before their eyes every damn day. Our voices raise a curse for the ages.

"*Maledicam tibi. Atram mortem patimini vos stulti.*" *Suffer the black death, you mortals.*

Rats pour from under the platform, spreading their invisible pestilence throughout the crowd. Before the day is through, countless will be ill, some even dead.

This plague we unleashed will be our crowning glory.

Our mission done, Elisaria and I drop our protection and submit our bodies to the cleansing flames willingly. Our sisters wait for us beyond the veil, beckoning us with open arms as we transcend into their warm embrace.

Sisters. Maidens. Witches.

THE BISHOP

Jeani Rector

"The failed crops are warnings from the Almighty!" Bishop Godfrey shouted at them with his booming voice. "People are selfish; they live only to seek the sins of the flesh. They lie and blaspheme. We need to get on our knees to beg the Almighty God to forgive us! We must repent from our sins! The great Lord God will no longer look past our transgressions!"

He paused for effect, then continued in a newly calm voice. "Now there is word of a great pestilence coming out of France."

He savored the effect his words had on the congregation as they recoiled in shock almost as a single body. He felt powerful, as though he alone could shelter the village from any evil miasmas that demons could send out. He understood that he projected a sense of strength which reinforced the intense fear he knew his congregation experienced. The church was the backbone of society, and the bishop knew the life of the villagers revolved around his sermons.

Although his was a larger village than most, he believed fear would keep his many followers in line. After all, he alone had the power to excommunicate.

Bishop Godfrey told them, "In Avignon, rumors abound that masses of the population are beset with tumors in the groin and armpits. In Normandy, it is said that people are erect and healthy one minute, then falling to their deaths on the ground the very next minute. In Burgundy, tales are told of mass graves that are filled to overflowing with countless dead. And in the medical facility in Paris, Pope Clement IV has requested that the doctors prepare reports on ways to reduce the spread of this great pestilence."

Again, Bishop Godfrey paused for effect. Then he thundered, "But still it spreads!"

The chapel was incredibly still, waiting for their leader in the faith to continue. Not a sound was heard; it was as though no one dared to move.

But when the bishop spoke again, his words were shocking. "There have been reported cases of this fearsome pestilence in Dorset. That is south of here, on the mother soil of England!"

All around, pandemonium erupted. Cries of fear and shouts of denial flowed from pews both on the ground and in the balcony.

"Listen to me!" shouted the bishop, and the people settled back into their seats, trembling but quiet once again. "We must beg the Lord's forgiveness. Each of you! Beg the Lord right now! Get down on your knees right now and pray with me for your own salvation and for the salvation of England!"

The entire congregation immediately dropped to its knees, while the bishop bellowed a prayer at the top of his voice, beseeching God to have mercy and to forgive his sinful flock. He could hear the people praying reverently, some moaning softly and others brought to tears.

The inside of the medieval church featured a long, rectangular nave with a separate area at the front known as the chancel. The altar area from where he preached was richly decorated with fabric hangings and candles, the overall visual effect aiming to be impressive and awe-inspiring. Throughout the church were stone carvings, stained-glass windows, and wooden pews. It was the bishop's domain.

Did he really believe his own words? Perhaps somewhat, because there was definitely something unusual happening, but he saw it as an opportunity. The church was all-powerful, with the ability to collect taxes, and he wanted to keep it that way. He needed to keep his congregation bound in fear. Fear was a great motivator to keep himself in charge, because they believed he was their only hope. As for himself, he wasn't worried because he completely believed that no sickness could touch a man of God.

He ended the service.

People began leaving, dazed, vacantly staring ahead, seemingly numbed with shock.

He escorted his flock outside, then felt unsettled as he watched them wander off.

As they dissipated, it seemed as though some began noticing how normal their surroundings still appeared. The sun still shined and the breezes still rustled the branches of the trees. No one appeared sick. Back in the environment of everyday life, Bishop Godfrey wondered if they thought his sermon was meaningless.

He was incensed with anger when he overheard one departing person say, "Bishop Godfrey may be a man of God, but he's still a man. And men have been known to be wrong."

Another said, "Aren't we already giving a great penance by living with such unusual rainfall and widespread crop failures? Surely the good and righteous people of England are in God's favor!"

He was furious. He knew a great pestilence was coming, and it was coming because his flock was still sinning by disrespecting him.

The rat was in its death throes.

Its nest was one of many nests in the thatched roof of a cottage, hidden among the straw, rushes, and sod used as roofing material. Under normal circumstances, the cottage roof would have provided ideal conditions for rats to live and multiply as the thatch could easily be gnawed and tunnels would go unnoticed by humans. Under normal circumstances, the darkness of nightfall would have provided excellent cover for rats to venture into the living quarters of humans and thereby steal food.

But that rat would never gnaw tunnels or steal food again. The dying animal shuddered as it gasped for breath. Blindly snapping at the air, it experienced progressive paralysis until, one by one, its internal organs shut down.

Suddenly, it lay still.

From the rat's cooling body, desperate fleas emerged, sensing their host was dead. The fleas, all infected with *Yersinia pestis*, found themselves in the roof of a peasant household. They deserted the lifeless rat in the quest for new hosts whose fresh blood could be consumed.

In the search for new hosts, some of the fleas fell from the ceiling straw to the cottage floor below. Unable to seek out their preferred rat hosts, the fleas turned to the only warm bodies they could locate, which were the humans who were sleeping in their beds. And the fleas' bites would transmit the most deadly bacterium of all time.

Gradually, the deadly disease traveled northward from the tiny cottages of Dorset. *Yersinia pestis* was making its way across the land.

It finally reached Bishop Godfrey's village.

The sickness had arrived.

The telltale signs began subtly—a few less villagers attending church here, a few more rumors there.

Then the pace quickened. Bishop Godfrey noticed people began wearing handkerchiefs over their noses and mouths, and they filled their pockets with sweet-smelling herbs. They refused to shake hands and avoided displays of grief as they mourned lost loved ones; others retreated into the dark holes of their cottages to grieve alone.

But the worst was the man with the pushcart that traveled the streets once a week. "Bring out your dead!"

The call for the dead would reverberate through the village, and the bishop cringed when he heard it.

He had to somehow take back control. He had to save his flock from God's wrath. He sent word to the congregation that there would be a special church service to cleanse the village and everyone needed to attend. He changed "needed" to "mandatory" in his message.

But on the day of the mandatory service, the church had only meager attendance, which further infuriated him. How could he save people who were unwilling to be saved? Didn't they understand their immortal souls were at risk? Didn't dying of the pestilence pale in comparison, so they should take the risk of going out and possibly getting sick to ensure their own salvation? Apparently not.

He wondered if it was a sign from God that he was a failure. He searched within himself to see if he could discover the reasons why. What was he doing wrong? What was he missing in his self-evaluation?

He was shocked to find himself lacking. He wasn't able to convince others as to what he found obvious. He wasn't able to force his flock into attending his services by his will alone. He wasn't able to save those who were already dying.

And he had tried to save them. Wouldn't that mean something to God?

He turned his focus upon one man with whom he was particularly close.

Kenric often stayed after church services to help clean the large chapel. He and Kenric took to praying together when the sickness began, and Bishop Godfrey felt that this servant of God was as untouchable as he was.

Then, suddenly, Kenric was stricken by the pestilence.

Bishop Godfrey was stunned. If it could affect a man such as Kenric, could he possibly be next? Such a thought would have been unheard of just a few weeks before. Yet …

He made his way to his friend's cottage. It was dark

and empty; the family had fled in fright. The bishop had not intended to stay, but Kenric pleaded with him, and the bishop could not find it even within his own selfish soul to walk away. He spent the night reading to his friend from the Bible.

Dawn lightened the room, and the bishop wiped Kenric's forehead with a damp cloth. The sick man burned with heat and moaned for water. When Godfrey tried to help him drink from a glass, Kenric couldn't seem to make his swollen tongue function and the water dribbled uselessly down his chin.

Dark blotches were beginning to form on Kenric's cheeks, and the telltale buboes appeared in the armpits. Periodically, Kenric's body jerked in spasms as his motor functions went awry. The sick man sighed and lay back against his pillow, and the bishop resumed wiping his brow with the cloth.

The bishop sat back on his chair and meditated. How trivial life's everyday problems appeared compared to all of this. How for granted he had taken his life! He had followed the rules to the exact letter, yet the rules turned out to not be set in stone. The rules had an unstable foundation, and he was devastated to learn he was tumbling, falling from the grace of God. Was he a sinner? Was that why his whole life was crashing down?

Then a foreign thought slapped him. Was this not about only him? Was he not at the center of attention? As he did his best to care for Kenric, he realized that no matter how much he believed that he alone could save his flock, he could not. Was his complete reliance upon God's favor a mirage?

He began thinking thoughts that were out of character for him. He regretted his restraint, how unnecessarily he had followed the rules that society dictated so closely, rarely questioning their purpose.

So many thoughts ran through his mind as the sun continued to fill the room with light. How odd it was that the sun would continue to shine daily, but all things made of flesh might cease.

If all the people in the world were to die, the sun would rise and set upon an empty landscape. Houses would fall and fields would be reclaimed by wilderness. Would anything be of any consequence if the only life forms that could comprehend the meaning of life were no longer around to contemplate it? Or was that an arrogant position, to take the stance that nothing was important in the world if humans were not part of it?

Bishop Godfrey thought of his own mortality. Was he ready to face death, to discover what, if anything, lay beyond? Would God really be there to welcome him, or had he been dismally misguided?

It was shocking that a man of God was questioning his faith.

A week ago, he would have been terrified to think he could possibly stray in his beliefs. But at that moment, it was strange to discover his thoughts wandered into the realm of doubt over and over as he tried to deal with the horrific events happening all around him. It seemed absurd at how normal his questions seemed. It was like he was getting used to the idea that not all was as it appeared. How much more could the mind get used to when exposed to such abhorrent circumstances?

Sitting in the bedside chair, Bishop Godfrey looked at Kenric. He felt his heart freeze in his chest at what he saw.

Kenric was sitting up, his mouth gaping, the skin melting off the bones of his face before the bishop's very eyes. The sick man threw back the covers, revealing bedclothes that were stuck to his skin from the oozing, open sores and from the rancid sweat of his body.

A bony arm covered in boils and black blotches stretched out as he pointed directly at the bishop. "You're next," Kenric croaked. "You're next!"

Kenric dragged himself out of the bed and stood on unsteady, bare feet. Still pointing his finger, he lurched toward the bishop. "You will be just like me!" the man cried as he reached the bishop.

Bishop Godfrey tried to get up from his chair, but Kenric grabbed his shoulders with his bony, diseased fingers, then with stinking, rotted breath, he said, "You already *are* like me!"

Bishop Godfrey woke with a start. He was still sitting in the chair.

His heart raced in his chest, pounding against his ribs. He was afraid to look at Kenric, even knowing it was only a dream that Kenric had risen from the sickbed. The bishop had to use a strong will to force himself to look at the man whom he considered a friend, perhaps the only real friend he ever had.

Kenric was not getting out of bed and coming for him.

Kenric was dead, lying still and silent under the covers. The large, dark buboes that had strained the skin underneath his armpits had burst, darkening the blanket with blood.

It was the bishop's breaking point. He jumped up from the chair and rushed to the cottage door. He flung the door wide open and didn't bother to shut it as he raced out into the empty street. His robes fluttered around him as he raced toward the church, dropping his Bible into the street as he ran.

The bishop felt remorse for his actions but did them anyway.

He knew that to leave his flock in a time of dire need was cowardice, yet he packed a small traveling bag. He was ashamed of his deficiencies but felt powerless to change. He couldn't bear to look into one more desperately ill face, to read the Catholic rites over one more diseased body, or to mouth the religious words in which he no longer believed.

One by one, he had watched his congregation sicken and die terrible deaths. He had searched inwardly for reasons why all of this tragedy was taking place, but all he found was his faith waning and his soul wanting.

Sadly, he continued to pack even though he knew there were people waiting who were hoping to receive his prayers. He ignored them; he couldn't bear to face them.

Times of trouble tended to bring out the real person within everyone. In himself, the real person was self-centered and cowardly. He intended to sneak out the back door of the church and to flee to London, but first he raided the coffers. The church wouldn't need money any more. And one of the villagers would no longer need his horse, because that villager was long dead.

As he buttoned up his satchel, a piece of parchment fell out and fluttered to the floor. The bishop ignored it and walked away, leaving the paper on the floor of the rectory.

The paper contained a message that was delivered to the bishop just that morning. The paper was from the church leaders, and it said:

Because the pestilence is so wide-spread, many people are left without priests to give God's comfort to the living and to issue the Holy Sacraments to the dying. Therefore, we decree that if men are near death without the presence of a priest, they now have the permission of the church to make confessions to each other. If fate deems it that no men are present, then the dying may make confessions to a woman, or even to children who are beyond the age of twelve. We are, in these desperate times, giving the layperson the ability and the permission to acquire the ears of God, which would normally be sanctified only from ordained priests.

The bishop had obviously agreed with the letter, because he was gone.

The people waiting patiently for his prayers waited in vain.

Bishop Godfrey arrived at one of the seven gates on the outskirts of London. The gate was so large that it housed a prison inside.

Once he entered the city, he realized people were everywhere—he had never seen so many people! They were all milling about, and each seemed to be rushing to complete some sort of urgent errand.

He had also never seen such buildings; they towered over the streets and blocked the sunlight. Some had flags hanging in front to mark shops or were decorated with signs containing paintings of lions, eagles, rams, and other animals. Many shops appeared to have apartments on top, on the second or third floors.

He guided his stolen horse through the crowded streets, which were narrow and dark, with houses overhanging everywhere.

Bishop Godfrey found the city both amazing and bewildering. He felt apprehensive, yet strangely excited—London was certainly an awesome sight for a country visitor.

Children were everywhere; they ran and darted

between horses and carts. Dogs and poultry were abundant, wandering around at will, and an occasional pig was seen rooting in the dirty streets.

In London, it appeared as though all classes of people were intermingled, because regal people dressed in finery walked the same streets as people in rags.

But it was the stench in the air that the bishop noticed most. A smell of rot predominated. He looked at his surroundings and saw that gutters from the roofs carried not only rainwater runoff but also kitchen refuse that people unloaded into them. Filth that obviously had been dumped from chamber pots lay in open trenches alongside the roads. Anything and everything that no longer had a use was simply discarded in the streets to either be picked up and reused by another or to merely lie there until the elements or the rats disposed of it.

Bishop Godfrey felt a growing sense of dread as he viewed the filthy city. Yet he was comforted by the idea that there were still people there. Certainly it meant the city was untouched by the pestilence?

As he continued to ride the horse into the center of the city, he heard a commotion coming from the next street.

A group of flagellants was approaching. He could see the band of about fifty people coming in an odd procession from around the corner.

He knew that flagellants were penitents. They took it upon themselves to give penance for the sins of the rest of the world. They had the hopes that by doing this, God would provide forgiveness and spare His children from the Great Dying.

The penitents repeatedly thrashed and flogged themselves, all the time singing mournful religious songs. Women ran beside the men and caught any spilled blood in their hands, then rubbed the blood over their faces. Some of the flagellants would strip to the waist in order for the beatings to take place directly upon naked flesh. They seemed unmindful of the severe chill of winter and only replaced their coats during breaks in the floggings.

The group of flagellants had cat-o'-nine-tails knotted with nails on the end. Blood flowed freely as they flogged themselves and each other. They beat themselves and exposed their flesh to the elements in extreme demonstrations of martyrdom. They beseeched bystanders to join them in their martyrdom, telling London's citizens that giving penance was mankind's only hope of salvation.

Their actions were abhorrent to watch, yet Bishop Godfrey could not seem to pull himself away. He had known about the existence of flagellants, of course, but even for him, they seemed extreme. The bishop believed that the body was a sacred temple and should not be abused. Yet here were people that were perverting the teachings of God.

Then he stopped himself. Wasn't he also going against the teachings of God by having a lack of faith? What was true and what was untrue? What was real and what was simply the result of a situation so horrible that it defied any reasoning?

Bishop Godfrey couldn't stand it any longer. He rode on, seeking lodging for the night. He found it in a dark tenement. How far he had fallen!

After two days in his new home, he saw that rats roamed the streets freely, but he didn't know they were taking their infected fleas from dwelling to dwelling. All over in the crowded and stinking tenements, people would go to sleep at night appearing healthy only to awaken the next morning bearing the telltale buboes.

The bishop realized fear was the predominant

emotion, for although medieval Londoners were well acquainted with mysterious diseases caused by their living conditions, never had death been so unrestrained in its rampage.

Death became an obsession of the people, and the ones that didn't flee the city were reduced to cowering in fright.

After two days became a week, the bishop saw that the graveyards in the church courtyards quickly filled, and the few bishops and priests that remained in London raced against time to consecrate more ground for new places to bury the dead. Services were held for multiple deceased, and funerals were held back to back to accommodate the ever-increasing numbers of the dead.

London became a city of horrors.

Animals had no one to feed them, so some fed upon their dead masters. Healthy babies perished because no one looked after them, so they were left to starve in their cribs. Many people who weren't sick ran away. Husbands left wives, and mothers left children.

Of the healthy people that remained, some paid penance by living frugally, while others partied freely, drinking and dancing. Social structures fell apart, and eventually law enforcement became nonexistent.

Then the rains came. The seemingly unending downpours washed some streets clean but pooled as deep puddles in others, creating cesspools of filth and breeding bacteria.

Orphaned children still roamed the streets, and too often the ones that were spared from the pestilence died anyway of dysentery or cholera from the dirty rainwater.

All the while, the rats traveled from dwelling to dwelling.

THE BISHOP

He considered leaving London. But to go where? By that time, Bishop Godfrey understood that the Great Dying was everywhere, in both cities and villages. He wondered if he was still able to pray. He looked inwardly very carefully, seeking answers, hoping he still had some semblance of a soul.

He was pretty sure he could not escape the terrible pestilence. He was surprised at how calm he felt once he understood he was most likely doomed. He realized that one's mind could accept anything if that anything kept occurring on a daily basis. It was as though the bar kept getting lowered, and his mind lowered accordingly.

He felt as though Christian virtues such as piety, devotion, and selflessness were no longer accepted as unfailing methods to achieve God's favor. Instead, there seemed to be no explanations or justifications for the tremendous suffering and loss of life.

He had nothing left. Or did he? Since he would probably die anyway, perhaps he could spend his remaining days doing good works. It was ironic that he had lost his faith yet the teachings of the church still remained engraved into his very being. He continued to live his life automatically, acting upon reflex and shunning any questions as to the "why" of things. He was reduced to his inner core; the outside world would go its own way.

But perhaps he could atone and find some meaning in his existence. Perhaps he didn't have to die in vain.

He would go to the great St. Paul's cathedral. He would help those who helped others. He no longer wanted to help people to prove to God that he was doing His bidding. He wanted to help others because it seemed to be the right thing to do.

Bishop Godfrey made arrangements to move to the cathedral. He would begin his service work the following day.

But the next morning, he woke up feverish and had a terrible headache. He was unable to get out of bed. At first, he panicked. This could not possibly be happening! Not when he finally found himself humbled! Not when he finally realized the real meaning in life, which was to dust off ambition and greed and try what little he could to better the world. He finally understood that in the end, people were all the same whether they were of the cloth or the lowest peasant. All were flesh and all could perish equally.

Most of all, he was not better than anyone else. His thinking that turned out to be a sad delusion.

His body began to twitch: the danse macabre. Then movement stilled and a flush of perspiration flooded his face. Eventually, that too ceased as dehydration overtook him.

He didn't want to die alone.

Suddenly, he was calmed with the idea that perhaps he wasn't alone after all. He felt a presence, and it soothed him.

His last thoughts were that with the millions of bright stars, the sky's luminescence would not be dimmed if a single light was extinguished. Somehow, the world would go on without him. And maybe that was where God really was: not in the church, but in the beauty of the universe and in the resilience of nature.

FORGED IN BLOOD

Elizabeth J. Brown

Lindisfarne, England, 850

The clang of hammer against iron rang out, sharp and rhythmic, as Aedric bent over the glowing red blade on his anvil. His strong, calloused hands gripped the hammer tightly, each strike sending a cascade of sparks into the dimly lit smithy. The heat of the forge wrapped around him, sweat soaking through his linen shirt until it clung to him like a second skin beneath the leather apron.

He paused for a moment, lifting the blade with tongs to inspect his work. The edge was taking shape, smooth and deadly sharp, ready to serve as a scythe for the harvest. He wiped at his brow with his forearm, his breath steady but labored.

The air was thick with the smell of metal and ash,

a familiar scent that clung to his clothes, his skin, as much a part of him as the blood in his veins. Behind him, the fire of the forge blazed, its light flickering on the soot-streaked walls like restless spirits.

Inhaling deeply, Aedric plunged the blade into the trough of water beside him, the hiss and steam filling the room with an almost ethereal sound. For a brief moment, the world shrank to the task at hand and the rhythm of his own breath, but then came the distant sounds of shouting.

Forehead creasing, Aedric removed the blade from the trough and set it down on the anvil. Wiping his hands down his apron, he stepped out of the smithy and into the glaring light of the midday sun. With the woods at his back, he followed the dirt path toward the heart of the village and the source of the noise.

A crowd had gathered by the time he reached his destination. Men, women, and children alike, were all jostling to catch a glimpse of whatever was hidden from view. The mass of bodies pressed together, creating a barrier that buzzed with an air of excitement and curiosity, though Aedric recognized concern among some of the faces.

He approached, his broad frame cutting a path before him without the need for words. Still, he nodded his thanks to those he passed.

"A heathen ship," Edwin muttered, pulling a hand down his greying beard, his lips pressing together in a thin line. "Or at least, part of one."

Aedric knew little of ships, but he knew enough to recognize that what was left of the battered hull—long and narrow—had overlapping planks, unlike the flush edges of the boats he had seen in his lifetime. He had heard whispers of these Northman ships, ungodly in their speed, built for raids that struck without warning, leaving villages in ruin, but he never expected to lay eyes on one.

He cast a sideways glance at his friend. "Who found it?"

"Hrothgar," Edwin said. "Playing down by the shore with the rest of them. Hauled it up here themselves."

Shaking his head, Aedric scowled. Northmen were savages. The children had no sense of caution, no care for the danger they invited. If a Northman had been nearby, they would have been slaughtered without a second thought. His jaw tightened. His kinsfolk had enough to worry about without these reckless fools tempting fate.

As if reading his thoughts, Edwin clapped him on the shoulder. "They're young. I remember what you were like when you were their age."

Aedric grunted in response.

"Besides, it's a wreck," Edwin continued. "Washed up after last night's storm. Not a man, beast, or demon could've survived those seas."

"Anyone checked the woods?"

"For what? Like I said, the ship was destroyed, the heathens drowned."

Perhaps Edwin was right. There was little left of the Northman ship, after all. Even so, a knot formed in Aedric's gut that he couldn't ignore.

"I think a few of us should, just to be sure. Where's Beorn?"

Edwin lifted his thick-set shoulders in a shrug. "Haven't seen him since this morning."

Aedric gave him a pointed look.

With a sigh of defeat, the old woodcutter met his gaze. "Go bank the forge. I'll fetch my ax and gather a few men."

When Aedric returned, it was with a hammer in his hand and a knife sheathed in his leather belt. He considered bringing a sickle too, but it felt unnatural in his grip, too light and awkward—he preferred the familiarity of his other tools.

Besides himself and Edwin, there were two other men. Aedric was disappointed Beorn wasn't among them. The woodcutter's son, who often brought timber to feed Aedric's forge, matched him in both height and brawn. And while Edwin could still swing an ax better than half the village, Beorn had the edge in speed and raw strength. Still, Aedric was glad to have the older man by his side.

The two men behind Edwin exchanged a grin, their postures loose and casual. It was clear they didn't share his concerns about the potential threat, dismissing it as little more than a way to pass the time. In truth, they were probably right, but it didn't stop the scowl from settling on Aedric's brow as he locked eyes with them. Their smiles vanished.

"I want to see where the ship was found first," Aedric said, turning his focus instead to the woodcutter.

Edwin gave him a nod, and in silence, the men headed toward the shore.

"This is where Hrothgar said they found it," Edwin said, his shoes crunching over shifting pebbles as he pointed to the scattered fragments of oak plank.

Aedric scanned the horizon, frowning at the endless expanse of grey water. The sea stretched, empty and unbroken save for faint ripples stirred by the wind. No boats, no sails—nothing to hint at anything amiss.

Turning, his gaze swept to the edge of the woods that loomed near the shore, their tangled mass of trees casting long shadows beneath the cloudless sky. If a Northman had survived, that was where they would have gone, seeking cover beneath the dense canopy. His grip tightened on the hammer as he calculated their likely path, his thoughts dark as he stepped forward to lead the men.

Branches clawed at Aedric's sleeves, snagging the linen fabric and dragging across his skin in thin red lines as he pressed deeper into the trees. The undergrowth was thick and tangled underfoot, the roots and brambles making every step more treacherous than the last. Their progress was slower than he would have liked, the silence around them heavy and watchful. Worse, something metallic wove into the thick scent of sap and earth, something that set his teeth on edge.

"Here," one of the men said, stopping near a tree with a freshly hewn stump. Chunks of chopped wood lay scattered around it, logs half-split and left unattended. A second tree bore the marks of an ax, deep cuts biting into the trunk.

"Beorn was here," Edwin murmured.

Aedric nodded. The sight of the stump in the absence of his friend unnerved him, and it was clear from the faces of the other men that they too felt the weight of unease.

Aedric crouched, his fingers brushing over a dark smear on a low-hanging branch. Blood. His heart began to pound, an icy knot tightening in his gut. He straightened and gestured to the others. "This way."

The trail was faint but unmistakable: broken branches, trampled underbrush, and scattered drops of blood that grew more frequent the farther they went.

Aedric quickened his pace, urgency driving his steps. Then they saw him.

Beorn sat slumped against the base of a large birch, his limbs twisted unnaturally, as though they had been wrenched and broken in ways that defied nature. His right arm hung limply across his torso, snapped just above the wrist, the jagged bone protruding from the mangled flesh. It twitched lightly. Then again.

A gruesome realization crawled through Aedric's mind. *He's still alive!*

"Beorn?" Aedric rushed forward.

Beorn's arm jerked again, then fell lifeless to his side. A rat, its fur slick and matted with gore, darted from the wide gash that cut across the young woodcutter's gut. Beneath the bloodied tatters of his tunic, Beorn's innards were exposed, glistening wet and bulging against the open wound as though they might spill at any moment.

His mind struggling to comprehend the horror before him, Aedric froze.

Edwin howled, his grief exploding out of him in a bellow so loud it sent the birds scattering from the canopy above. The other men muttered prayers under their breath, crossing themselves as they drew closer.

Coming to his senses, Aedric knelt beside his fallen friend, his jaw clenched.

Beorn's face was locked in a contorted grimace as though he had died screaming in agony. His mouth hung open, eyes wide, staring at nothing, the whites still visible beneath the lids.

Aedric reached out and closed them with a shaking hand, his chest tight.

"His ax is gone," one of the men said, his voice grim.

"The Northman must've taken it," the other said quietly. He pointed to a single set of bloodied boot prints leading away from the corpse, deeper into the woods.

Aedric stood, his voice as cold and hard as steel. "We're not leaving until we find the savage."

"We're not abandoning Beorn here," Edwin growled, glancing down at his son's lifeless form. "You two," he gestured toward the other two men, "take him back to the village. Get more men, and bring weapons."

"Edwin." Aedric stepped forward, his voice low but firm. "Maybe it's better if you take him?" As much as he didn't want to cause the older man any offense, he knew first-hand how fury could blind a man, make him reckless.

Edwin's face darkened. "No," he snarled, shoving Aedric back roughly. "There's blood to be spilled, and I'll be the one to see it done. I'll not rest until my ax meets the throat of the bastard who did this. I'll see him dead before the day is over."

Aedric gave him a single nod.

With that agreed, the other two men bent to lift Beorn, their faces grave as they turned back toward the village.

Aedric and Edwin watched them leave. Neither one of them spoke, their shared resolve saying more than words ever could.

"Let's go," Aedric said, gesturing for Edwin to follow.

The woodcutter grunted in agreement, a shadow passing over his features.

When darkness smothered the last of the dying light from the heavens, Aedric and Edwin were forced to admit defeat. They had expected others to join them before the woods were swallowed by night, but still, no one had arrived. It was possible they had just missed one another among the dense trees, that his kinsfolk had spread themselves to cover as much ground as possible in the fading daylight. Somehow, he doubted it. The thought gnawed at him with equal measures of frustration and concern. He chose not to voice it; the woodcutter had enough on his mind.

Edwin's fury, once a blazing beacon of vengeance, had been snuffed out under the unrelenting weight of a father's grief, leaving him hollowed and broken.

Aedric recognized it all too well. He had worn the same look when his own son had died during childbirth, then again when his sweet Aeaba followed not two days later.

Their search for the Northman had yielded nothing. Still, at least the woodcutter could find comfort in seeing Beorn laid to rest.

The moon hung low in the sky, its pale light pooling on the narrow dirt path ahead. Only the sound of their muted footsteps broke the silence between them.

Smoke curled languidly from the thatched roofs of the huts as they approached the village, the smell of broth drifting through the night, mingling with the earthy scent of wood smoke. It did nothing but turn Aedric's stomach.

He lowered his gaze to the ground, his eyes following the flickering shadows cast by the warm glow of firelight spilling from the wooden shutters and cracks in the walls.

They made their way to the reeve's hall, where Beorn's body would be being prepared for burial.

Edwin's shoulders hunched, his face drawn.

Aedric's eyes flicked to the large building, his unease growing with every step. Something was nagging at the back of his mind, though he couldn't quite put his finger on what. Then he realized. There were no voices coming from the hall, no sounds of movement, no flickering glow of torch light.

Just as he was about to speak, Edwin pushed the heavy doors open. The wood creaked on its iron hinges, revealing an empty room, Beorn's body nowhere to be seen.

"They haven't returned," Edwin said quietly.

Aedric didn't answer, the knot in his gut pulling tighter.

A blood-curdling scream ripped through the village.

Without conscious thought, Aedric increased his grip on his hammer and sprinted toward the sound, Edwin a pace behind him. Just as his lungs began to burn, the screams reached their peak. He pushed his way past the few people gathered, each step heavier than the last, until he saw it: the grotesque remains of one of the men tasked with taking Beorn back to the village.

The smell hit him immediately, but it wasn't the copper reek that made his jaw drop—it was the way the body had been mutilated.

Lying face down in the dirt, the man was shirtless, his back a yawning mess of torn flesh and muscle. His ribs had been severed from their attachments, his lungs pulled through the openings and left to rest upon his back in slick pools that dribbled down his sides to stain the earth below.

Aedric's bile rose, and he swallowed hard, fighting the burn at the back of his throat. Icy fingers clawed their way up his back despite the cloying heat of the night.

More and more people spilled from their huts, their panicked whispers rising into a clamor of fear and anger.

A figure emerged beside Aedric, a sharp intake of breath betraying the man's usually calm demeanour.

Oslac, the village reeve. If anyone could restore order amidst the chaos, it was him.

"Northmen?" Oslac kept his voice low.

Aedric nodded.

"How many?"

"We found a single set of tracks in the woods."

Oslac turned, raising his voice for all to hear. "Everyone, gather in the hall." He held up a hand, forestalling the score of voices that rose in unison. "Now is not the time for questions. Wake anyone who's sleeping, and help the elderly or infirm to their feet. Move quickly."

He turned to Aedric and gestured to the mangled body at their feet. "You and Edwin take him to the barn and cover him well. We'll deal with the dead once the living are safe."

Aedric nodded, laying his weapon at his feet and watching as the reeve directed the villagers to disperse. Once the last backs were turned, he motioned to Edwin to take the legs. Together, they hoisted the corpse between them.

The lungs shifted slightly with the movement, sliding and tugging at the flesh beneath, bobbing faintly with each step they took toward the barn. More than once, he heard the older man gag. He couldn't blame him; the sight caused his own stomach to roil, his morning bread sitting heavy and perilous.

What fate had befallen Beorn's body Aedric couldn't say, but he saw the same unspoken question etched into the deep furrows of Edwin's brow. The idea that the Northman was out there, watching them from the outskirts of the village, made his blood turn from fire to ice and back again in quick succession.

The heathen was toying with them, mocking them for his own depraved amusement.

The rumors he had heard—about what had happened to other villages, the gruesome murders, the rapes, the wanton destruction—bayed inside his mind, all fighting to be heard. He squared his shoulders, heat igniting in his chest once more. Despite the vile act he had committed, the Northman was just *one* man. Alone. Cut off. A stranger in hostile lands. Come daybreak, Aedric would see him hanged for his crimes.

By the time Aedric and Edwin returned to the hall, Oslac had already stationed men outside. The village reeve was not fool enough to leave his kinsmen unprotected, and each man stood within sight of at least one other.

Aedric noted the assortment of axes, pitchforks, and clubs and was relieved to see at least a few hunting knives at their belts. No torches were lit; the flames would have overwhelmed their senses, blinding them to any danger lurking in the night. Better, then, to rely on the moon's silver light and keep their positions hidden.

As they approached, the wooden door creaked open, releasing a burst of light from the sconces within. Oslac stepped out, followed by five others, his features tight as he closed the door firmly behind him, cutting off the frightened murmurs of the villagers inside. "Another body was found while you were at the barn," he said solemnly.

'Beorn?' Edwin asked, his voice cracking.

Oslac shook his head.

Relief and wretchedness warred on the old woodcutter's face; his grief was raw enough without the thought of his son's body being defiled.

"The Northman can't be far," the reeve continued, his tone sharpening. "Holed up in the woods, most likely. That's where we'll start—two men to a group. Be on your guard. These Northmen are ruthless barbarians. You've seen what they're capable of. Keep your weapons ready and your wits sharp."

Oslac waved one of the men forward. The man reached out, passing a hammer to Aedric, the familiar weight settling in the blacksmith's hand like an extension of himself. Edwin's ax followed, the polished blade reflecting the silver moonlight.

Aedric's eyes shifted toward the hall and the men standing guard outside. His brow furrowed. "Will they be safe? The women and children?"

The reeve followed his gaze and gave a curt nod. "There are more men inside, all armed. They wanted to be out here teaching that heathen bastard a lesson, but their iron will hold fast should he dare breach the walls."

Satisfied, Aedric gave a low grunt of acknowledgment, and they set off toward the treeline, where the shadows loomed like spectres, ready to decide their fate.

The plan was simple: spread out, cover as much ground as possible, shout if they found the Northman.

Exchanging a quick glance, Aedric and Edwin strode into the darkness. Without so much as a candle to guide them, their progress was slow. Every knotted root, every skeletal branch, reached and grasped for them as they walked.

They heard nothing of the others as they ventured farther into the trees. In fact, there was no sound at all. Aedric stopped, raising a hand to halt Edwin as well. Silence pressed in around them, thick and unnatural. Not the hoot of an owl, nor the rustle of a small creature in the underbrush, nor the distant howl of a wolf. Not even the whisper of leaves stirring in the wind.

The hairs on the back of Aedric's neck prickled. He clenched his fist around his hammer, knuckles straining, while the fingers of his other hand slid over the hilt of his knife, ready to draw.

Something whistled through the air and struck the ground before him with a scatter of dry leaves and twigs. His breath caught, his mouth dry as he stared down.

In the dappled moonlight lay Beorn's severed head, its empty eyes fixed on him.

Edwin cried out, his voice an incoherent mix of horror and rage.

With inhuman speed, a hulking mass tore from the shadows, launching itself at Edwin in a blur. The sharp glint of steel trailed in its wake.

Edwin flung up his arms, raising his ax in a desperate attempt to shield himself from the sword slicing through the air. Wood splintered with a sharp crack as the blade sheared through the handle. Before he could react further, the weapon struck true, burying itself with a sickening thunk into the thick column of his neck.

The Northman yanked the sword free, and Edwin crumpled to his knees, clutching at his wound as blood spurted between his trembling fingers.

Aedric roared, the sound tearing from his throat as he hefted his hammer and hurled himself at the savage. Fury ignited his veins as he brought the weapon down, landing a glancing blow on the Northman's shoulder.

The man bared his teeth—not in pain, but in a feral grin. He barked something in his foul tongue, the words guttural and incomprehensible, then began circling Edwin, who sagged forward, collapsing against the dirt. The wild brute was putting distance between them, his movements calculated.

The man before Aedric was unlike any he had encountered. His towering stature and broad shoulders marked him as a warrior, his frame forged for conflict, not toil. Pale-blue eyes, colder than winter's frost, bored into Aedric's own. They blazed with unyielding fierceness, wholly devoid of fear. His hair, paler than

Aedric's, was bound into a long braided tail that swung down his back, the sides of his head shaved in the heathen style. Draped over his shoulders was a wolf's pelt, its head resting against his chest, yellowed fangs frozen in a perpetual snarl, a grim echo of the predatory smirk that twisted the Northman's lips.

Yet despite all of that, it was his belt that held Aedric's focus. Hanging from one of the leather loops was an ax. A plain, ordinary ax, its handle worn smooth with use, a notch missing from its shaft. Aedric had forged that ax himself—for Beorn.

Aedric's breath quickened, blood thrashing in his ears.

The Northman shifted his stance, the sword held at the ready.

But even as fear clawed at his chest, fury burned hotter in Aedric's heart. He would not cower before the ungodly bastard. He strengthened his grip around the hammer, pain flaring in his palm as the handle threatened to splinter beneath the force of his fury. He lunged, bringing the hammer down in a crushing arc, but the swing faltered as his boot caught something beneath him. He stumbled, his strike veering wide, and the Northman laughed—a sharp, mocking bark.

Twisting the sword in his hands with calculated ease, the heathen slashed forward.

The blade bit into Aedric's arm, slicing deep. Hot blood surged beneath the torn fabric of his shirt, and Aedric snarled, adjusting his grip on the hammer despite the searing pain.

The Northman surged forward, his sword cutting the air in a silver blur.

Aedric jerked back, the blade grazing so close he felt its cold kiss against his throat.

Then the savage spoke. His words came in jagged

bursts, harsh and guttural, like stones grinding in his throat. Though they made no sense to Aedric, the scorn in his tone was unmistakable. The man sneered, gesturing with his sword as if Aedric was little more than a nuisance.

Then he bellowed—a sound so raw it seemed to split the night.

It took a moment for Aedric to understand. Then he saw it—the shift of Edwin's body as the old woodcutter pulled the hunting knife free from the meat of the Northman's calf and drove it down again.

The heathen growled, raising his sword high, and Aedric froze as the blade came crashing down.

The crack of bone shattered the silence as the blade struck the back of the woodcutter's skull, splitting it like firewood. Blood spattered across the ground, Edwin's body pinned to the earth by the sheer force of the blow.

Aedric's stomach lurched.

Shouts rang out from the trees behind him. His body moved instinctively, twisting toward the sound before his numbed mind could intervene. Too late, a surge of cold dread flooded over him. He threw up his arms, spinning back to face the savage, bracing for the killing blow.

But the bastard was gone.

Oslac crashed through the underbrush, another villager close at his heels. They halted beside Aedric, their chests heaving, their breathing ragged.

Aedric gaped. How had the Northman moved so fast with an injured leg? This was no man, but a devil.

"Quickly!" Aedric bellowed. "He can't have gotten far—come on!" Trusting his gut, he tore through the woods, the others keeping pace behind. Once or twice, he thought he caught a glimpse of the fiend only for shadows to take his place. All the same, be it instinct or some divine intervention, he knew he was on the right path.

The Northman was headed toward the shore.

A wild grin split Aedric's face. The shore was open. The devil would be exposed, nowhere to hide, nowhere to run. They had him!

His feet pounded the cracked earth, his lungs burning, muscles screaming in protest. But still, Aedric ran, pushing himself harder as the ground gave way to loose pebbles beneath his boots.

And there, bathed in the pale light of the moon, staring out at the black waters, stood the Northman.

The savage turned at their approach, but with the sea at his back and Aedric, along with the others, cutting him off from the treeline, he was trapped. It was over.

With a snarl, Aedric sprinted forward. He heard Oslac's bellow beside him.

The Northman smiled as the head of Aedric's hammer glanced off his sword, sparks igniting where iron struck steel in a clash of fury. The savage pivoted, ignoring Aedric, instead swinging his blade at Oslac.

Oslac jerked back, unscathed.

The man at Oslac's side didn't fare so well, the weapon biting into flesh as it reached the end of its brutal arc. The cry of agony that burst from his lips cut off in a gurgle, the barbarian driving the blade through his throat and out in a crimson spray that misted the night air. Clutching at his wound, the man's eyes bulging, he collapsed back with a dull thud.

Fire alighting inside of him, Aedric bellowed and swung his hammer once more, muscles straining with the force. It struck the heathen, but the Northman rolled with the impact, rendering what should have been a crippling blow into something all but useless.

In an instant, the Northman's eyes locked onto

Aedric's, his face, twisted with fury moments before, now settled into an eerie calm.

Something about that look stirred some primal part of the blacksmith, an animal warning for him to flee. But there was too much at stake.

The savage had slain his kin; if he made it back to the village, made it past the men guarding the hall...

Aedric set his jaw, adjusting his stance.

With a sudden roar, the Northman charged, slashing at Aedric with reckless abandon.

Aedric barely managed to twist away in time, feeling the raw edge of the blade as it sliced his shoulder.

The devil's fury was unstoppable, his strikes faster than Aedric could have ever anticipated. Every swing forced Aedric back, step by step.

Aedric's hammer felt awkward in his hands. Slow. Clumsy. No match for the heathen's sword. The heat that had blazed so fiercely in his chest was beginning to wane, giving way to the cold hard shock of desperation. Still he swung with all his might, hoping to land a blow, but his every strike was deflected. The ice in his blood was working its way into his muscles, robbing them of their speed, each attack wider off the mark than the last. Sweat beaded down his brow, blurring his vision. He blinked rapidly, the world focusing just in time to see the Northman's sword come down again.

The blade bit into Aedric's left hand. Three fingers—little to middle—were severed in that single swipe.

Aedric roared, something inside him snapping. Gritting his teeth, he swung the hammer, rage burning through the pain. It hit true, colliding with the heathen's sword and sending it flying from his hands. Aedric had the advantage.

Before he could raise his hammer again, the savage

lunged forward with terrifying speed, crashing into him. Aedric's back hit the ground hard, the weapon flying from his grasp. The Northman's weight pressed down on his chest, pinning his right arm beneath him. A strangled gasp caught in his throat as the air was crushed from his lungs.

His knife. He had to get his knife! But with three fingers missing, his grip was useless, his hands too slick with his own blood. He gritted his teeth, snarling into the face of the demon on top of him. Bucking beneath the savage, Aedric shoved the bloody stumps into the Northman's eyes.

The savage recoiled, but only for a moment before he sank his teeth into the soft flesh of Aedric's throat.

Aedric thrashed, pain exploding through him, as the Northman tore chunks from his body. He tried to scream, but the heathen's hand was gouging into his jaw, forcing his head to the side to better expose his ravaged neck.

Suddenly, the crushing weight on Aedric's chest was gone. He gasped, coughing as he sucked down a desperate breath, the world spinning around him. For a heartbeat, he couldn't understand what had happened, his body frozen in shock and agony.

Then he saw them—Oslac and the Northman, locked in a violent struggle on the stony shore. The reeve had tackled the savage from behind, and the two thrashed and grappled in the tideline, fists flying as they landed punches wherever they could find purchase.

Aedric stumbled drunkenly to his feet. His hammer lay not far away. He staggered forward, reaching for it with his good hand, his fingers closing around it numbly. Hefting it with a grunt, he lurched toward the men. Neither one looked up at his approach. With all the strength he could muster, he swung.

The blow landed with a sickening crack against the Northman's skull, throwing him off the reeve. The heathen crumpled to the ground, dazed, but before he could recover, Aedric was on him again, swinging the hammer with unrelenting force. Each blow jarred Aedric's arm to the shoulder, sending a shudder through his bones. Every violent crack spattered him with blood and pulp as the savage's skull gave way. The very ground beneath Aedric's feet seemed to tremble with each strike, his vision flashing red with every impact. The dull, meaty *thunk* of strike after strike rang in his ears like the toll of a death bell. And still he refused to stop, not until there was nothing left to ruin, not until he returned the bastard to dust.

"Enough." Oslac placed his hand on the blacksmith's shoulder, causing him to jump. "Enough," the reeve repeated. "It is done."

Aedric let the hammer drop. His body shook with exhaustion. He sank to his knees, his blood-soaked hands trembling.

Oslac sat beside him, tearing a strip from his shirt. "Show me your hand."

Chest still heaving, Aedric did as he was asked, holding the dripping stumps of his fingers out for the reeve's inspection. As Oslac bound his injuries, Aedric stared out at the blackened horizon. There was no comfort in the quiet. The night felt too still, too heavy, with the weight of all that had been lost.

"There. That should hold until we get back to the village."

Aedric didn't respond. The strip of linen around his throat was already damp, clinging to his skin as he swallowed. He was covered in blood, the metallic smell thick in his nostrils. Even the sharp scent of salt from the sea couldn't cut through it.

He glanced at the Northman's pulverized head, then spat, a globule of saliva hitting the soup of flesh and bone.

The reeve patted Aedric's back gently. "Come, let's get going—" Oslac's words died on his tongue.

Eyebrows knitting together, Aedric followed the man's gaze.

And then he saw them.

Shapes rising from the water with a hollow, otherworldly sound that seemed to lap across the waves as though the sea itself was whispering a warning.

Ships. Northman ships.

Scores of them.

The blacksmith reached for his hammer.

SAXON FODDER

KIMBERLY NICOLE

As the soldiers made their way through the lands of Northumbria, there were fewer and fewer animals for the locals to hunt. Food had never been so scarce. It had become a thing of wealth, food. Meat in general had become a precious delicacy. Their mouths salivated at the thought of it.

Elfric always knew he wasn't quite like the other men, he just didn't realize exactly what that meant until the war began.

His wife, Edith, was the one in charge. She demanded he stay home and help care for their large family—seven children—and he obeyed.

The soldiers came knocking once, and he managed to temporarily delay his summons, with his wife being sick and so pregnant that she was likely going to give birth at any given moment. But that would only last for so long. They knew they would be back for him; it was just a matter of when.

After countless nights of Elfric coming home empty-handed from his hunts, Edith finally put her foot down. "Quit failing us and use what's available to you," she demanded. Elfric wasn't quite sure what she meant by that, but was determined to not return home before figuring it out.

As he continued down the path, he passed dead body after dead body. "Those poor men," he muttered to himself. "Use what's available to you." He repeated Edith's words, feeling ambitious. *The men. The bodies. They're what's available to me!* Elfric thought.

The utter repugnance of the aroma clouding over him was damn near unbearable, but a man is not a man if he can't keep his family fed. There were more dead bodies than he could count. None of them appeared to be even remotely clean and healthy, so he chose the one that appeared to have been dead for the least amount of time.

Lifting up the ax that he had only used in the past to split wood—to keep his family warm during the shivering white seasons—he aimed it carefully, closed his cowardly eyes, then grunted as he hammered it down with all his might.

He opened his scared eyes. It was done. The dead man, that was nothing but roadkill, was one less leg than before. He and his family would eat that night. He dragged the removed leg behind him and made his way back home.

He wasn't exactly feeling a sense of pride for what he had just done, but he was thankful to the universe for the food, nonetheless. He also felt a level of gratitude at the knowledge that Edith would not be yelling at him again the moment he walked through the door. There had been so much tension between them as of late. The hunger had become almost unbearable, not to mention having to watch his children grow thinner and thinner over the past several months.

Elfric finally made it back home with his not-so-fresh freshly severed leg and was fully prepared to feed it to his family.

"Elfric, is that you? You better not be empty-handed again, or I swear to—" Edith began, and stopped speaking abruptly when she came face to face with Elfric and the meat that he carried. "Oh, I see," she said. "Alright, well, let's prepare dinner, then," she finished.

The meal was ready and the family sat down to eat. The children's eyes grew wide at the mere sight of the meat. There was so much of it they couldn't believe their eyes.

They dug in, and everyone excitedly filled their mouths with the delicious meat. It was completely quiet in their home aside from the slicing and chewing.

Their bellies were finally full, and it was oh so magical. None of them could remember the last time they had such a large feast.

Edith couldn't help but smile. Elfric noticed and

smiled, as well. Their children would no longer have to starve.

Several days, almost weeks, had passed and they carried on eating that way. The bodies were easy to come by, almost as if the universe was begging them to use them to their voracious advantage.

Their children were less lethargic and happy again, frolicking about and giggling among themselves. Life was good again. But they knew it wouldn't last long. It was bound to be disrupted eventually. It was only a matter of time.

Then the day finally came, the day they had been dreading. Well, Elfric feared it. Edith seemed prepared for it.

There was a knock, no not a knock, a pounding, at the door.

"It's time. Don't fret, my love, for I have a plan. Just answer the door and let the men in. It will be okay," Edith instructed, maintaining a clear level of calmness in her authoritative tone.

Elfric swallowed a hefty gulp, then slowly made his way toward the door. He found himself trembling as he approached the doorknob. He began to open it as the pounding announced itself again, somehow more aggressive that time around. He couldn't help but to be nervous.

"Hello, sirs. Please, come on in. To what do we owe this surprising pleasure?" Elfric enquired, attempting to hide the fear he felt all the way to his core.

"It's time to pay your dues, lad. It's time to fight with your brothers. It's time to bear arms and defend our families and lands," one of the two knights commanded, the one with the heavier armor.

"Welcome, gentleman. Yes, of course he will go with you. Thank you so much for letting him stay with us through my sickness. It was a close call for me. Could we offer you a hot meal before you go, to show our gratitude?" Edith chimed in, warmer and more charming than ever.

"That would be fine, peasant, thank you," said one of the knights, realizing his level of hunger was becoming more and more difficult to ignore.

The men sat down, placed their swords beside them, and prepared to feast.

Edith brought the food out and put specific plates down in front of everyone.

Elfric thought nothing of it as they all dug in. He trusted Edith had something planned but wasn't quite sure how she planned to get them to leave without him.

Before the food was even halfway eaten, Elfric noticed that the two other men were acting dizzy and appeared to be on high alert. It wasn't long before they both collapsed in a dramatic frenzy and stopped breathing.

Edith had poisoned them.

"What are we supposed to do now? We'll never get away with this!" Elfric blurted out in an obvious state of panic.

"Now we continue to eat, my dear," Edith responded as she began undressing her prized future feasts.

It didn't take long for Edith to finish preparing the fresh human meat she just acquired. She knew she had come into more than what her family could eat before it went bad. So, what to do with it, she pondered.

Elfric helped where he could, but per usual, Edith took the reins. Once it was all said and done, Elfric was still very much on edge. They burned the clothes and buried the armor, bones, and swords. Once all of the food was eaten, there would be zero evidence that anyone had come back to summon Elfric. The question remained, though: how would they consume all of the meat? Even with as many children as they had, it was still too much for one family.

"We'll share it. The rest of the village is bound to be hurting for food just as much as we once were. So why not share the bounty?" Edith said to Elfric, a proud expression planted upon her face.

"I guess we could do that. They wouldn't have to know where or how we came upon it or *what* exactly it is. Yeah, this could work. We could make a giant stew and spread it about. That'll take care of it very quickly. Smart thinking!" Elfric responded.

As everyone in the village sat down to feast on the stew—the gifted bounty—more knights stormed in, demanding answers.

"Where are our men?" one of them yelled, anger spilling out of his tone.

Another one of the knights helped himself to some stew, pushing villagers out of his way. "This is phenomenal! I haven't had meat this delicious in ages!" he said as he grabbed more bowls and handed them to the other men. They were starving and immediately dug in.

"I'm so glad you like it. It's a very old family recipe," Edith said, pride oozing out of her demeanor.

The first knight that spoke up had yet to grab a bowl and sternly asked again, "I demand answers immediately!"

"I'm not sure what you're talking about. No one has shown up here," Edith responded, her manner far more timid than before, as she swallowed down the bite of stew that was lingering in her mouth.

"Don't lie to me, peasant. I know they came here. They were two of my best men. Now, where are they?" he asked again, spittle flinging from his angry lips.

A sudden cacophony began around them. People gasped for air, reaching for their throats and gagging. They couldn't breathe. Their faces hastily turned bluish-purple, and they fell over—villagers and knights alike.

"What the hell is going on here?!" the main knight—the one who didn't try the stew—demanded. He had a family of his own waiting for him at home, and quite frankly, he didn't want to deal with that shit.

Edith gasped for air as she watched her children and her husband keel over. She made eye contact with Elfric as tears rolled down both of their guilty faces. They realized—at the same exact moment—the mistake they made. They accidentally poisoned everyone, themselves included. The meat was tainted...

In poisoning the original two men and feeding them to the village, they inadvertently poisoned everyone around them, as well as their children and themselves.

We should have known better, was Elfric's last living thought.

Only one living human remained in the village—the knight. He stood there in utter shock, having no clue what happened or why he just lost more men.

"What happened here!?" he said to no one.

He was in complete disbelief as he fell to his knees and cupped his hands over his face. He had seen some bad things—hell, he had caused some bad things—but that sight was nearly too much to bear. Everyone was completely dead—the men, the women, and even the children. So many children...

He stood up and left. He wandered aimlessly through the land with no destination in mind. He was still in shock.

Early the following day, more men showed up at the village in hopes of finding their lost men. They couldn't afford to lose them. They had already lost far too many.

What they found shook each of them to their core.

They couldn't believe what they were seeing. So many dead people... So many of their men gone.

"What in the hell happened here? An entire village dead, and our fellow men," one of them said, sorrow in his tone. He found it difficult to continue looking at all of the poor corpses, so he averted his gaze.

"Look over there. All that food! We'd be heroes if we brought that much food back with us. Better than letting it go to waste," another one of them suggested to the others.

They gathered all the food they could carry and morosely made their way back to their dilapidated camp, looking forward to feeding their remaining men. It had been too long since their bellies were full.

Little did they know they would all be dead by morning...

THE RIDDLE OF THE BONE WITCH

CHRISTY ALDRIDGE

A SINGLE CANDLE FLICKERED in the corner of the humble cottage, its light casting shapes across the walls. Rhea knelt beside her mother, the mattress creaking each time her mother shifted. Her frail body trembled beneath a coarse woolen blanket, her cheeks hollow and her lips dry. For days, she had grown weaker, consumed by her illness that even fervent prayers couldn't cure.

"She can't hold on like this."

Rhea glanced up at the open door. Mara, her mother's friend, stood inside. "I've known her all my life, child. Never seen her this ...sick."

Rhea's heart twisted. She had never been one for tears, but they threatened to overflow. She gathered her mother's hand against her chest, feeling the faint beat of life. "There must be something more," she whispered. "Some medicine or charm we've overlooked."

Mara paused, her gaze darting toward the open window as if fearful of listening ears. "Have you considered ..."

Rhea's blood went cold. Like all villagers, she knew the tales—dark fables meant to frighten children away from the crumbling tower in the north.

"Of course."

"The Bone Witch is a dangerous risk though," Mara answered. "I've heard she makes bargains with the dead. Witchcraft, and you know what dabbling in that will do to you."

She knew. Rhea knew exactly what conversing with any of the occult would do to you, whether you practiced it or enlisted the help from it. She stared at the hearth instinctively.

She pressed her mother's limp hand to her heart. "If there is any chance, then I must find her. I cannot let my mother slip away without trying."

Old Mara's fingers twitched around the lantern's handle. "They say few who go to that tower ever return. At best, they come back changed, torn away from the warmth of the living. You'd risk that?"

Rhea lifted her chin. She felt the weight of unspoken terror, yet her mother's labored breaths strengthened her resolve. "I would risk all I have," she said. "She is all that's left of my family."

Mara studied her a moment, then reached into the folds of her cloak. Her gaze flickered to the figure on the pallet. "Hasten, child. The night only grows colder and she only grows weaker."

Rhea leaned over her mother one final time, pressing a gentle kiss to her burning forehead. Then she rose, every bone in her body protesting as though she had been running for days.

"I'll return soon," she breathed, forcing confidence into her words. "Hold on, please."

She strode out of the cottage, letting the darkness enfold her. Clouds rolled across a pale crescent moon, and the distant silhouette of the old tower loomed somewhere to the north. Rhea's heart pounded against her ribcage as she made her way beyond the village fences, guided by a path known to few travelers. She thought of the stories, the whispered rumors—of spirits who roamed the moors under the Bone Witch's command.

It could all be just stories. That was what she feared most. It was why the Bone Witch still existed in such times, because her very presence was unconfirmed.

Yet she pressed on, each step carrying her farther from the safety of her world and closer to that forsaken tower. The wind's lament rose around her, and in it, she fancied she could hear the echoes of unspeakable secrets, or perhaps the faint, agonized cry of those who had gone before and never returned.

Cold moonlight illuminated the twisting track Rhea followed. Each step pressed into the damp earth, the mud pulling at her worn boots as if to swallow her whole. The wind whistled low through brittle reeds, carrying the faint hint of decay—a reminder that those lands had once hosted terrible conflicts, long abandoned by both armies and hope.

Her cloak, a threadbare shield against the biting chill, fluttered around her legs. She moved in silence. The gloom seemed almost sentient, shifting at the edges of her vision.

A faint memory flickered: her mother's voice, soft and musical, telling stories of far-off cities where banners flew bright as dawn and princesses who never knew hunger. *"Someday,"* her mother had said, *"we will see such places."* But that day never came, and Rhea journeyed through a nightmare.

Beyond the willows, the land sloped upward, unveiling a sweeping vista of mist-shrouded hills. And there, perched like a raven on a dead branch, stood the tower. Time had ravaged it, leaving jagged edges that pointed accusingly at the heavens. A lone light flickered high in a window.

She pressed a hand to her throat, feeling the flutter of her pulse. The Bone Witch. Never had she expected to see the witch's lair with her own eyes. Fireside gossip in the village painted the witch as a living horror, a being carved from nightmares who could command the spirits of the departed. Yet there Rhea stood, only steps away.

Her heart hammered. She remembered Old Mara's warning: *"Few who enter the tower ever return."* Perhaps those unfortunate souls had walked those very steps.

She closed her own eyes, inhaling the acrid scent of damp stone. Somewhere in her mind echoed the hollow sound of her mother's labored breathing.

"Just a little further," she whispered, as though reassuring herself. "For her."

The tower door stood as black as midnight, bearing carvings that resembled the twisted skeletons of ancient beasts. Rhea braced a hand on the iron latch—still warm from the fleeting heat of day—and pushed.

It yielded, releasing a draft of stale air that smelled of incense and something fouler, unnamable. She stepped into the gloom, swallowing the knot of fear in her throat. The door drifted shut behind her with a heavy thud, sealing her inside.

Darkness enveloped her, broken only by the glow of scattered candles perched on sconces along the circular walls. The faint scratch of something moving—rats or worse—slithered through the hush. Gooseflesh crept along Rhea's arms, and she fought the urge to sprint back into the open air.

Yet she stood her ground. If the Bone Witch could save her mother, then she would face whatever horror lurked within those walls, even if it meant offering more of herself than she dared imagine.

A single voice, low and scratchy, emerged from the upper landing of a winding staircase. "You came," it said with a cruel trace of satisfaction.

The words reverberated through the tower. Rhea raised her gaze toward it. There, half veiled by shadows, stood a figure.

Rhea did not flinch. Instead, she lifted her chin. "I have come for my mother," she called, her voice steady despite the quiver in her chest.

Silence stretched out. Then, at last, the figure moved, the light revealing a hint of bone-white hair and a thin-lipped grin.

Rhea's heart thundered in her chest. She peered upward, narrowing her eyes to see the figure descending, her footfalls a soft, scraping sound on each step. The Bone Witch moved with a slow, deliberate grace, as though every motion carried the weight of countless secrets. A single candle in a wall sconce flickered violently, and in its tremulous glow, Rhea caught a better glimpse of the witch.

She was tall—taller than any woman Rhea had known—her frame draped in a robe of tattered silk the color of old ashes. Strands of silvery hair fell loose around a gaunt face that seemed almost skull-like in its contours. Pale skin stretched tightly across angular cheekbones, and her dark eyes glimmered with an otherworldly sheen. On her narrow lips rested a slight smile, yet it carried no warmth.

Bones—real bones, from creatures Rhea couldn't readily identify—adorned the witch's hair like macabre ornaments. Some were carved with strange symbols, others bound with sinewy cords and bits of thread. Around her throat, she wore a necklace of delicate finger-length bones that clattered faintly with each step. In her hand, she gripped a long staff, its gnarled top affixed with a single skull no bigger than a child's fist, the empty eye sockets glaring blindly into the gloom.

"You are braver than most who come seeking me, girl," she said, her voice like the rasp of leaves in a graveyard. "Or more desperate."

Rhea forced herself not to recoil from the bone talismans or the sharp, unholy scent of incense clinging to the witch's robes. She cleared her throat, struggling to keep her voice steady. "I ... I come for my mother. She's gravely ill. The village healers can do nothing." She swallowed the lump of fear lodged in her throat. "They say you—"

The witch raised a hand, rings made of bone clicking softly together. "I know what they say," she interrupted, her tone at once impatient and gently mocking. "That I bend life and death. That I speak to spirits in the netherworld. Is that not why you stand before me with terror in your eyes?"

Rhea clenched her fists at her sides. Her nerves trembled, yet she raised her gaze to meet the witch's. "I came here because there's no other way. If you can save her, I will pay whatever price you demand."

The Bone Witch stepped forward. The bones in her hair clattered like a chorus of whispers, and the staff's skull let out a faint, hollow rattle. She circled Rhea in a slow, predatory arc, her robes stirring the stale air like a gathering storm.

"You speak of *price*," she said softly, voice echoing through the cavernous space. "Yet you do not comprehend what such a payment entails. Are you prepared to carve out your own heart if that is the cost? To chain your very soul to the shadows?"

Rhea's voice wavered, but she held firm. "I said I would do anything."

A low chuckle escaped the witch's lips, humorless and cold. "Then hear me well, for I do not conjure my powers lightly, nor do I grant mercy to those who fail me." She tapped her staff against the floor, and a faint, tremoring ring pulsed through the stones. "If you desire my aid, you must pass three trials—three riddles that test your devotion and your courage. Complete them and I shall wrest your mother from the jaws of death. Fail, and the penalty will be dire."

Behind Rhea, the tall door to the tower slammed shut of its own accord, the iron latch groaning like a living thing. She whirled around, heart pounding. A hush fell once more, broken only by the subtle hiss and crackle of unseen energies in the air.

Turning back, she found the witch smiling, that same predatory glint in her eyes. Rhea felt a chill skitter down her spine at the quiet menace in those words. *What have I done?* a frantic voice in her mind asked. Yet she remembered the sight of her mother's body, wasted away on the straw pallet, the shallow pull of her breath. That memory flared within her, kindling a desperate bravery.

"I accept," she said, her voice only slightly shaking.

The Bone Witch raised her staff, triumphant, and her voice took on an eerie resonance. "The first riddle is just this," she began.

"*What lies below yet knows not the sky,*
Born of old bones but never shall die?

*Bring me its token, wrested from earth's tears,
Or remain in this tower for uncounted years."*

The last echo of her words died away, leaving Rhea breathless with unease. She tried to gather her thoughts, forcing her mind to wrestle with the riddle's meaning. Beneath her initial dread, a tentative curiosity flickered—some part of her drawn to the puzzle as much as she was repelled by the witch.

The Bone Witch traced one talon-like finger across the staff, turning back to Rhea with dark satisfaction. "You have until the stroke of midnight to answer each riddle and present it to me," she said, her hollow voice filling the space like a hiss of wind through a graveyard. "If you cannot, then what you love most shall be claimed by the shadows."

Rhea swallowed. Her mouth tasted of ash, and beads of cold sweat gathered at her temples. She wished to ask what the cryptic lines meant. Yet something in the witch's gaze warned her that no further counsel would be given. The riddle was hers alone to solve.

As if on cue, the iron door groaned and swung inward, leading to the moonlit courtyard. Rhea turned, heart hammering at the thought of plunging once more into the dark moors. Still, it was a reprieve from the suffocating menace pulsing within those walls.

Rhea pulled her cloak tightly around her and fled out the door, crossing the courtyard at a near run. The wind whipped her hair, stinging her cheeks. Moonlight bathed the moor in a pale, ghostly glow as she departed the tower. The iron gate groaned shut behind her, sealing her once again in the forlorn countryside. Yet something had shifted; the air felt heavier, as though bearing witness to the oath she had sworn. Even the night wind that had sliced through her clothing—always so quick to whistle and moan—dropped, seemed subdued, reluctant to stir the tall grasses that trembled beneath the moon's baleful gaze.

Rhea pressed a palm over her racing heart. The Bone Witch's first riddle echoed in her thoughts. A chill wrapped itself around her, and not just from the cold. Her mind spun with questions. *What could be 'born of old bones' but never die?* A creature? A plant? A cursed remnant of bygone wars? She exhaled shakily, resisting the urge to hurl the riddle into the night out of frustration.

Yet she had no choice but to solve it. Her mother's life depended on it.

Like a distant memory, she recalled an ancient battlefield that lay not far off. The villagers whispered that the land there still writhed with unease, littered with bones bleached by countless seasons. *"Born of old bones... never shall die."* Her mind returned to the possibility that the riddle pointed to that place of ghosts and half-buried relics.

Though her heart pounded with every step, she veered off the familiar trail and ventured northeast, guided only by a faint memory of where the cursed field might lie. She trudged onward, the land slowly rising and falling beneath her. The wind picked up. The moor gave way to a swath of open ground. Rhea's nose wrinkled at the faint scent of decay—a stale bitterness that clung to the fields even then. An uneasy recognition prickled at her memory. Yes. It was the place rumored to be haunted by the spirits of fallen knights and soldiers, whose final cries once mingled in the air.

She climbed, her cloak tugging at her shoulders as if urging her to reconsider. But at the crest of the hill, the battlefield spread out before her: a hollow basin of land strewn with broken spears, rusted armor, and half-sunken grave markers. Many of the bones had long since been scavenged by animals or claimed by the shifting earth, yet here and there, a bleached rib cage or fractured skull jutted from the soil, sorrowful in its silent testimony.

Is this what the witch meant? She descended cautiously, boots crunching over gravel and the occasional splinter of bone. The scattered debris of ancient battles turned the ground into a tragic tapestry of lost hopes.

Crouching beside a fallen banner-pole crowned with a rusted finial, she found a skeletal hand protruding from the soil like a final plea to the heavens. Her stomach twisted at the sight, but she gently touched the back of the hand. The bones felt cold, timeworn. Something about the tang of the air here felt older than death itself.

"What lies below yet knows not the sky, born of old bones but never shall die," she murmured to the vacant darkness. *What in all creation fits that description?*

Her gaze drifted to a nearby crater—a large, sunken place where the ground had collapsed into a shallow pit. Tendrils of mist coiled from its edges, as if the land breathed in pained slumber. Heart pounding, Rhea inched closer, peering into the hollow. By moonlight, she saw a gleam of something white and glossy half-buried amid the rubble.

She slid carefully down the lip of the pit, each step sending loose stones skittering. The closer she came, the stronger the bitter stench became. At last, she crouched and brushed away loose soil, her fingers trembling. There, nestled among a tangle of shattered ribs, lay a cluster of pale fungal blooms—spindly stalks topped with smooth, bulbous caps. They glistened as though coated with dew, or perhaps the oily tears of the earth itself. The entire cluster seemed to pulse faintly with life, feeding on the ancient marrow that lay beneath.

A swirl of dread and fascination washed over Rhea. *Fungus—born from old bones, living on them, never truly dying.* Did that match the riddle's words? She recalled hearing tales of mushrooms that sprang from battlefield remains, said to glow in the dark. Soldiers once called them "ghost lights" or "the bone's promise." Some believed them cursed; others insisted they bore secret healing properties.

Could that be the token the witch demanded? If so, Rhea would have to claim it—for her mother's sake, she would do anything.

She pried a short blade from her satchel, hands shaking. The moonlit metal glinted as she carefully sliced through the thick stems of the fungal blooms. A noxious smell wafted up, and she bit back a gag, breathing shallowly through her mouth. When she had severed a decent cluster, she wrapped the stalks in a bit of linen to keep them intact.

With the bundle of eerie fungus cradled in her arms, Rhea scrambled back up the crater's rim, nearly tripping on a loose rock. When she reached the top, she paused, panting softly. The moor stretched out around her once more, unfeeling and vast. In the distance, the warped line of pines beckoned her away from the silent graveyard.

She set her jaw and pressed on, navigating carefully over the broken spears and bleaching shards of bone, hoping against hope that the mushrooms were the correct interpretation of the Bone Witch's riddle.

At last, she stood before the iron gate. A battered gargoyle glared at her from a crumbling pillar, its stone features eroded into a twisted sneer. Rhea's heart hammered, and she lifted a trembling hand to the gate, half-expecting it to swing open of its own accord. A gust of wind rattled the rusted iron, and indeed, the gate creaked open just enough for her to slip inside.

When she reached the door, she hesitated, then raised her hand to push. Inside, the glow of scattered candles painted twisted shapes across the floor. Immediately, Rhea sensed the presence of the witch—somewhere in those rooms, waiting with an unnatural stillness. Gathering her courage, she stepped fully into the tower's gloom, letting the door thud shut behind her.

Silence stretched. The shadows danced. Then from above, that dry, whispery voice spoke out, dripping with dark amusement. "Brave child," it said, the words floating down the spiraling staircase. "So eager to present your offering." A pause—then a low, rustling sound, as if bones clacked together. "Let us see if it will suffice."

"I found these," Rhea whispered, steadying her breath. "They grow from the bones of soldiers long dead. They feed on marrow that's turned to soil. If ever something was born from 'old bones' yet never truly dies, it is this."

For a heartbeat, the Bone Witch remained silent, her expression inscrutable. Her bony fingers hovered over the fungi as though reading energy that pulsed beneath the surface. Then she made a low, nearly inaudible hiss. "Yes," she murmured at last, trailing a fingertip across a bulbous cap. "This will do."

A gust of wind hissed through a high window slit, extinguishing a nearby candle. Shadows rushed in, cloaking half the chamber. In that shifting gloom, the Bone Witch turned, her robes brushing the cold floor. She motioned with a brittle hand for Rhea to follow. Torchlight flickered, illuminating passages of stone draped in centuries of dust and spider webs. No windows graced the corridors; only the feeble glow of sconces marked the way.

At length, they emerged into a smaller room—a vaulted alcove scattered with parchment, broken quills, and half-finished drawings of cryptic symbols. In the corner stood a large brazier, glowing with coals that emitted a red, wavering light. The witch approached it, staff tapping the floor in an ominous rhythm. Then, with a curt nod, she beckoned Rhea closer.

"You have passed the first trial," said the witch, "but your mother's life is yet far from saved." Her eyes gleamed with sudden intensity. "If you mean to wrest her from the grave's embrace, you must succeed twice more. Fail, and the cost shall be dearer than you can conceive." Her voice dropped low, each word reverberating in Rhea's skull. "Attend now—here is the second riddle I lay upon you."

*"A memory wrought in flesh,
a tether between lost and found.
Surrender a fragment of what once was,
lest all be left unbound."*

Rhea's lips parted, questions tumbling unspoken through her thoughts. *A memory wrought in flesh?* Could the Bone Witch truly demand a piece of her own body? Or something symbolic of her history—an heirloom, perhaps, that carried great personal meaning?

Before Rhea could speak, a rush of air snuffed out every torch, plunging the alcove into pitch-black darkness. She stifled a cry, her pulse thudding in her ears.

When the torches sputtered back to life on their own accord, the Bone Witch stood inches away, her talon-like nails nearly grazing Rhea's cheek. "Heed this, girl," she hissed. "Each task delves deeper into your spirit. The gifts I craft do not come without sacrifice—blood, bone, or something more intangible."

Rhea fought the urge to recoil. Yet her mind flashed to

her mother, pale and feverish, dwindling in their small cottage. Summoning her courage, she looked into the witch's eyes. "I understand," she managed.

A brittle laugh escaped the Bone Witch's lips. "You echo the vow of every lost soul who's come here. Let us see how far your devotion extends." With a swirl of her ragged robes, she stepped away, leaving Rhea swaying in the brazier's ruddy glow. "The riddle is yours to solve. Give me the essence I demand—or linger forever in my domain."

Rhea's mind reeled, but much like the battlefield had entered into her thoughts, her bag suddenly felt more aware by her side. Rhea slid the small pouch free from its binding. Her heart thundered, but her hand remained steady. She loosened the leather cord, revealing a single lock of hair from her infancy—golden strands tied with old thread, dull but once radiant as sunlight. Their significance to her mother was beyond measure.

Stepping forward, Rhea placed the lock upon a stone table in the center of the chamber. The table was stained with shadows and ringed by half-melted candles; their flames wavered in the draft, uncertain witnesses to ancient sorceries.

"This is part of me," Rhea said, her voice hushed. "Cut from my head when I was just an infant. My mother kept it as a token of hope." She swallowed. "It's all I can offer to prove my devotion."

A long silence followed. The Bone Witch bowed her head as if in contemplation. Her bony fingers drifted over the delicate strands, nails clicking faintly against the tabletop. Then she lifted her staff, and the skull at its tip caught the candlelight, magnifying it into a pale glow. Rhea clenched her teeth, recalling how the unearthly glow had illuminated so many horrors in that tower.

A swirl of power seemed to coil in the air, stirring

Rhea's hair away from her face. Gooseflesh prickled up her arms. She felt a presence pressing in, like countless invisible eyes observing this dark transaction.

"So much love, so much sorrow, dwells in these strands," the Bone Witch murmured, her tone almost reverent. "A link between your mother and you, a bridge across time."

She straightened, the staff's glow fading. "Place your hand over it."

Rhea obeyed, heart pounding. Her skin brushed the dry, fragile threads of hair, and a rush of memories unfurled—childhood laughter, bedtime stories, gentle arms cradling her after a nightmare. Tears gathered at the corners of her eyes, an ache opening wide in her chest.

"You have given your memory, child," the witch said, that dangerous undercurrent curling in her tone. "But know this: memory and love are not lightly parted from the soul. In forging this link to save another's life, you have broken a seal upon your own heart."

Rhea swallowed, unwilling to let fear best her. "Does this mean the second riddle is fulfilled?"

A slow nod. "The second riddle is satisfied." The Bone Witch's lips curved in a thin, humorless smile. "Your mother's breath grows stronger even now. But she remains tethered between worlds, for the final chord is yet unstruck."

A shiver ran down Rhea's spine, half relief and half foreboding. "What must I do next?"

Silence, jagged as broken glass. Then the Bone Witch's staff thudded softly on the stone. "There is a third riddle," she said with dreadful finality. "The most perilous of all. Prepare yourself, child." Her eyes burned like embers. "A life borrowed must be repaid in kind."

Rhea's heart lurched. A sense of impending doom

clawed at her. Yet she forced herself to stand tall, ignoring the faint burn in her palm and the hollowness yawning in her chest. "Tell me."

A soft, mirthless chuckle issued from the witch's throat. "A mother's life is a powerful tether, indeed." She lifted her staff, and the courtyard torches flared, casting wild shadows that leaped over the walls like restless spirits. "Very well. You shall have the final riddle—though it is less a riddle than a reckoning."

The witch raised one pale hand, and in the torchlight, Rhea saw runes carved into the witch's very skin, etched like scars of ancient secrets. The woman spoke, and her words curled around the tower courtyard like a living serpent.

"When blood has bound what death unbound,
No breath is gained unless breath is drowned.
A life borrowed must be repaid in kind—
Which soul will you offer, that yours be left behind?"

The final line stung like a lash across Rhea's heart. She heard the echoes of it in the hush that followed, as if the tower itself repeated the words in a mournful, sub-audible chant. *Which soul will you offer?*

Fear hammered through her veins. The witch's meaning was plain enough. *To save her mother completely, another life must take her mother's place.* A savage exchange, a final bartering in the ledger of fate.

She swallowed, her voice low, tremulous. "No," she breathed, shaking her head. "I won't sacrifice an innocent life for hers."

The Bone Witch's eyes gleamed like black mirrors. "Then your mother's recovery shall wither beneath the next dawn, and your efforts shall be for nothing."

A storm of anguish and determination flared within Rhea. *I can't betray someone else to the grave.* She thought wildly of Old Mara, her neighbors, the vulnerable children of the village. Every life was precious. The witch knew that, relishing the monstrous bargain.

But what if ... Rhea closed her eyes, fighting the rush of tears. *There is a life I can give—my own.* Blood thundered in her ears as she raised her chin, meeting the witch's gaze. "Take me," she said, her voice catching on an unsteady breath. "Let my mother live. I will pay the price with my own life."

For a moment, the courtyard's torches seemed to gutter, drawing in the night's breath. The Bone Witch watched her, head tilted as if weighing the offer. Then she gave a slow, dangerous smile. "A life given in love, or in desperation? No matter. It shall suffice." She slammed the staff against the stones. "Swear it on the blood that flows between you and she."

Rhea's hands clenched into fists. *It is the only way.* The prospect of surrendering her life burned hot and cold all at once, but better that than to damn another soul. "I swear it," she said, tears forcing their way down her cheeks, "by my blood, by the bond of my mother and me."

Thunder rumbled in the distance, though the sky above remained free of storms. The witch's lips parted in silent incantation, and the torches flared higher, spitting embers that drifted around them like malevolent fireflies. Rhea's throat constricted, yet she did not flinch.

A shard of moonlight fell upon them, and the Bone Witch raised a dagger carved from animal bone, its edge polished to a vicious gleam. She extended it toward Rhea's trembling hands. "Then take this blade," she hissed. "Offer me a single drop of your blood, and your vow shall be sealed."

Rhea grasped the dagger. Its handle felt unsettlingly warm, as though alive. With her free hand, she bared her forearm, her breath ragged. She paused a heartbeat—imagining her mother's gentle smile, her laugh long before sickness claimed her. *This is worth it.* The blade bit her flesh in a swift line, stinging her skin and releasing a crimson bead that rolled down her arm.

The witch's staff glowed with an eerie luminescence as she chanted in that strange, ancient tongue. The courtyard swam before Rhea's eyes. She felt her heartbeat pulsing in her ears, in the earth beneath her feet, in the shimmering torchlight. Every sound twisted into a dull roar.

Then—silence. The dagger clattered to the ground. Rhea swayed, pressing a hand to her bleeding arm. She locked her gaze on the Bone Witch's gleaming eyes, breath coming in shaking gulps. "It's done?" she whispered.

The witch lowered her staff. A cold smile lingered on her lips. "Your mother's fate is bound to life," she said, voice echoing. "You have sold your own tomorrows to buy her future. The final riddle is answered. The circle closes." The torches guttered, as if inhaling the last of the magic. "Take your leave, child."

Chest heaving, Rhea tried to speak, but only a hoarse rasp emerged. She clutched her wounded arm, warm blood trickling between her fingers. Turning on unsteady feet, she stumbled toward the courtyard gate. The Bone Witch made no move to stop her. In the torchlight's dying glow, Rhea glimpsed the tower's high windows—dark and silent as a tomb.

Beyond the gate, the moor spread out under the solemn light of the full moon. Rhea's vision blurred, her body aching with both terror and relief. *It is done. She will live.* Yet at what cost? Her own life?

No matter. She could think of nothing except reaching her mother, confirming with her own eyes that the woman's strength truly endured. So she staggered forward, crossing the moorland with the moon trailing overhead, a silent witness to the great debt she had taken upon her soul.

And behind her, in that courtyard of old bones and flickering torches, the Bone Witch lingered—her staff's skull glinting beneath the moon's pallid glow, a keeper of grim secrets and bartered fates.

Rhea stumbled across the moors as night surrendered to a pallid dawn. Clouds draped the sky like torn veils, the sun's first rays hidden behind their gray shadows. Despite the stiffness in her legs and the dull ache in her bleeding arm, she pressed forward, compelled by the singular hope that had sustained her through the Bone Witch's grim demands: *My mother will live.*

At the village boundary, she paused, gasping for breath. A chill wind lifted her hair, and she felt it then—a thin, spectral tug behind her ribs. It was as though an invisible hand had reached inside her chest and taken hold of her heartbeat. She sagged against the rough wooden fence, sweat beading at her temples. *Did I truly give up my life?* An echo of the witch's final incantation pulsed at the edges of her memory, sharp and inevitable as a dirge.

She gathered the frayed edges of her resolve. *One step at a time.* By the time she reached the humble cottage, the sky had lightened to the palest gray.

Within, a single lantern burned, illuminating Old Mara's worried face peering through the shutter slats. At the sight of Rhea's haggard form, Mara flung the door wide, skirts rustling.

"Child," she exclaimed, voice trembling with relief and alarm. "Your arm. What have you done?" Her gaze flicked to the blood-streaked tear in Rhea's sleeve.

Rhea swallowed. Her lips felt chapped, her mouth

desert dry. "Is she awake?" she managed, ignoring the question as Mara rushed to support her weight.

A step into the cottage brought her into warm lamplight—and the sight of her mother rising gingerly from the pallet. The older woman's face bore a subtle glow of renewed vitality. Though still thin, she moved with a care that suggested strength was returning to her limbs. When her eyes landed on Rhea, tears gathered, reflecting the lamp's flicker.

"My darling," she whispered, pressing a trembling hand to her mouth. "You're hurt. Sit."

Rhea's throat constricted. She stumbled forward, letting her mother guide her into a nearby chair. Dizziness wove through her mind, but the joy of seeing her mother upright, breathing, kept her conscious. Gently, her mother examined the wound, her brows pinched with worry.

"It's just a cut," Rhea murmured. She winced as cloth met her raw skin. Blood matted her sleeve, sticky and dark. "I'll be fine."

Old Mara set about gathering clean rags and a bowl of water. Her hands trembled as she dabbed at Rhea's arm. "What have you done?" Mara repeated, voice low. "You were gone all night. And now?"

A ragged breath escaped Rhea. She glanced from Mara to her mother, uncertain how much truth she could lay bare. The Bone Witch's riddle clung to her heart like a chain of ice: *A life borrowed must be repaid in kind.* At last, she met her mother's searching gaze.

Her eyes flicked to her mother's wrapped forearm—where the fever once raged, the skin looked clear. There was no sign of the fatal ailment. "Your strength is returning. That's all that matters."

A tremor passed through her mother's lips. She reached out, cupping Rhea's cheek, a gesture so gentle it made Rhea's eyes burn with unshed tears. "But at what price, child?"

Rhea hesitated. *How can I speak of the vow—offering my own life in exchange for my mother's survival?* Something in her chest twisted, an ache deeper than the throbbing wound.

The first days of Rhea's return passed in a soft glow of relief. Her mother, once pale and fever-stricken, walked freely about the cottage. She held steady in her voice and step, occasionally pausing to marvel at how the sickness had failed to claim her. Old Mara, too, relaxed her constant vigil, confident the threat had lifted for good.

But not so for Rhea. Though her heart still beat, she felt increasingly like a stranger in her own skin. At times, a dull ache gripped her chest, and a creeping chill brushed her spine. Night after night, she woke gasping from dreams of hollow-eyed specters prowling the moors. Whenever she closed her eyes, the Bone Witch's final words haunted her: *"A life borrowed must be repaid in kind."*

Midday arrived on a bracing gust of autumn wind. Rhea's mother spent the morning sorting linens, humming a half-remembered lullaby that once soothed Rhea as a child.

Rhea watched from the doorway. That was exactly what she had fought for—her mother's life, delivered from the edge of the grave. *If only I could share fully in her joy.* But a constant weight pressed at her ribcage, as if a chain slowly tightened around her heart.

For a fleeting moment, Rhea forgot the quiet dread gnawing inside her. A gentle breeze set the branches swaying, and sunlight glimmered through leaves turning orange and gold. Her mother's laughter rang out, free of pain for the first time in many months. *All is well.*

Then it happened.

Rhea felt a stabbing force tear through her chest. She cried out, staggering backward. An overwhelming agony seized her lungs and spread in a wave of cold that numbed her limbs.

Her mother rushed to her side. "Rhea!" she yelled, voice frantic.

Rhea opened her mouth to answer, but her throat locked, words strangled by pain. She sank to her knees, her vision swimming in a haze of white. Heartbeats thundered in her ears, each one an impossible weight. She had no breath to speak, only a choked gasp.

Somewhere in that throbbing fog, she heard a faint, echoing laugh—an old, rasping voice that scratched at her mind. *The Bone Witch. She's come to collect.* Deep within her memory, the final riddle rang out in a mocking refrain: *"No breath is gained unless breath is drowned."*

Her mother frantically cradled Rhea's head, tears flashing in her eyes as she begged her daughter to hold on. But Rhea felt her pulse sputter, skipping beats, every rush of blood a torment in her veins.

Skin clammy, Rhea coughed and tasted blood. Sharp agony burned behind her eyes, then everything blurred. Her mother's desperate sobs rang out, but Rhea could no longer focus on the shape of her mother's face. Coldness seeped under her skin, an icy tide that spread from her heart outward. Her lips moved in one last effort to speak. *I love you.* No sound emerged.

She collapsed against her mother's arms. Rhea's body tensed, then slackened in a final, violent jolt.

In that moment of abrupt horror, she felt a *pull*, as though something wrenched her spirit free. A final spasm wracked her chest, and all warmth fled. Then, a hush. No breath, no pain—only dim, receding light.

Rhea's last thought was of the riddle, echoing again in her mind. As her senses faded and the light waned, she surrendered to that final truth: *A life borrowed... must be repaid... in kind...*

IF I COULD JUST SPEAK

MJ Mars

The door to Janet's cottage was pushed open without warning, and Gertrude Hinkle, Janet's sister-in-law, strode into the house. Janet pushed a tightly wrapped bundle of fresh herbs into a cupboard, hurriedly closing it to keep the contents from her relative's prying eyes.

"Sister!" Gertrude greeted her, a gust of autumn winds carrying the crisp, orange stars of sycamore leaves in behind her. She closed the door and shuddered, wrapping her shawl around her shoulders. "The winds grow colder still today."

"Winter is surely on its way," Janet agreed.

"Let us pray it does not bring about as much misfortune as last winter."

Janet nodded, her thoughts lingering momentarily on her husband, who had fallen in the fields and frozen the previous January. The widower forced a smile. "What brings you out in the colds today, sister?"

Gertrude looked exaggeratedly around the small cottage, her eyes falling on the stairwell. "Is my nephew here?"

"No. Thomas is away collecting wood for the fire." Janet observed her sister-in-law's face fall, the visit clearly not intended for her. An uneasy sensation iced her chest. "My brother spoke of your struggles. I hope you don't mind me speaking of it."

Clearing her throat, Gertrude's chubby fingers flapped around her face, a failed attempt to distract from the heat that bloomed on her cheeks. "Alas, the village's ongoing misfortunes have manifested as a quiet home without the laughter of children for your brother and I."

"I am truly sorry to hear it. Hopefully you will be blessed before the winter is out."

Gertrude's eyes sharpened. "Perhaps that is something you may be able to assist me with."

Hesitant, Janet gestured for the woman to sit.

The chair creaked under Gertrude's weight, and the woman folded her hands over her apron front. "I have heard it told that you have helped the villagers with maladies using skills learned in your gardens."

Janet shook her head. "There is no plant that can bring about a child, sister."

The door opened once more, and Thomas came through, a pile of sticks cradled in his arms.

At the sight of the seven-year-old, Gertrude leapt to her feet and clasped her hands under her chin, her eyes brimming with adoration. There was a longing in her expression that tore into Janet's heart.

While Thomas set the wood by the fire and allowed his aunt to fuss over him, Janet snuck to her cabinet. She reached inside and pulled out an egg and a bundle of dried thyme and basil wrapped tightly in golden thread, then concealed the items in her apron pocket. "Go on upstairs now, Thomas. Rest yourself before supper."

Watching the boy until he was out of sight, Gertrude's tears flowed freely. "Forgive me, sister. Of all that this village has been through in the last ten years, my one loss seems small compared to many. But my heart breaks every day I return to an empty house."

Janet moved to her brother's wife, her good nature fighting against the trepidation that brewed within her the closer she got to the woman. She was an intuitive empath and knew better than to ignore the feeling of dread that grew with every step. However, her sister-in-law was clearly in need, and Janet felt she had a duty to heal. She took the small bundle from her pocket and pressed it into Gertrude's clammy hands. "Eat the egg, take the dried shell and boil it with these herbs. Wrap the brew in this golden thread and place it under your marital bed. If the gods decree it, a child will be yours."

Gertrude enveloped Janet into an elated embrace, her gratitude radiating into the space around them and forcing the dark thoughts from Janet's mind. "Oh, sister! You have given me just what I needed, as I knew you would."

"Best not to inform my brother of my assistance. He dislikes such practice, as you know." She walked Gertrude to the door.

As she opened it, the wind carried with it a grunting roar, the noise chilling both women and causing them to freeze for a moment. Janet stepped out ahead of Gertrude and faced the rolling hills past the marshland to the left of the cottage. Unseen by Gertrude, she waved her fingers, muttering to herself. The dark shadow that she could see lurking behind the old rock formation slunk back.

"Did you say something, sister?" Gertrude asked, moving close behind her.

"Nothing." Janet turned and gave her a brisk smile. "I didn't speak a word."

The manor court trial was held in the village's wealthiest estate. In a reception room that seated fifty spectators, the county assize, Lyle Cornthwaite, and his assistant, Brogan Hart, faced the crowd as they deliberated. Janet was standing in the dock, a curved wooden panel separating her from the baying crowd. Her hands were tied at her front, and the blue spectre of a bruise grew in hue on her cheek as the day progressed.

Lyle Cornthwaite habitually tugged the left side of his moustache before he spoke, an odd little twitch Janet soon learned to dread. The magistrate had reveled in his new role, and his assistant was eager to prove himself to his master. That meant both men in charge of Janet's fate were cruel, unrelenting, and driven by the need to impress—a combination that would surely prove dire.

"I call witness Joseph Hinkle!" Lyle called without looking up from his papers.

Janet watched her brother leave his seat and walk to the front of the room. Although she kept her eyes locked on him, he never once had the courage to look toward her.

"State your name and relation to the accused," Lyle drawled.

"My name is Joseph Hinkle, and I am the brother of the accused, Janet Barbery."

"And it was your concern that instigated this court to be held."

"It was, My Lord."

"Describe your concerns in detail, if you please."

Joseph's eyes drifted to the ceiling, where they remained throughout the first of his claims, as though the words he spoke had been painted above by an unseen hand. "On the afternoon of October 3rd, my wife paid a visit to Janet, uh, the accused. Once there, she witnessed terrible maltreatment of our nephew, whom we have now taken into our own loving embrace."

Janet forced herself to look at the pew where her brother had sat. Gertrude had Thomas in a hug that bordered on strangulation, a possessive, predatory factor in her demeanour toward the boy. In order to assist the courts, her in-laws had been only too happy to attend her arrest, proclaiming they would take the boy into their own home until the sordid matter came to a conclusion. Brazenly, Gertrude stared back at Janet, a look of triumph in her eyes.

"But that wasn't all that was witnessed that day. Continue, please," Lyle encouraged.

His gaze never leaving the ceiling, Joseph went on. "I found a strange bundle in my wife's possession that night. My sister had promised that the use of these objects would give us a child of our own. In constant mourning of the fact that we have not yet been blessed, my wife was carried away by the idea, not once considering this to be the sign of wicked witchcraft that it is. I had heard rumours about my sister's practices but had never once believed them to be true. Once I had this evidence, I immediately brought it to your attention, Sir."

"And for that, we are eternally grateful. You may sit."

Brogan addressed the assembly. "Upon the arrest of

the accused, we discovered some items within the home that we consider to be damning. In a small cupboard in the living area, we found a number of belongings that can be seen as nothing other than devilry."

Lyle lifted a sack onto the table and proceeded to tip the contents of Janet's cupboard out for all to see. The congregation let out a series of gasps and hisses when they took in the objects. Bundled herbs, carved idols, and jars containing various trinkets from nature had spilled out, enough to fill the shelves of any traveling apothecary cart.

Janet met the crowd's gasps with one of her own. "Sirs, you are making a terrible mistake by removing those from my home."

"Silence!" Lyle slammed down his fist.

"But my purpose in the house by the hills has been intentional and necessary for the wellbeing of this town."

"Wellbeing? This town has faced ten years of ruin and devastation."

"And I assure you, Sir, had my husband and I not been residing in that property and undertaking the practices I did with those items, this town would no longer stand."

Brogan advanced on her. "Preposterous! We will not be privy to your wicked lies any more. We will reconvene tomorrow, but from now on, the accused will only be brought to the public eye wearing a branks."

At the thought of wearing the tongue-stilling contraption, Janet held up her hands, pleading. "Mr. Hart, you must not do this, for the sake of this town and everyone in it. It may already be too late to save us, but I must be able to retain the ability to speak or we will all certainly be doomed!"

Brogan looked to Lyle Cornthwaite, and both men dissolved into guffaws. The congregation followed suit, and soon the room was full of malicious laughter aimed at Janet. "Woman, I'd put the bridle on you this instant if I had it to hand. Now, away with you!"

Rough hands grasped Janet's shoulders, and she was forcibly removed from the pulpit. Dragged past the table of her belongings, Janet managed to free her arm for one moment. She grabbed one of the bundles and held it toward her son, shouting a protective spell that she hoped would be enough to protect him from what was coming. With all the best will in the world from her pitiful position, she could not have mustered the power to protect the villagers. If there was one thing she could hope to leave behind in this cruel world, it was her son.

Upon the utterance of her words, the audience's laughter fell to screams.

Lyle Cornthwaite slapped her hard across the face, and the bundle fell from her hand. The man who was due to host her short trial loomed over her. "Witch! There can now be no doubt of your guilt. We will reconvene tomorrow, where the punishment for your crimes of devilry will be meted out. Take her away!"

With the terrified screams of the villagers behind her, Janet knew she would be hearing the sound again all too soon.

Brought to misery by the injustice she was facing, something deep within her looked forward to it. Ashamed, she buried the feeling and said a prayer for the souls of the ignorant villagers as she was dragged deep into the dungeons of the manor house.

The guard sneered at Janet through the door of her

makeshift cell and spat at her. His aim was true, and a thick smattering of mucus landed on her forehead. The foul liquid slowly slid down her brow, tracking the side of her nose until it came to pool against the tight metal bars clasped against her cheeks.

The scold's bridle, branks, or brankit, as the guard had called it when he had clamped it unceremoniously over her skull, comprised of a metal cage that was unnecessarily tight. It cut deep into Janet's cheekbones and pressed on the back of her skull, causing a headache that prevented any hope of sleep no matter how exhausted she became. More torturous still was the bit that was welded to the front bar. She had struggled for a moment when the frightening hunk of metal had forced its way through her lips but froze when her movements caused the iron to smash through her two front teeth. The compress tasted of corroded metal and manure, an additional surprise no doubt added by the awful men who were tasked with her incarceration. The spike on the underside of the metal bit dug into her tongue even when it was still, preventing her from swallowing, let alone eating or drinking. The shattered pieces of her teeth were sharp gravel in her mouth, and saliva pooled in her jowls and dripped over her chin, making her feel as dignified as a rabid dog.

Starving, dehydrated, and freezing, there would be no sleep for Janet that night. Knowing the end was nigh was some small comfort as she sat huddled against the stone wall.

Her husband's family home was purposefully erected next to the moorlands below the hills and had been so for generations past. Nobody else knew of the strange creature that resided behind the moors; they only knew of the dreaded misfortunes the village faced at certain points of the year when the moon was a crescent and the winds blew from the west, when its power grew enough to cause a certain amount of mischief. It was ancient, a spirit of pure sinful rage that could consume anything in its path. If it wasn't for the spells conducted at the cottage between it and the people, no man or beast could have lived there. They had sworn to protect in secret, spells cast and passed down through the ages, keeping a veil between the monster's world and their own.

Without Janet to continue the relentless protection rites, the beast would soon discover it was free to roam.

When the guards had shuffled away, she tried to speak, wondering if there was any chance she may be able to use her words to vanquish the beast if it appeared prior to her execution. Her tongue was forcibly pressed down into the deepest crevasse of her jaw, and when she tried to drag it to the side in an effort to evade the silencing method, the spike cut deep into the muscular flesh. Any sound she managed to utter was muffled and could not possibly be formed into a coherent word.

The village had doomed themselves with her silence.

Although true sleep had been impossible, Janet must have been in the midst of a semi-conscious stupor when the guards entered her chamber the next morning. She startled to, momentarily forgetting she was trapped in the branks. Sour saliva, thick through lack of water in her system, slopped from her parched lips. The urge to swallow overcame her, and her throat constricted painfully, muscles jumping deep in her gullet as her brain panicked, trying to complete what had been such a simple task for the previous thirty years. Stiff from being forced into the same unnatural position overnight, her jaw ached, burning deep in the hinges. Janet's tongue was torn and bloodied, the sharp spike under the bit feeling like a giant thorn in her open flesh.

Without bothering to speak, the guards hoisted Janet to her feet, forced a sack over her head, and pushed her out of the dungeon.

Some time later, she was thrown onto a cart, the mode of transportation made clear when it began to move. She could hear the horses' hooves on the track and was aware of the uneven surface of the road when she bounced against the hard wood, her bound hands preventing her from shielding her battered body.

Before long, the sound of a crowd filtered through the sack over her ears. The guards hauled her into a seated position so she might be seen by the spectators who had gathered. The baying grew louder, and she startled when something soft and wet exploded against her chest.

The scent of rotting onion wafted up into the burlap, and more items were thrown, pelting the sides of the cart. Few objects were a direct hit, thankfully, but those that made contact did so with stinging ferocity, leaving trails of rancid liquid dappling her cold skin.

Cringing at the increasing volume of the crowd, Janet knew they were coming to her final resting place. All too soon, the cart wheels crunched to a halt and the guards grabbed her under the armpits.

More rancid vegetables were thrown as she was hauled to the ground, her feet unable to gain purchase on the earth as she was half-dragged, half-carried to her fate.

Moments later, the bag was whipped from her head, the harsh burlap snagging the bridle and yanking it, sending the spike jerking sideways in the open flesh of her tongue. Her eyes swam with dizzy stars as she fought the urge to faint at the raw sting of pain in her already swollen mouth. Lyle Cornthwaite's face appeared through smudged sight, his head tilted to one side as he appraised her dishevelled appearance. Brogan, standing a few paces beyond his master, had the good decency to look shocked and somewhat sympathetic to her plight. Lyle twitched his moustache, evidently pleased.

"Tie her to the post!" he instructed.

The weight of the metal cage was excruciating. If it would have been possible, Janet would have let her head loll against her chest, but the torture device kept her neck in the perpetual agony of erection.

Rough hands forced her against a wooden post, and her bare feet were scratched by the hay and twigs that had been piled beneath it.

When she was bound tightly to the post, her captors moved away and the excited crowd fell into anticipatory silence. A cool breeze slipped through them, coming from the west.

Lyle began to put on a show for the witnesses, his words aimed at Janet but his back to her, his arms outstretched and punctuating every word with a flourish. "Janet Barbery, you have been convicted of the crime of devilry. The sentence of death at the stake has been allotted to you in a fair court of village peers after we were all witness to your witchcraft."

Janet's eyes scanned the crowds, searching for Thomas. Although her brother stood near the front, his expression unreadable, neither Gertrude nor Thomas appeared to be there. Janet hoped they had the decency to keep him away from her execution, and she dared to muse that Gertrude may have taken Thomas away to another town on a visit to relatives. If her protection spell had worked, there was every possibility that had happened.

While she was relieved Thomas may have been saved, Janet could not help but feel anger that her sister-in-law had also escaped the coming onslaught.

The creature was close. She could feel it. It would be drawn to the venomous hate of the crowd, as surely as a dog was drawn to a bone. Janet and the ancient beast had built something of a connection over the months, both enemies yet tied in the simple knowledge of what the other one was. That they existed together when nobody else knew the truth of either of them tied them somehow. It was a bond she would rather not have been forced to form, but it was a bond nonetheless. Shivering against the post, seeing the hatred in the eyes of people she had kept safe from the sacrifice of her duties, Janet seethed.

Brogan lit a torch and passed it to Lyle.

At the sight of the flame, a rumble went through the crowd.

Then came the first of the screams.

It began at the back, to the west of the baying curve of spectators. The first scream was shrill with terror, cutting off after a second, at which point more screams erupted. From where she stood tied to the post, Janet saw limbs fly, bodies ripped inside out and flung into the air like dandelion seeds being blown from the plant.

The monster was a black smudge of smoke, similar to the smog that poured from the torch held at Lyle Cornthwaite's side, his body frozen in fear as he watched the crowd fall. There was no escape. Before the thought of running entered the heads of the villagers, the black tendrils of the monster reached them, turned them inside out, ribs exploding through chests and tearing through clothing, thigh bones splintering through legs, and brains spilling from noses like soup. The creature was at full power without Janet there to stop it.

In a way, it was marvelous.

Lyle turned on her, terrified. "You have done this! What creature from the depths of Hell have you dredged?"

Janet, the scold's bridle clamping her swollen and infected tongue, could only scowl. *If I could just speak*, she thought, *I could have saved you all*.

Terror drawing all color from his face as Brogan's scream erupted behind him, Lyle struck out with the torch, hoping to vanquish Janet before the monster's rampage came to him. But just before flame met straw, he froze. Black slipped around his body, tendrils like algae wrapping around lakebed stones.

Janet watched in delight as bones exploded through flesh.

The torch tumbled from a bloodied and broken hand, igniting the straw.

Bracing herself for her torture to end, Janet thought of Thomas. *At least I have saved him*, she thought. Although he would never have gratitude for her sacrifice, he would not carry hatred toward her, and that would have to do.

But before the flames could touch her feet, the black was upon her. It rose up, its shadow cutting out the carnage of the village square. Blocking the flames and the smoke, the creature appeared to suspend time, keeping them both within a pocket of existence that no other creature was privy to.

It did not speak out loud, but she understood it.

These people turned on you, though you did nothing but nurture them.

In her head, she answered, not knowing if the monster

would know. "Yes."

Your sympathy has become rage.

"Yes."

And we are one.

Janet hesitated. For all of her adult life, her job had been to protect without anything in return. Through the agonies of illness or injury, her grief at being widowed, the days when she felt she could stay in bed and hide, she had to push on and perform her duties. It was her role, and she had always accepted it without qualm for the good of the people.

Her swollen tongue burned with a pain that could only have been matched by the flames of the pyre consuming her body. And yet she managed to speak to this being that now felt more kin than foe.

"We are one."

The ties that bound her hands suddenly loosened, and Janet hoped for one tantalising moment that the monster would remove the contraption around her head. Instead, the flames began to grow, coating her skin. She felt no pain.

She and the creature moved together, slinking back to the hills behind the marshland, the bond of rage a shackle that neither of them could break. With her tongue held tight by the contraption, there was no way for Janet to control or stifle the monster, and so it allowed her to roam with it, eternal companions.

They were seen on occasion, rumors told by rural shepherds or lost hikers on their way back to civilization over the years, the few witnesses who survived an encounter. The black creature that moved like smoke and the blazing woman, her head encased in a cage, a sigh of furious indignation the only sound coming with the winds from the west.

BLACK DEATH

Ali Jane Sweet

A CRISP WINTER WIND blows the dead leaves around the base of the lone oak tree standing guard at the entrance to the cave. Its imposing height suggests it has been there for eons. A faint golden glow emanates from the oak, whispering of magic.

Inside the cave, the crone hovers over her cast iron cauldron. It is her most prized possession, a tool that she uses for all types of spells, for mixing, cooking, heating. But now she uses it for its most important purpose—scrying. She peers into the water and watches as the thief decides whether or not to brave the thick woods surrounding her village.

The thief, unaware he's being watched, wades into the woods. The dense pine boughs mixed with bare oak and alder branches make it difficult passage. Their long limbs grab at his clothes, attempting to catch him, *snare* him. His feet snag on roots and become tangled in the underbrush. Branches whip his cheeks, and he raises his arms to protect his face from the sharp needles. He huffs heavily as he twists and turns, clawing his way blindly forward. His progress is slow, and he's unsure what lies on the other side of the thicket. But whatever it is, it can't be worse than what he leaves behind.

The forest encircles the village, keeping it hidden. The villagers are a self-sustaining community. Their fields lie dormant now that winter has settled in. The livestock are safely asleep in their sheds. The whole town lies sleeping, not just because it's night, but because they are under a protection spell.

The thief is unaware of the village's existence, knows not that it's under the protection of a powerful witch.

Dusk has fallen, and the greenery appears black in the encroaching darkness. He has made it halfway, though he does not know that, either.

How long has it been since I first stepped into these woods?

He's beginning to tire, when suddenly he's met with a resistance stronger than the boughs of the trees. Thinking he must have walked into a large oak, he lowers his arms and sees the nearest tree is more than a foot in front of him. Confused, he looks around. The forest has thinned here, the boughs no longer fighting each other for space. He extends his hands slowly in front of him until they hit something solid. But there's nothing there.

Nothing there that I can see, in any case.

He holds his hands out flat and pushes against the

invisible wall. His palms tingle through his gloves. He slides his hands back and forth across whatever is blocking his path.

As if put there by magic.

He draws his falchion. The sword quivers in his hand, and the jewels on the hilt glow a soft red. It was a gift from the sorcerer who raised him. He was taught how to properly wield tools of the craft with magical intent. He knows its capabilities are far greater than a mundane blade. He raises it above his head and whispers, "See me through, that I may see it through." Though he sees nothing in front of him, he feels the sword slicing...something. It is ethereal, invisible, yet it's there. Something...magical.

I hope this doesn't come back to haunt me.

It's a protection spell. He has read about them in his book and knows how to bypass them. But he has yet to come across one outside of his practice with the sorcerer. He senses that this one is strong.

He takes a deep breath and steps forward.

He keeps the blade pointed in front of him and pierces the magical barrier, then pushes himself forward. The blade sparks. He drops one shoulder and pushes hard with his hind leg.

The Crone gathers the last of what she needs and makes her way back to the cave. She still thinks of it as *the cave*, though she has lived there for more than a century. With fondness, she recalls her time here. She has been waiting for so long, preparing for *something*. The oak tree has kept her steady over the years, comforting her with its warm essence and reminding her that she will know what to do once the time comes.

That time is now.

She thinks back to the day in the forest when she was a young girl, out foraging for berries when she heard a whisper. It was faint at first. Unsure she had really heard anything but the wind, she dismissed it and continued picking her berries. As she moved deeper into the woods, she heard it again. That time it was stronger, clearer. A voice calling to her.

Gwendolyn...

The call of the oak tree.

If she had known all these years that *this* would be her objective, she would not have befriended the people of the town. But she realizes that if she had not done just that, the thief wouldn't be able to do what he needs to.

The thief is exhausted, unsure how much longer he can keep this up, when suddenly there is a loud *snap* and the resistance falls away, pitching him forward onto his face. He rolls over and lies on his back, looking up at the cloudy night sky. It's hard to breathe as the cold air fills his lungs, but he's also filled with a sense of accomplishment. He has successfully broken through the protection spell to the other side of the woods. He lies there until his breath becomes steady and he feels able to move again.

The clouds part in the sky above him, uncovering the full moon and allowing him to see. He is at the edge of a village, and if this one is like the one that came before, it will be littered with the dead—unlucky folks taken out by the plague. The Black Death.

A bitter wind, the kind only born on a December night such as this, snaps at the thief. He shudders against it, wrapping his woollen cloak tighter around himself. He peers into the village, looking for any signs of life. The only thing that moves is the wind and the leaves. All is silent and still.

He sheathes his sword, switching it out for the dagger required to complete his mission. He glides through the shadows, his back against the wall of the first stone house. He crouches by the entryway and takes a small bottle from his satchel. He drinks the glowing elixir, one of his own concoctions that allows him immunity to the disease that plagues the country. He pockets the empty bottle and, with a quick glance over his shoulder, slips inside.

He's light on his feet, a rogue well versed in stealth and deception. He thinks back again to the sorcerer who taught him how to move undetected, showed him how to be one with the shadows, to lean into the silence of night. And how those lessons had never been enough for the thief. He has always been hungry for more than simple healing and protection spells.

He is reminded of the first time he felt the power of magic flow through him. How he knew in that moment he was destined for something great. When he held the dagger, it filled his mind with endless possibilities, showing him the infinite extent of his abilities—the potency of his power. No one could keep him from his true purpose.

He moves across the floor like a wraith, advancing toward the man sleeping in the bed under the window. His weapon gleams in the moonlight cast through the window as he slides it across the lone sleeping man's throat. The man doesn't even twitch. His eyes remain closed as blood pours out of the wound and pools onto his chest.

That's odd, not even a flinch.

The thief sweeps the small room, pocketing the few coins he finds and grabbing a loaf of bread, the freshest he has found in days. The next house bestows him the same luck. He creeps in and swiftly and silently kills the man. He's on high alert, prepared for the man to jolt and shout, to wake the rest of his family. But he does no such thing.

Again, not a flinch.

The same goes for the man's wife and their two sleeping daughters. Their serene faces are angelic in the soft glow of the moon. Their bodies don't even tremble or shudder after he slays them. He collects fresh cheese and milk and puts it with the bread in his satchel. His lips turn upward in a sly smile as he moves on, violating every home in the sleeping village, one by one.

The crone walks slowly and with purpose to the church at the edge of the village. This is where the thief will end his reave. She climbs the steps, carrying her basket of supplies in her right hand, careful to keep it steady. Making her way up the center aisle, she lights the candles along the walls with a simple flick of her left index finger. The soft glow will allow her to see as she works.

Such a waste.

As she grinds the herbs and mushroom stalks with her mortar and pestle, she thinks of the kind and loving members of the church, how they welcomed her into their village and would visit her, asking for advice when the crops failed or for potions when sickness befell the population. They would also visit to bring her fresh milk and cheese, baked bread and freshly churned butter. She would brew tea and listen to the women of the village complain of their disobedient children. They, in turn, would listen to her sage advice, which always came from love and light.

"If the children feel safe with you, they will heed your words."

The children, too, adored the crone and visited often when free from their chores. They would crowd around her, sitting on the stone floor, listening raptly as she spun tales from the old world.

So, this relationship, fostered over the years, is the reason the villagers and their livestock now come to be frozen, safely shielded from the plague that has ravaged the country over the past four years. The pestilence which has caught England off guard, as it advances undeterred, ruinously, and without discrimination—noblemen and peasants alike fall victim to the Black Death.

She thinks of the clergymen and when they came to her with their fears three years before.

"It is coming. We have heard tell that it moves in our direction."

She had told them not to fear. She would protect the village and keep anyone from trespassing within. She assured them that once the plague was extinct, she would wake them.

A tear escapes as she thinks of these compassionate, good folks who have always trusted her to keep them safe, religious people of the church who fear their God but also understand the magic of the earth.

And now she must betray them.

She snuffs the candles out as easily as she lit them and waits.

The thief has come out of the last house, his satchel bulging. A second bag, procured from one of the houses, hangs over his other shoulder and is also stuffed with goods and trinkets. He tires now; the elixir has worn off.

The village church looms on the other side of a small field. Its hulking frame is ominous in the distance. Despite its foreboding exterior, he knows that churches are places of sanctuary, and he feels its call. He shivers in the frigid wind, hiking the heavy bag tighter over his shoulder, then makes his way across the frost-coated grass to seek shelter for the night.

The crone stands at the altar looking into her mortar at decades worth of preparation. She waits for the thief to enter. She wishes the village could have been spared, but this was divine providence. Just as it is the thief's fate to commit the sordid act of murdering those who lie innocent and sleeping in the village, it is hers to execute the consequence. It is a destiny written in a prophecy spun by The Fates themselves.

The front doors groan and a blast of icy air rushes up the aisle toward her.

He turns and pushes the doors closed, shivering against the wind that has followed him across the field and into the church. He stomps his boots and drops his bag, waiting for his eyes to adjust to the darkness.

Suddenly, the room is awash in light as the candles along the walls ignite. He is at once disoriented. He feels as though he has been here before. A long-forgotten memory itches at the back of his mind.

"Thief!"

An old woman is rushing down the center aisle, directly toward him. Instinctively drawing his dagger, he prepares to defend himself. Her irises blaze with violet fire and he's frozen in place. He tries to raise his weapon and step forward to meet her head on but is unable to move. It isn't fear keeping him immobile, no; he's under a spell. She stops but a foot in front of him, and her eyes bore into his soul. He is overcome by the feeling that she knows him, that he knows her. But he's sure he has never met this woman before.

He is stricken by fear as his hand suddenly moves of its own volition, guiding the knife to rest against his throat.

She chants something in a language he doesn't understand, something ancient, and then he feels the bite of the blade as it glides across his throat.

He is powerless as he watches his lifeblood dripping from the end of the dagger.

The witch holds out a golden chalice and collects it. Her face has changed. The fire in her eyes is gone, replaced with something else... Is that sorrow?

He watches the witch take the goblet back to the altar and pour its contents into a small bowl. His body is stone; he's unable to move even his eyes, and he can feel his energy fading.

He thinks back to the night he gained the sorcerer's power. As he was creeping along the hallway to his mentor's room, he was struck with a vision. It was so powerful he fell against the wall to steady himself. In the vision, he saw a witch killing him in a church. This witch, in this very church.

At the time, he had dismissed it as strong apprehension. He loved the sorcerer, who was like a father to him, but the thief knew if he wanted to reach his full potential, he would have to do so on his own. And he would need the dagger.

The thief had slipped into the sorcerer's room, and after removing the dagger from the cabinet it was always kept in, he had taken the sorcerer's life. He escaped the village, taking the sorcerer's dagger and book with him. That was the first time he had taken a life, and he felt the surge of power as the soul transferred into the blade. It was also the first time he stole something that was not his to take. But it quickly became a matter of course.

He watches as the witch flicks her hand at him, then he drops to the ground. He lies there as the last of his blood flows from his wound. He's too weak to even reach up and attempt to stop the flow. As his consciousness fades, his last thought is one of disbelief.

How is this to be my fate? I was supposed to do something great.

The crone finishes her incantation then releases the thief from her spell. She watches as he collapses to the floor, the life draining out of him. It seems such a squander, all these lives lost. It is beyond her how The Fates operate, and it is none of her concern. She will cast the spell that will cure England of the Black Death, a plague so great it has killed almost half the populace.

Once she is done, she gathers her belongings and leaves the church, flicking the candles out as she goes.

When she reaches the cave, she deposits her things on the table in the main cavern. She spins in a circle and sighs. She will miss this place, but her labor is finished.

She can now rest.

She exits the hollow in the rock and sits at the base of the ancient oak. She lies down, curling her knees up into her chest, and closes her eyes. The tree thrums and the bark at the base of the trunk cracks open. A golden glow illuminates her as she's pulled inside.

WEB OF TRUTHS

ELIZABETH DEVECCHI

I LOOKED AT MY watch—five minutes until class let out for the weekend. My fingers tapped against my jeans pocket, crinkling the folded paper tucked inside. My list. Places I wanted to see during the three week adventure the Art Department had organized. We were at the last stop, the most important one.

Professor Ganz looked around the room then set her notes on the desk and sighed. Most of the other students were chatting and already packing up their things. She had lost them. She looked at me, and I cinched one corner of my mouth and shrugged.

"Ok, looks like you are all ready to head out to bathe in the culture of this beautiful city. Don't forget to check out the Torre Civica at some point. Your tickets are in the packets I gave you on the bus. I look forward to seeing your sketches on Monday. Remember, pick a buddy, and if I text you, please text back. I get that you are all technically adults, but most of your parents beg to differ. And I would hate to lose any of you ... Well, *they* would hate to lose you." The corner of her mouth curled into a smirk, and a few malicious chuckles echoed through the room.

Professor Ganz raised a hand, waving it to redirect attention back to the front of the room.

I tucked my notebook and pen into my backpack.

"Remember, I'm going on a walking tour at two. Meet me in the hotel lobby if you want to tag along."

"Right," someone mumbled with a voice dripping in sarcasm.

I knew where my classmates were heading. I heard whispered bits of the plan all morning. They—and I was fairly certain that *they* included most if not all of the rest of the class—were heading into the city for the weekend to party. One of them, Robert, had a family villa there.

I had been invited but declined. I wasn't there to party. I could party back in Massachusetts. I was there to learn, to explore. From the moment I found out about the trip, I knew I had to come. And I worked my butt off to raise the money, taking extra shifts at the restaurant then pulling all-nighters to get my homework done.

"I'm so proud," my mom had said, brushing my cheek with the back of her hand. "So proud of you."

"You will see where our family comes from," added Nonna Gina, her ever-piercing stare softening just a bit.

Mom had picked up the pamphlet about the trip and pointed to the page describing the very place the tour was at now: Cuneo, Italy.

"Here. Right, Mamma?" she said, pointing to the last stop on the tour. The one I was at.

Nonna Gina's eyes had drifted upward, taken on a blurry, dreamy film. "Close by. In a little town close by."

She had wandered to the fireplace mantel, removed a frame, and brought it to us. "Here," she said, pointing to the yellowing image behind the glass. It was an image of her grandmother standing in front of the Town Hall of Rifreddo.

"Change your mind?" The deep syrupy voice snapped me back to the classroom, or perhaps it was the blast of a freshly chewed breath mint assaulting my sinuses.

I slid out of my seat and took a step back, regaining the personal space Robert invaded. He winked, shooting me a smile that would have made the Cheshire Cat blush.

"No, thank you. I have my own plans," I said, not disguising my disdain. Subtlety might leave him thinking he had a chance.

"What plans could be better than camping out in an actual villa overlooking Turin and partying all weekend ..." Robert slid an arm around my waist and pulled me closer. He leaned in, positioning his lips just above my ear, "...with *me*." He was obviously not used to being rejected. I could honestly not understand why he kept bothering me, unless in his warped mind he was trying to live out some sort of rich boy/ poor girl trope. No thank you.

I shimmied and ducked under his arm then walked toward Professor Ganz, who had been quietly observing the interaction from her podium while she shuffled papers and stuffed them into her satchel.

"Hey there, Katerina," she said, projecting her voice, a sort of wall to keep Robert at bay. When I was closer she whispered, "If he's still bothering you, I will gladly intervene."

I shook my head. I could handle a blowhard like Robert. Besides, Robert liked to brag about his family being the main source of funds for the College of Fine Arts at the university. I didn't want to get Professor Ganz into trouble.

"I'm good," I said.

"Are you coming along on the tour after lunch?" she asked, fastening the buckle on the worn leather satchel.

I shook my head again. "I'm going to do some shopping, pick up some gifts for my mother and grandmother, and explore. There's a small town called Rifreddo that I want to visit."

"That's not too far from here. It's about a forty-five minute taxi ride," she said. "There's actually a festival going on there now. *Le Notti Delle Streghe*, The Nights of the Witches. I went during last year's trip."

"That sounds cool, but I'm mostly going because my mom's family supposedly comes from there, or somewhere near there." I pulled out my phone and showed her the picture I had snapped of the photo of my great-great-grandmother.

"A descendant of one of the famous *masche*, perhaps?" She winked.

"The *what*?" I asked, scrunching the bridge of my nose.

"The *masche*. A secret society of witches. Hunted, tortured, put through bogus trials during the Dark Ages. There was a famous trial in Rifreddo, at the monastery. A big part of the festival takes place in its ruins. It's kind of touristy now, a big party of sorts. But the history behind it is fascinating."

"So kind of like Salem?"

"Somewhat, though the *masche* were around hundreds of years before the town of Salem even existed. Strong women have been vilified throughout the centuries, sadly." She sighed and shrugged, then tipped her head and looked at me over the rim of her glasses. "Who is your buddy for this excursion of yours? Remember, there is safety in numbers."

"I'm going to sign up for a walking tour of the town right when I get there," I said. "I'll probably only be there for a couple hours. Then I'll head back."

I pictured gears spinning in her head as she mulled this over, knuckles flashing white as she tightened and loosened her grip on the handle of her satchel. Then she set a hand on my shoulder.

"Come with me. I think I may have a solution. Let's grab an espresso at the cafe."

Great, I thought, chewing the inside of my cheek. She was probably going to try to pair me with one of the other students, maybe one of the younger ones who would feel obligated to go and secretly hate me for making them miss a party with upperclassman in an Italian villa.

We walked toward Robert, who was lingering near the exit. He reached out and squeezed my ass as we passed, and I shot him a side-eye loaded with knives. He sauntered away, a satisfied grin pocking his face.

"You know," said Professor Ganz as we walked along the sidewalk, "the monastery in Rifreddo would be a wonderful subject for your weekend sketches. An eerie combination of ruins and local vegetation."

This lightened my mood, and not only because the statement assumed I would, in fact, be heading to Rifreddo. It sounded like something I wanted to capture on my sketch pad.

"You should get there well before the ceremony kicks off, though, so there aren't quite so many tourists."

I nodded, once again grateful I was able to come on the trip and grateful my academic path had led me to Professor Ganz. She helped me secure the meager travel scholarship that not only made up for the funds I was unable to raise, but left me with some spending money on top to buy souvenirs and participate in the extras that interested me. She was my favorite art prof, hands down. She had welcomed me into her drawing class though I knew absolutely nothing about art. My major was in botany.

"The next Maria Sibylla Merian. Or perhaps a Jeanne Baret," she had said when she found out. "Though *you* won't have to pretend you're a man to explore the world."

"*Eccoci*," she said when we arrived at the cafe. "Here we are."

Instead of heading to the counter to order, she veered to a table just outside the establishment, where one of our tour bus drivers, Paolo, was sipping a cappuccino and reading a book.

Paolo was the son half of the father/son driving team chauffeuring us around the continent. Unlike his father, who loved to spend his driving time chatting over the loudspeaker, Paolo preferred to surrender the mic to Professor Ganz or his dad during his shifts.

I had barely heard his voice and only spoken with him once, when I needed to get some motion sickness meds from the bag stored under the bus. He had very kindly pulled the bus over and helped me to retrieve it. His English, like his father's, was impeccable.

"*Ciao, Paolo. Come va? Hai ancora piani di andare a Saluzzo oggi? Hai mica spazzio per un passeggero?*" Professor Ganz smiled at me. "Are you still heading to Saluzzo today? Any room for a passenger?" she translated, in case my limited Italian wasn't up to par. I had understood the gist of what was said but was grateful for the consideration.

Paolo lifted his head. He looked from the professor to me. Then he closed his book, sliding a receipt in between the pages to keep his place, and motioned to the two empty seats on the other side of the table.

"Please," he said, "have a coffee with me."

Professor Ganz pulled out one of the empty chairs and gave the back of my shoulder a pat. "Have a seat. I'll get us some cappuccinos." She headed into the cafe.

"So," said Paolo, taking a sip of his coffee while sizing me up. "You want to see Saluzzo?"

"I'm actually heading to Rifreddo," I said after pausing to decide if I wanted to attempt some Italian. "My mother's family comes from there and I wanted to explore. I guess there's a bus that runs from Saluzzo to Rifreddo?" Professor Ganz had said as much on the way over. "But I can take a taxi if I need to." I didn't want him to feel obligated on his weekend off.

The professor arrived at the table with three cappuccinos and set them down. "A refill for you, my friend," she said, sliding one of the cups toward Paolo.

"Or," said Paolo, finishing off his first cup and pushing it aside in favor of the new one, "perhaps a little bribe?"

A sudden blush burned in my cheeks.

"*Scherzo*," he said. "I joke, of course."

I relaxed and picked up my coffee, sipping at it to distract from my embarrassment.

"I would be happy to give Ms. Katerina a ride. I need to drop off some things for my mother in Saluzzo, then I can bring her to Rifreddo. It is very close."

"Are you sure?" I felt bad about imposing on his family time when their business probably kept him and his father away from home for such long periods of time.

"Really, it's no problem at all." He looked at the professor and gave her a nod. "I can bring her back safe and sound when she is done exploring too."

We finished our coffees, and Professor Ganz pushed up her sleeve to peek at her watch. "Well, I need to get going. I can't be late for my tour. I've been promised access to parts of the Town Hall that are generally closed to the public." She stood and pointed in my direction. "Have a wonderful time exploring, and say hello to the dark forces for me." Then she turned to Paolo. "*Grazie mille*! Tell your mom I said hello."

"Ok," said Paolo standing and stretching. I helped him gather up our cups and saucers, and we brought them to the counter inside. "*Mia zia*, my aunt, she owns this place. I will be in very hot water, as you say, if I don't clean up." He winked as we set the dishes down.

"What time would you like to leave?" he asked when we were back outside.

"Whenever is good for you. I just have to grab my pad and more pencils."

"How about we meet here in ten minutes. Does this work? We stop in Saluzzo for a minute, then on to Rifreddo."

I nodded and headed for the hotel to get my stuff.

The ride to Saluzzo was pleasant, if a bit awkward at first. I hadn't realized Paolo was so close to my age. And we had more in common than I expected. He liked a lot of the same bands I did, and I knew he wasn't just saying so, because he not only nodded when I named a band but would then proceed to name his favorite albums and tracks. The drive took a little over half an hour, and by the time we got there, I had a new appreciation for the man who had been driving our tour bus half the time.

When we pulled into the driveway of his home, I said I would wait in the car. I didn't want to intrude.

"Nonsense," he said, waving for me to follow. "My

mother will want to meet you. She is an artist too. This is how she knows Professor Ganz, how we got this job. Here, it is all about *conoscenze*, who you know."

We walked up a cobblestone path to the front door of Paolo's home, a two-story villa of beige stucco, topped with a traditional terracotta roof.

"We will climb to the second floor," he said, opening the door. "The lower floor is the home of my grandmother."

I followed him up the marble stairs, each step spawning a hollow echo. Past the first door to the second. He pointed up to where the stairs continued. "My house," he explained. "The attic."

He knocked three times, then opened the door. "Mamma," he called. "*Abbiamo un ospite*. We have a guest, one of Professor Ganz's best students, Katerina." He grinned at me over his shoulder. I shook my head.

"Welcome, welcome," said an energetic woman who looked to be about the age of my mom, but half her height. She bustled out of a side room and gestured at us to follow her into the living room, just off the foyer. "Come. Sit." She gave a deep-red loveseat a pat on the way by and instructed Paolo to fetch us all some coffee. "Oh, you have the medication for Nonna?" she asked as he made his way to the kitchen.

"*Sì, Mamma*," he answered, giving his pocket a pat.

"You leave them on the table, please. In the center or Romeo will knock them down." She turned to me. "Romeo is our cat. He is a pest."

I smiled, not quite sure what to say. Should I ask about the cat? About the grandmother? I wasn't good at making small talk with strangers, never mind the cultural divide.

"You will stay for lunch. We have plenty. My mother will be up soon, and we can all sit to eat. She doesn't speak much English, but Paolo and I can translate."

Paolo appeared, holding a tray topped with three steaming espresso cups, a tiny container of milk, and a bowl of sugar. He set the tray down and placed two tiny spoons beside the sugar. "*La devo portare a Rifreddo, Mamma,*" he said, explaining the plan.

"Oh, you are going to the Nights of the Witches? Very nice."

The front door opened, and a sullen-looking older woman with a cane wandered in, squinting then adjusting her glasses when she noticed me on the sofa. She looked at the other two occupants of the room with lifted brows as if waiting for an explanation.

Paolo's mother rose and walked to her. "Mamma, *questa è una studentessa della Professoressa Ganz. Si chiama Katerina,*" she said, explaining who I was.

The elderly woman sized me up and gave a singular nod.

I stood and extended a hand, which she promptly took, holding it clasped tightly in hers while she gave me another once over with hawk-like eyes.

"*Paolo porta Katerina alla festa a Rifreddo, Mamma,*" said Paolo's mother, telling her I was going to the festival in Rifreddo.

"I actually just found out about the festival today," I said, flashing a meek smile. "I want to see Rifreddo because my mother's family comes from there."

"Ah, wonderful! It is important to study one's origins," Paolo's mother said, smiling. "*Hai sentito, Mamma? La famiglia ...*"

"I am understanding," the elderly woman said, her English hesitant but clear. She was still holding my hand. The strength of her grip and the force of her eyes as they continued to take me in was a bit concerning.

"Nonna," said Paolo with a gentle chuckle, "*basta. La spaventi.*" (Enough. You will scare her.)

His grandmother smiled at me, released my hand, and waved him away. "The name of your family?" she asked.

I reached into my pocket and pulled out a small piece of paper, folded into a tight square. I smoothed it and handed it to her.

"Borella," she whispered, turning the *r* over on her tongue with a pleasant half-trill. She looked up at me, lifting a brow. "One *air*?" she asked.

It took me a second to understand what she meant. "Oh, *r*," I said, nodding. "My mother said that an *r* may have been dropped when the family left Italy during WWII."

I looked to Paolo, waiting for him to translate, but it wasn't necessary. I wasn't surprised. So far, every time an Italian had told me they didn't speak much English, their proficiency had far out-paced my Italian. When *I* told people I didn't speak much Italian, I meant it.

"Hmmm," she said, her voice soft like the purr of a cat. "The families, *come foglie al vento*."

"Leaves in the wind," Paolo whispered next to me.

"Yes, Mamma," said his mother with a slight roll of her eyes her mother did not catch. "The world is big, and we Italian women make it better by flying to every corner." She laughed at the smirk that dimpled my cheeks. My Nonna was always saying things like that.

"Come," said Paolo's mom. "We sit and eat."

I looked at Paolo, hoping he would remember I needed to get to Rifreddo early so I could draw the ruins before the crowds arrived for the ceremony. Italian meals at any time of the day tended to involve multiple courses and hours, and I didn't want to be rude. He gave a reassuring nod.

"Mamma," he said, smiling and looping an arm through hers. "We really need to go. Katerina should get there before the afternoon crowds. I am certain that

Professor Ganz has given her drawing homework for the weekend. Too many bodies spoil the view."

His mother gave his arm a squeeze, pulling him closer. "Then, my son, we will go prepare some sandwiches for the trip. Katerina, sit and wait with Nonna." She winked at me and pulled him to the kitchen, not giving any time for resistance.

I looked over at Nonna, who was already seated in one of the armchairs. Her eyes were closed, and for a moment, I thought she had dozed off, that way elderly people often do.

"Sit," she said, giving me a start. She reached out a spindly arm of crepe-paper skin and patted the chair next to her. Her eyes remained closed.

I walked over, and the moment I was seated, she opened her eyes and turned to me.

"Your family is strong and dutiful," she said, an odd grin on her face.

My shoulders and brows lifted in tandem. I had no idea what that was supposed to mean.

She didn't seem to mind, nodding at me with a broad, confident smile. Then she reached out and set her hand on mine, her expression sliding from confident to curious. "You come here alone?" she asked, her free hand drifting up to scratch a spot just above her ear.

"Ummm," I said, my gaze roaming as if to find the answer she wanted somewhere in the room. "I mean, I'm here with a group of students. But they aren't *here* with me. Professor Ganz said there are interesting plants to sketch, to draw. I'm studying botany."

Again, Nonna nodded. This time her brows furrowed deeply against the top of her eye sockets, pushing her gaze to a squint.

"Mmmm," she hummed. "*Botanica*. You know the magic of plants."

I shifted on the chair, a little unnerved by this woman who seemed to be conversing on a different level, one to which I was not privy. My eyes turned toward the entry to the kitchen, where I could hear the muffled voices of Paolo and his mother. I sent desperate, silent prayers into the air for them to hurry.

"No worry, Kat," Paolo's grandmother said, catching my attention. Nobody called me Kat except for my own grandmother; my mom thought it sounded trite. "You are not here alone. Not really. We are, how you say, a web? Connected."

"A network," was all I could think she might mean.

"*Ecco i panini*, the sandwiches have arrived." I jolted upright in my seat as Paolo's mother strode into the room, one hand raised like a ringmaster waving on a parade.

Paolo followed close behind, holding a tray stacked high with Italian rolls packed with a variety of meats, vegetables, and cheeses. I wondered if maybe she, too, thought the rest of the students were waiting outside.

"You pick the ones you want, Katerina. The rest I give to Paolo's sister for her children. They eat like ..." She paused and looked back at Paolo, who shrugged. "*Ooo, come si chiamano*. What is the name? The ones that look like the hoppers."

"Locusts?" I asked, heat rushing to my cheeks at the sudden thought it might be rude to call someone's grandchildren locusts.

"Yes! The locusts! *Brava*, Katerina." She gave a satisfied nod. "You pick what you want, the rest go to the locusts."

A relieved smile graced my lips, and I thanked her for her trouble. I picked out a couple sandwiches, and Paolo did the same. Then I thanked his family again and we headed for the door. Just as Paolo took hold of the handle, his grandmother called out.

"No worry, Kat. You are not alone." She waved and closed her eyes, sinking back into her seat.

"You really made an impression on my mother and grandmother," said Paolo on the drive to Rifreddo. "We may just have to adopt you." He laughed at my awkward grin. "I hope my grandmother didn't spook you too much. She gets spookier every year. My mother says that when we approach the other side, we begin to speak the language."

"Is she very sick?" I remembered the medicine he was dropping off, the reason for the stop.

"Yes. But she is a tank, my *nonna*. Don't worry." It sounded like he was saying this more to himself than to me.

When we arrived in Rifreddo, Paolo found a place to pull the car over and proposed a quick picnic in the car.

"This way you do not have to carry the sandwiches around and you have a warm place to eat. Then, I *get out of your hair* and you explore." He sure did love using English expressions and continued to pepper them in anywhere he could while we ate.

When we finished, I picked up my backpack and he waved me on my way, pointing to the road that led to the ruins.

"Text me when you need a ride back," he called as he drove away.

Rifreddo was a checkerboard of the present and the past. Freshly built villas with their pristine walls of stone and stucco alternated with the crumbling walls of long abandoned homes. The new outnumbered the old as I strode farther from the town's center. Neatly groomed lawns drew the eye from the exposed layers of the neglected walls of another time.

Evidence of the festival at hand abounded. The streets bustled with activity. Guides dressed all in black, their faces covered by black screens attached to their hoods, led groups of tourists through town. People popped in and out of the little shops that lined the streets, paper sacks gripped in their fists.

Many had dressed for the occasion, and I had to smile each time a small verdant witch *alla* Wicked Witch of the West scurried by. But the costumes which most impressed me were those tending toward authenticity, featuring long tunics, puffy sleeves and pant legs, funny hats of all shapes and sizes. Some among them were more serious than others in their portrayal of the gloomy times we called the Dark Ages.

Another thing that surprised and impressed me was the number of owls—live owls upon wooden perches or gripping the gloved arms of their handlers. So many different shapes and sizes of the raptors. Owls, the gods of darkness.

I found myself wondering what the streets looked like on normal days. Was the town always filled with shoppers, families living out their lives in fairytale fashion? Meeting in the square for coffee, stopping at the bakery each morning for bread and a dose of town gossip? A warmth filled me despite the chilly fall air. I imagined my ancestors walking these roads in darker times and felt a pull, a sense of belonging I had not yet experienced, not at school, not even at home.

A man passed, sending a shiver through me like static when his arm bumped mine. I turned to apologize, but something about his cold, probing eyes choked the attempt. He tipped his head slightly and moved on, his inquisitor robes flaring in the breeze.

Right behind him, a joyous group of women danced up the street in their colorful tunics. Each wore a pointy black hat atop her head. They held trays of large red plastic cups. One made eye contact with me and rushed over.

"*Americana?*" she asked, giggling. "I am right, yes?" Her friends followed close behind.

"God, is it *that* obvious?" I asked, looking down to see what had given me away.

"Is the clothes," she said.

"And the look!" one of her friends blurted, grinning.

"You have fun?" the woman who had first noticed me asked. "You are come to the party tonight, yes?"

"Oh," I said, "thank you. But I am here to draw the ruins. I'm an art student." I swung my backpack around and unzipped the top to show a large sketch book and a case of pencils. "It's my homework, my *compito*."

The girl glanced back at her friends, pointing to my bag and nodding. "We meet a famous artist," she said, but not in a mocking way. "Here, you take this with you. Is good medicine for art." She winked and handed me one of the cups. "*Cin cin!* Cheers!" they all called out, raising their cups.

I raised my cup to theirs and took a sip, ignoring the valid fear of open beverages implanted by my mother. This felt different. My new friends gave me a pat on the back and took off toward the next unsuspecting tourist.

I continued on my way, enjoying the barley flavor tinged with something fruity as I walked. I allowed the festive atmosphere to sweep me along, lighten my steps as I advanced. By the time I reached the ruins, I was wearing a permanent grin.

I decided on a portion of the ruins away from the main façade and the tourists admiring it and sat on a stone wall. Professor Ganz had been right—the tangle of weeds reaching up to trap the crumbling ruins, climbing around and through them, created a sense of drama that mere stone alone could not have managed. I took out my supplies and began to sketch, letting the scene flow through my hand and onto the page.

"Need a refill, babe?"

I looked up from my work, grimacing at the sound of the familiar, annoying voice. Robert's voice.

"What?" he asked with an innocence we both knew to be fake. "I heard you were coming here, and it sounded cool. And damn if you didn't find your own fun little party." He raised a plastic cup toward me, sloshing a small wave of beer over the side. "What say we hit the dance floor they have set up downtown, do a little grinding?"

I sighed, tucking my sketchbook and pencils into my bag. Then I stood and swung the backpack onto my shoulder. "I'm not sure how I can be any more obvious, Robert. I am *not* interested."

He took a step, closing the distance between us. He lifted his cup and downed the rest of his beer with a gulp. A creepy smile spread across his face like oil through water.

"Come on, Katerina." His warm breath pushed waves of hops at me. "I'm tired of your little games. I know you want it as much as I do." He dropped his cup and reached out to brush my chin with the back of his index finger.

I pulled my head away, my pulse quickening when I realized he had maneuvered me into one of the remaining walls of the monastery. He pressed closer, trapping my legs between his, and leaned in.

"It's cool to play hard to get, but don't be an outright tease." He reached around and gave my butt a squeeze, drawing me against him.

Bile rose in my throat as I lifted my hands to push him back, but he anticipated the move. Grabbing my wrists, he moved his head forward to attempt a sloppy, beer-infused kiss.

"Fuck off, Robert" I hissed, bringing a knee swiftly into his groin.

He bent forward, sucking in a gulp of cool, crisp air through his crooked scowl, his body still blocking my path. When he was finally able to focus his glare on me, he snickered and straightened, but not fully. Pushing against me again, this time with much more force, he jammed his knees between mine. I looked around, hoping to make eye contact with someone exploring the ruins, remembering to my horror that the location I chose was tucked behind the area marked for the tours. I opened my mouth to scream, but he forced his over mine, choking me with a wave of beer-flavored spit.

"Nobody likes a tease," he said, sliding against me, enjoying the control he thought he had over me.

He reached down to unfasten the top of my jeans, but I took advantage to swing my hand up and slapped him as hard as I could with one hand while shoving with the other. Then I dropped to the ground and crawled away. "I said fuck off!"

He looked over at me, rage bright in his eyes. I turned to run but was grabbed by two masked figures dressed as inquisitors.

"Thank god," I said, letting them straighten me. "This man, *quest'uomo*. This man won't leave me alone," I finished, hoping they understood.

"Who the fuck are you talking to?" asked Robert, his face contorted.

I furrowed my brow, opening my mouth to ask if he was blind, when I felt a yank backward. The world went dark, launching me into a nightmare of screams and pleas.

No! screamed a woman's voice from somewhere nearby. *No, I did not sleep with the Devil.*

No, I am not his vessel, yelled another.

I will not confess. I have done nothing wrong, cried yet another.

Weeping filled my head, and cold fingers of darkness spread inside me.

When I was finally able to open my eyes, to focus on my surroundings, a horrifying scene greeted me. Three women lay naked on the floor, bleeding. Their arms were tied behind them at the wrists and fastened to a sort of pulley.

"I didn't sign up to participate in a reenactment," I yelled, trying to make sense of it all. A thin, shadowy figure sat behind a desk just beyond the pale dancing light cast by candles lining the floor.

I whimpered and stumbled backward as three hooded figures approached.

"Child," said one of the forms as they pushed back their hoods to reveal their silver-white faces and long black hair. They were women. "You have nothing to fear with us. You have done your duty."

Your family is dutiful. The words of Paolo's grandmother floated through my mind.

The women drifted over to tend to the battered women on the ground, untying wrists, bandaging wounds, providing fresh tunics. When they were helped to their feet, the injured women smiled at me and bowed their heads in nods. I smiled back, uncertain of what was happening but warmed by the tender scene.

Then their faces turned dark as their eyes drifted, turning their attention to something behind me. Someone. I spun around to see two hooded figures dragging Robert into the cold stone room of the monastery as it had been. He was stripped naked, scratches running down his arms and legs. He was growling, cursing at his captors, calling them bitches and sluts.

The figure behind the desk stood, the candles illuminating her graceful features. A sly smile crept across her lips as she examined me.

"Like flies to honey," she said with a laugh. "They have scattered their hateful seed throughout the world. But so, too, has our web spread. And vengeance has no expiration."

"Katerina?"

I opened my eyes, narrowing them against the biting bright light of the sun.

Paolo was standing above me, a worried look etched onto his face. "Everything ok? I got home and saw you left this in the car."

I blinked hard, focusing on the pencil case in his hand. My spares. Before I could answer, he reached down and picked up my sketch book, which lay open on the wall next to me. I watched him follow the flow of my pencil strokes, his brow smoothing, eyes softening. The hint of a smile brushed his lips, widening when his gaze turned to mine.

"This," he said, turning the pad toward me, "is beautiful."

I regarded my sketch of the monastery ruins. The original façade of the building acted as a backdrop to a tangled web of vines, their forms suggesting that of three women holding hands.

THE WITCH AND THE SERPENT

Lisa Vasquez

Constitution Criminalis Carolina deemed acts as heinous as murder, manslaughter, arson, and witchcraft were to be executed with fire, laying the foundation for mass witch trials between 1580 and 1680.

FIRES OF FATE

APRIL 1602

Clara stood, staring out at the crowd around her. Hate filled their eyes as regretful tears filled hers. Her gaze landed on the only face who mattered in the sea of vitriol, her father.

Harold's face was filled with shame. Her father

appeared to have aged as he shook his head. Humiliation was heavy on his brow. Harold lowered his chin in defeat, his head resting on his chest between his slumped shoulders.

He could no longer look at his daughter, whom he once revered on his knee at night. He recalled brighter days of teaching Clara about plants and their medicinal properties. Harold was once the village Apotheker; his knowledge of herbalism and remedies was unmatched.

And now? Because of *her*, he was a pariah. Dispossessed from the favor he once held.

I should've known better than to think a woman could handle the knowledge of a man, he thought to himself. *I was stupid to think it might enrich her.*

Harold sneered as he stared at the ground. He might have been ordered to be there for his daughter's punishment, but he would not ever set eyes on her again. If he could, he would wipe her image from his mind.

Behind her father, a cloaked figure slithered in the sea of bodies until it disappeared. Clara's eyes caught movement as the body crawled on the ground unnoticed as if it was invisible. The figure curled within the cloak before it shifted form. A serpent, black as night, was now coiled around a boy's feet in the front row.

Clara expected to see its presence. She actively searched for it while she was being tethered to the post. It was there in the beginning, tempting her with promises of fulfilling all of her wishes, and it stayed with her until the end, when it all fell apart.

Because of her relationship with the *Serpent*—one of Morrigan's forms—Death would come collect her soul today.

As she stood on the platform, alone and frozen, Clara closed her eyes as if testing the reality of the moment. When she opened them again, everything was still there—the smell of shit and rotten vegetation thrown at her by the people she once called neighbors and friends. The remnants of both clung to her nightdress, made of hemp to burn faster.

Food was too expensive, she thought. *They wouldn't waste it by throwing it on a woman who was accused of murder.*

"Murderess! Harlot! Witch!" a woman cried from somewhere in the crowd.

From behind, another woman cursed Clara's name, shaking her fist as if to exorcise some demon. Beside her, a young girl—no more than twelve—spat on the ground before her mother's arm pulled her close. They were all complicit in their judgment, each one a knot in the noose woven from the village's fear.

Clara's chest tightened; her breath hitched as she pressed her lips together. She held back sobs which threatened to escape. She blinked rapidly, the gesture blurring her vision until the sea of angry faces dissolved, replaced by sunlit memories of her father's garden.

They were far below her as her thoughts drifted. While the crowd's jeers grew louder, dripping in its venom and loathing, a boy broke through the line. He ran up to the platform, where Clara was shivering with her eyes squeezed tight.

"Let's see if she's got a third tit!" the boy shouted out. No older than thirteen, he spread his lips in a malignant smile and drank in the condemned woman's figure with his adolescent eyes.

"Go on, Tom," his father belted out in laughter. "Don't be shy, lad. Check for that Devil's tit!"

Encouraged by his father, Tom did as he was told. He thrust his dirty, cold hand forward and grasped Clara's left breast. His claw-like grip was like a vice as he squished her flesh between his fingers.

"Get outta here, dog!" One of the guards gripped the boy by the back of his coat and tossed him off the platform to the ground. The wiry teen rolled in the mud until he came to rest before his father's feet. The crowd erupted in laughter.

Embarrassed and angry, Tom threw his finger toward Clara and shouted, "I felt it! A third tit! She's a witch!"

The crowd took in a collective gasp and stepped back in unison, like roaches in the light.

Clara's tears were hot on her cheeks and left trails of salt down to her chin. She continued to travel in her mind to the days of innocence. The stench of the breath of the guard winding the rope around her legs faded into the background, lost on the wind that began to grow stronger around them. She could no longer feel the logs stacked around her feet and up to her calves.

Clara's mind immersed in the memory. She was back in the garden, her bare feet and toes sinking deep into the rich earth of Papa's garden. There she watched him as he tended to fresh oregano. In his hand was a small notebook where he wrote notes; any plant she could ever find was documented in it.

There, the scent of death could not reach her. She was no longer freezing. Clara's skin was warm under the summer sun. Her long reddish-blonde hair blew freely in the breeze like wheatgrass, and her white dress was clean. In the world she transcended to, Clara looked down at the elegant pattern of roses her mother hand-sewed along the hem. Stretching her fingers out, Clara's nails were long and clean, not broken and black with mud and dried blood.

"Clara."

A voice penetrated the meditation. It floated along the breeze with a soft caress of her skin. She could feel it like a lover tucking a lock of hair behind her ear.

"Clarrraaaa," it whispered again. Heated breath against her earlobe caused her to flinch and tighten her eyes in protest.

No, she thought and shook her head. *I will not come back.*

"You mussst come back," the voice said. It was detached from any physical form. Instead, it hung on the space between her ear and her shoulder. She could feel the sensation of slithering around her neck.

It was the Serpent. It was there with her in her final moments. It was the entity who gave her power. It gave her the love of a King. And her ultimate demise.

She reached too far, bit too much from the sinful apple in the Garden of Eden.

The Serpent's voice twisted around her thoughts like a tightening vine. She fought back, pushing against the heavy weight of the past.

Clara let out a sob and fluttered her eyes open.

The faces of the villagers were all pale and stoic. Black holes replaced their eyes, and their mouths were open caverns, like the opening of dark wells. Tendrils of ink-colored strands stretched out where tongues once wagged with blasphemous rumors.

A scream lodged in her throat.

Clara tipped her head back until she looked at the sky. Storm clouds rolled in. The smell of oak and ash kindling mixed with tallow and peat filled her nose, but oxygen could not reach her aching lungs.

I cannot breathe! her mind cried out in panic.

"You must breathe," the whisper said.

With a sharp inhale, Clara gulped air past the tightness closing around her throat like a chokehold. Guards wove their way through the demonic-looking audience whose eyeless gazes remained fixated on her. In their hands were torches meant to set her on fire and send her soul to Hell. The smoke and soot of her incinerated body would rise toward Heaven, allowing her to get so close before being pulled back to Earth.

Clara's remains would spread across the soil, bury itself in unconsecrated, barren land, only to crawl into Hell, where they condemned her.

MY CUP RUNNETH OVER
Let her meet her Master in his Kingdom of Hell!

The priest's words filled the court on the day of her trial. Then, like now, she was clad only in a thin, filth-worn nightdress. The guards were ordered to scrape her hair off; patches of scabs and wounds where their dull blades ripped at her scalp were wet with infection. She could smell the rot setting in. So could the rats which visited every night. Their tiny claws and sharp teeth took their share before scuttling into shadowed corners of her prison cell.

In the pitch-dark, the Serpent was there. It crawled out onto its slick belly until she could see it appear in front of her. The Serpent's oily scales would shimmer like onyx under the moonlight filtering in through the window of her cell. With the night came its frozen breath of freezing air on her shivering body.

"You brought this to me," she cried through chattering teeth.

"I brought you everything you asked for," the Serpent whispered.

"This?" Clara shrieked. "Why would I ask for this?"

"I promised you you would get what you asked for, but you forgot the consequence. What you put into the universe, it will deliver back to you."

"I never asked the universe for exile and shame."

"You did not put out anything to sow good, Clarrrra." The Serpent trilled its tongue over her name with its

exotic, otherworldly accent. "You took, but did you ever think about returning?"

Clara woke with a start. The dreams were growing more vivid every night. Beside her, Charles sat up and put his hand on her cheek.

"Clara?" Charles's hand on her cheek pulled her back from the precipice of her dreams, but the haunting images lingered in the corners of her mind, like shadows too stubborn to fade.

"I'm sorry, my love," she whispered, and put her hand over his before she turned to kiss the center of his palm. The heat met with her lips, and she savored the warmth of his touch. "It was a nightmare."

"That's the third one this week, Clara." Charles's brows knit together in concern. "Let me call the physician for a tonic."

Before Clara could protest, Charles rolled out of the bed, and his chamberlain was on his feet as if he never knew sleep.

"Your Highness." The chamberlain's voice remained low.

"Fetch a sleeping tonic from my physician," Charles commanded. When the young man exited, Charles returned with another blanket, made from soft mink. "You're shivering," he said as he placed it over her. "I will add another log to the fire."

Clara's teeth chattered, and she realized he was right. She felt cold down into her bones.

Death has visited me.

While she watched Charles stoke the fire, from the corner of her eye, she could see a figure in the shadows of the far corner. It was always lurking, draped in a cloak.

Clara remembered the figure being there as a permanent companion since she turned fifteen. The memory of sitting beneath an old oak rushed into her thoughts. The secret offering and prayer she spoke before dawn ... She could smell the moss under her feet and the dew on her cheeks, even at that moment.

Charles turned and watched her in silence for a moment before Clara tore her eyes away from the shadow, toward him.

"I'm fine, your Majesty," she said with a contrived smile.

Charles stepped back toward the bed, his doubt masking his otherwise flawless features.

She could feel the mattress lower under his weight, but the snapping of teeth just behind her was something she could never run from.

"You look as though you are in constant motion, running from something," he said in a soft voice of genuine worry. "Is there something I can do? Anything. Tell me what I must say or do."

Clara smiled; her eyes filled with tears. He was *everything* she wished for. Her dreams were within reach, but she would never truly hold them. She understood from the beginning she was reaching for them from the bottom of her own grave.

The physician's tonic arrived, and Clara stared into the cup. An itch at the back of her neck reminded her she could be forced to pay the toll at any time. Even in her sleep. What a cruel joke it would be to long for Charles's arms, only to expire in them.

Lifting the cup to her lips, she partook of the sedative. Her eyes closed before her head touched the pillow.

FIGHTING THE DARK TIDE
Morrigan's pull was a powerful magnet, drawing her into the Otherworld. A murder of crows fluttered around her as her eyes opened. The sound of their wings was

a deafening roar, causing her to cup her ears with her hands.

Disoriented, Clara turned in a circle in an attempt to gather her bearings before the crows dissolved into the night sky. She was left alone on the black-sand shore. The water rolled at her feet; white foam rushed over her bare feet before drawing back into the eternal abyss. From where she stood, the moon looked so close Clara took a frightened step back in fear it may fall on her.

Silence was unbearable in the wake of the chaos she arrived in.

I do not want to be here, Clara thought. It came with the feeling of isolation. Pressure on her chest made it hard for her to breathe. *I must get back. But ... Back where? Where am I?*

Clara looked at her hands with an overwhelming feeling of detachment. She turned as if to run and stopped in her tracks.

In the distance, the Serpent was there. It had many forms but only spoke to her in one.

It must be Morrigan.

Before she could think better of it, Clara ran toward her. The sand beneath her feet made it difficult. The harder she tried to run, the more sluggish she felt. All her energy was being sapped out of her, and she could feel her lungs burning to fill with air.

Please! Clara reached out for her and fell forward into the sand. The acrid granules filled her mouth. When she tried to spit it out, it soaked all the saliva from her mouth, and she began choking and coughing. She felt her body sinking into the sand farther, and unable to scream, Clara attempted to claw her way out.

Quicksand! No! Not now. Please!

The sand gave way, and Clara went under. Thick slops of it filled her nostrils, and fear lit her survival instincts on fire. Clara fought harder than ever. That was not how she wanted to die. Despite her body wanting to react in a panic, she fought for the opposite. She stopped moving and let calm come over her.

Relax, Clara, she told herself. The change was instant. Her body stopped fighting, and she stopped sinking. Clara arched herself back and began pulling her legs up from side to side to side and rocking her body until she began to rise. Despite wanting to move faster, the slower movements were working and she was able to breach the surface.

The quicksand oozed from between her lips, and the first breath of air was both painful and full of relief. Freeing one hand, Clara reached out for the dry edge of the shore and felt a hand grip her wrist.

A POISONED HEART
"Clara!"

Clara's eyes flew open. A lady's maid was shouting at her and giving rough slaps to her cheeks.

Having no idea what was going on, Clara was still in fighting mode. Her nails swiped across the woman's cheek, causing her to squall in pain and surprise. When the woman backed off, holding her cheek, Clara crab-walked backward until her back hit the headboard. She looked beside her and watched as the chamberlain did the same to rouse the prince.

"What's going on? What's happening!"

"Poison," the lady's maid said. Her eyes were wide, exposing the whites. "You were both poisoned, my lady."

The woman directed her eyes to the cup on its side between Clara and Charles, its contents half-spilled on the mink blanket.

"Charles didn't drink this," Clara said as she jerked her foot away from the spill. "His physician sent it for me to help me sleep!"

As she spoke the words, another man flew into the room and flashed an angry glance at her. "I have been fast asleep in bed, far away from the prince's chambers. I've ordered no such drink!"

Behind him, a woman wrapped in a gown thrown on haphazardly stood off to the side. His mistress, looking disheveled and fresh from coital exertion, turned her head in embarrassment.

The chamberlain, hearing the physician's words, backed away from the prince and glanced between the mistress and Clara.

"I swear," he stammered. "I sent a messenger to the physician! He brought the cup up straight away!"

"Get them out of here," the physician snarled. He pulled smelling salts out of his small bag and thrust the bottle under the prince's nose. After what felt like a lifetime, the prince's mouth opened and he sucked in a breath.

Clara was pulled out of the room by a large guard and escorted to the throne room, where the king and queen awaited.

Clara was thrown to the floor in front of them like a discarded piece of trash.

"Tell me what you know," the king hissed. "I want every detail. Who tried to assassinate my son?"

Clara righted herself to a proper kneel and lowered her head. The nightdress she wore fell off one shoulder, and she caught it as best she could to remain modest in public.

"I swear, your Majesty! I have no clue who might want to hurt the prince!"

She let out a sob, and the tears rushed to the corners of her eyes. Clara could feel them fall free like warm rain down her cheeks.

"He called for a tonic to help me sleep. When it arrived, I drank it. I remember nothing after the first sip. I woke up to being slapped by Lady Margaret!"

The king looked at the guard, who nodded, confirming her story was true.

"Take her to her room. Post a guard at the door. Nor she or her ladies may leave without my permission."

"Yes, Majesty."

"I want blood! Find who did this before I take yours!"

The king stood, and the queen stood in turn, her eyes rimmed in crimson from crying. She followed in the king's shadow as he swooped out of the room.

For hours, Clara paced her room while her ladies watched in silence. No one dared speak a word. They exchanged looks of uncertainty and suspicion. Slipping a powerful sedative and poison into the prince's chambers required planning and power. Regardless of who was to blame, someone would pay the price. It was always those who were lower on the ladder who would take the fall.

When the chaos became quiet, most of the ladies fell asleep propped against one another, and Clara continued to pace as the room fell dark except for the amber light pouring out from the low fire. It had not been stoked in hours. The stretch of its warmth grew smaller with the fading light. Clara stood in front of it, absorbing its embrace, her eyes darting from shadow to shadow for her companion.

Please, she thought. *Tell me the prince is alive. Give me a sign. Send me a message, anything.*

As soon as her prayer was complete, a knock at the door came, causing a jolt to her heart. She spun around and ran toward the door, passing the cloaked figure as she did. When she threw open the door, the prince was standing there, two guards in tow. He threw his arms around her, and she drew him in for a kiss.

"You're alive!" Clara said between meetings of their lips. She could not hold on tight enough.

"And you," he said, brushing her hair back from her face. "I cannot stay tonight. I am under physician's care for seventy-two hours. I wanted to see you for myself and let you know in person."

Clara's eyes filled with more unshed tears, and she was unable to speak.

"All will be well," he continued. "I have placed a taster in your service, and two more guards."

"The attack wasn't on me," Clara whispered. Her eyes looked past him to the figure watching. "I'm so scared. I cannot lose you, Charles."

"And you shan't," he said, lowering his chin and staring into her eyes. "I swear to you, now, all will be well. I will return in one piece."

As if to seal her lips from more protest, he leaned in and kissed her. When he pulled away, he nodded to the ladies who stared with relief at him.

"Handle her with extreme care, for I will be back for my love in due time."

The ladies all nodded and curtsied in turn.

When Charles pulled away, Clara felt as if her heart was torn from her. She watched him leave, and the doors closed, shutting him out of sight.

A CROWN OF CROWS
The weeks following Charles's healing were good ones. Clara was at his side in all his free time. Together, they would go for rides on horseback or practice archery. Like all good things, their joy would come to a crossroads with the announcement of Princess Calah's arrival.

In her heart, Clara knew it was inevitable. She could

not marry the prince. She would have to settle for the position of official mistress, but she did hope for more time. The past year felt as if it went by in the blink of an eye.

Whispers in the court reached her before Charles had a chance to tell her himself. When he entered her room, his shoulders dropped. Clara sat in front of her mirror dabbing her eyes as her shoulders shook in silent sobs.

"Clara," he started, then paused when he saw her sobs grew stronger. He rushed to her side and wrapped her in his arms. "Nothing changes for us. Nothing at all."

"Charles, everything changes. She will have your time, your attention ..." unable to speak without choking up, her voice warbled. "Your children."

Charles gave her a gentle smile and curled his finger under her chin. He tilted her head up until her eyes met his.

"Yes, I will have to give her and this marriage some attention," he confessed. "But you are my heart and my one true love. Marriages are transactional. Love is not. Calah is here to secure lineage and to keep peace among countries. I will love her with respect for her position, but I will love you as my Leannán."

Clara's smile widened when he used the secret term between them. In his tender moments of affection, he referred to her as Leannán—his fairy lover—telling her she came to him in a dream much like the famous playwright, Shakespeare's *A Midsummer Night's Dream*.

"It's dangerous to love such a creature," he whispered to her once.

The memory of the cloaked figure staring at them as they confessed such secrets reminded her of how fragile her life was.

Clara turned, facing the mirror. When she looked up,

she saw the cloaked figure melt into the Serpent.

"The time of light has passed you by," Serpent hissed. "No prayer, no plea, no last goodbyes."

A trickle of cold sweat trailed down Clara's spine. A sickness pooled within her bowels, and she went pale. Her reflection stared back, a death mask foretelling her destiny with Otherworld.

"There you go, again," Charles whispered. "Come back to me, Clara."

Charles reached his hand out and placed it over hers. "Your fears are unfounded." His voice softened, and he brought her hand to his lips to brush a kiss across her knuckles.

Tearing her gaze from the Serpent form of Morrigan, Clara turned her gaze to him and forced a smile on her lips. Her days were numbered. A desperate need to make the most of them filled her chest. Her heart fluttered like a moth around a flame.

"She arrives today," Clara said. "Kiss me before you leave to greet her, and I shall be quenched until next you come to me."

Charles smiled and leaned in to place a kiss on her lips. His arms wrapped around her, and he drew her to him. He held on tight as if she might fly away, and they remained locked in each other's arms until a knock on the door broke them from the spell.

Charles touched his forehead to hers, and she could feel the pain and conflict hanging between them like a pendulum threatening to sever their bond. His eyes, burning phosphorus blue in the half-light, caused her to curl her fingers into the fabric of his attire in hopes of keeping him by her side.

With a gentle pull, he stood. The knock came again, and he sighed.

"Enter," he commanded.

Lord William stepped in and bowed.

"Your Highness," he said with urgency in his voice. Allowing his eyes to flicker on Clara for a moment, he cleared his throat before lowering his head in respect. "The royal ship makes its approach."

Charles let Clara's hand slip from his, and he straightened himself and his clothing.

"Then let us greet the princess," he said. Charles turned toward Clara, and he offered her an apologetic smile. "You can do this ... And I apologize in advance for any injury to your heart which may result from this."

The lines on Clara's face smoothed, and a mask of stoicism replaced the emotional face reserved for him in private.

"Princes do not apologize," she whispered under her breath, before glancing toward Lord William. "I understand my position, your Highness."

Clara stood and curtsied before taking her place behind him. The two exited the private chambers, and Clara's ladies fell into line behind the entourage set out to greet the princess who was betrothed to the prince.

TO HAVE AND TO DESTROY

The royal entourage stood on the dock and watched the royal ship make its crawl and anchor. The princess was boarded onto a smaller ship donned with colorful flags, surrounded by guards and her closest lady's maid.

Seagulls cried out overhead, circling the shore. The smell of sweat and fish made Clara nauseated. She pulled out a small fan from her purse and fluttered it in front of her face. It had a small satchel of lavender and sage attached for protection and to fend off the stench of body odor in closed places such as those.

The queen, two rows ahead of her, dabbed a handkerchief soaked in perfume across her nose to ward off the smells and capture beads of sweat pooling on her porcelain skin. Even in the cool weather, the layers of clothing gave no reprieve. Bone corsets cinched her figure into place with brutal precision, forcing her to take shallow breaths within her imprisoned ribcage.

Time here seemed to slow to a crawl. Clara's toes, crunched into the delicate, unforgiving satin, were numb, and her shoulders ached under the weight of the fur cloak. The slosh of water surrounding them coupled with the sea spray heavy with salt caused her to force back a gag.

One of her ladies beside her placed her hand on Clara's back and leaned toward her. "My lady, are you well?" Her whisper was discreet and almost silent between them.

Clara gave her a tiny nod.

The young woman handed her a lace handkerchief, the smell of mint filled her nose, and an immediate sense of relief washed over her. Clara gave the lady a grateful smile.

It was an hour before the princess arrived and set foot on the weather-beaten wood of the dock. Clara's hope flew above with the gulls. She was as beautiful as the rising sun she arrived with. She could see the prince's smile widen as the princess came closer and offered her hand. Introductions were made, and the two were locked in a gaze of mutual attraction.

A hiss caught Clara's attention, and she watched as the Serpent slithered around her ankles. She lifted her head and forced her chin not to quiver. The Serpent moved its way up her leg, around her waist, and then around her neck, where it settled like a silk scarf.

"Threadsss of fate are never asss you wishhh them to be," the Serpent whispered in her ear.

Stop. Please ...

"Foolissssh hope clingsss to you ssstill," it continued. "A princcce'sss heart isss not bound by promisssesss but by whim."

Clara's throat clenched and tears stung her eyes as she watched the exchange between the king and queen and the new princess. They too, were enamored.

"Hissss heart wasss never yoursssss to keep," it reminded her. "Ssssee him now? A moth too clossssse to the fire will burn dessssspite itssss desssssire for itsss warmth and light."

A tear escaped Clara's eye, and she used the handkerchief to wipe it away.

You said we were destined, that our fates were tied together.

"And here you ssstand. The priccce of your own desssssiressss. Ssssuffering is not your fate. It issss your choiccccce. You chossssee the path that led you to thissss moment. I offered you your desssssiressss and you grassssssped at it. Now you musssst walk through the thornsssssss."

You are a cruel God. Does my suffering feed your black heart? Is this what you gather joy from?

The Serpent tightened around her neck in warning.

"There issssss alwaysss a way forward, child."

A hint of bitter mirth lined the words Morrigan whispered in her ear. Clara knew there was always a price, but as she watched her lover pull away from the princess, Clara was willing to pay any price.

I don't want to ... I don't want to be like you. I don't want to find happiness in others' pain.

"The heart isss a fragile thing," Morrigan continued. "But the mind issss a weapon."

The sound of the prince's laughter mingled with the princess's, and Morrigan's words sank deeper into his skin like barbs.

I cannot bear this.

There was only one option she could think of—being together in the Otherworld where no one but they existed. Clara began to sway and tremble to the thought.

The lady beside her tightened her arm around Clara's waist.

If I cannot be his queen in this life, then I will be queen and companion for eternity in the next.

The Serpent hissed and parted its maw in a wicked, reptilian smile.

"At lasssst you underssssstand. The only essssscape from the agony of love issss to ssssever the bond in thissss world and join him in the Otherworld asssss one."

THUS WITH A KISS I DIE

Days rolled past without a visit from the prince, and Clara sank into a deep depression. Ignoring the pleading from her ladies and the physician, Clara would not eat or rise from her bed. After a week, dehydration began to take its toll. There were rumors and reports of Clara speaking to some*thing* or some*one* no one else could see.

Concerns of her mental fitness were called into question, and the cause for alarm was raised when Clara's new skeletal appearance was seen wandering the halls late at night. Her nightdress hung loose off her shoulder; sharp points of her bones poked through her paper-thin skin.

The warm glow of the sun-kissed blush of her cheeks was replaced by a sickly pallor. Edged cheek bones disguised her from recognition.

Word reached the prince, who reacted with irritation and impatience.

"What is the physician doing? Must I take leave from my duties to perform his?"

Lord William bowed low in fear of the prince's wrath. It was out of character for him to lash out in such a way.

"Forgive me your Highness," Lord William said. "The physician has done all he can, but the princess refuses to eat until she ..."

Lord William paused.

"Until she what? Out with it!"

"Begging pardon, your Highness." he cleared his throat. "In the lady's words, she refuses to eat until you come to her."

The man bowed again in an attempt to avoid the offense of *demanding* anything from the prince.

Fury filled the prince's eyes and he stood, throwing his seat to the floor with the sudden momentum.

"She said this?"

"Yes, your Highness," Lord William said, still lowered.

Charles stormed past him with full intention to chastise his mistress for her overstep. Bursting through her door, his fury dissipated when he saw the condition of her. In a little over a week, she had lost so much weight her fragility frightened him.

The spell of the new princess snapped in the moment like a frayed thread.

"Clara?"

Charles's voice woke Clara, and she rolled over in the bed to face him. Seeing it was him, she sat up and extended her arms toward him like a child.

"Charles! Please, come to me!"

Without hesitation, the prince ran to her and took her into his arms.

"What have you done, Leannán?"

His eyes welled up with tears, and he realized his neglect had caused her to withdraw like this.

"I promised you and I failed," he whispered, and buried his face in her neck with shame.

In the corner, Morrigan stood watching.

Clara clung to Charles and sobbed against his shoulder. The beating of his heart against her chest made hers come back to life. She took his face into her hands and pressed her lips to his in a deep kiss. It was a kiss meant to seal both their fates together.

Charles poured his heart into the kiss and tasted her lips. The taste was ambrosia. The more he tasted, the more he wanted. He curled his fingers into tight fistfuls of her hair, unable to get enough of her.

Charles groaned into her mouth as desire consumed him. He leaned her back, no longer seeing the fragile degradation of her appearance but the woman he was enamored with.

"I'm here, my love, my everything," he whispered, pushing himself against her.

Morrigan smiled from the shadows, and it lit her features up, capturing the light of the fireplace and drawing heat from it. Her lips parted, exposing pointed teeth. A black, serpentine-like tongue slid out and flickered against her dark, wine-colored lips.

Clara's sobs grew more intense the more they kissed and embraced one another as she could feel the life leaving her prince and entering herself. Under Morrigan's spell, she could not stop herself until the prince took his last breath and fell against her. His features sunken in, he looked like a husk of his former self.

The door was still open, and one of Clara's ladies entered, unaware of the prince's presence. In her hand, she held a tray with Clara's tea. When she came upon the two, the woman stopped. At first, she was embarrassed, until the situation processed in her mind. Clara looked healthy once more, but the prince had taken on her hideous appearance and lay against her chest, blue in the face and eyes locked open.

The tray in the woman's hands rattled as her hands shook, and the porcelain teacup bounced and spilled over. In slow motion, the woman's jaw dropped, and her mouth opened wide to allow for the size of the scream to follow. The shriek flew through the halls, alerting every guard and person within its reach.

Clara closed her eyes and held on to her lover until the last moment.

BOUND BY FATE, LOST TO FLAME

The guard who bound her to the post stood before her and looked into her eyes. Clara nodded. It was a sign that she forgave him for taking her life out of duty. Her lady's maid stepped onto the platform and handed him a small purse of coins.

The executioner took the purse, then weighed it in his hand. Satisfied with its contents, he took a hood from his waistband and placed it over Clara's head. When he tied it, he slid a tiny bottle into her mouth. The clandestine act was practiced by the best executioners to numb the victims so they felt no pain.

Clara bit down on the bottle and felt the liquid contents spread across her tongue. The numbing sensation came fast. She could feel and hear her breath quicken beneath the hood. The executioner leaned in and whispered against her ear before disappearing.

"There is no mercy, only clarity. You shall feel every flame, witch."

The tincture wasn't a numbing medicine but one to paralyze her. She could not scream. She could not beg for death. She could only burn until her body disappeared into the ash.

THE LITTLE OLD WOMAN

ASIA BRITO GUERRERO

1650

Alice could feel the child inside her rolling around, its small, growing limbs pushing uncomfortably against the inner lining of her uterus. She placed both of her hands, palms down, on her stomach and held back the urge to cry, knowing what would come soon.

Like every other surrounding one, her village was suffering, and she was suffering along with it. She could barely keep herself fed enough, her nine-months pregnant belly appearing as a much smaller gestation, and she knew she would never be able to support any life she brought into this cold, grey world. How she made it so far along in her pregnancy was amazing.

After her parents died two years before, one from starvation and the other from a new, spreading plague,

Alice was left alone and vulnerable. Struggling to stay alive, she let a man into her life she hoped she could trust to take care of her. She quickly learned how wrong she was. No sooner than he took advantage of her he was gone, and she was left all alone again.

She realized she wasn't alone when the first feeling of life fluttered inside her. The dream of having a child warmed her heart, but the reality of it was terrifying. She wasn't well educated, but she knew enough to know that without enough food, she would never be able to make enough milk and the baby would perish before she could figure out another means of food for it.

She was unsure of what to do until a nearby neighbor confided in her. The woman, Agnes, had two children of her own, both lucky enough to be near adulthood themselves. What she told Alice that day shocked and intrigued her. She confessed to having given birth to nine children; two she kept and raised, three died in childbirth, and four she gave, out of desperation, to Matilda.

At the sound of the name, Alice shuddered. While she had never met the old woman, she had seen her many times.

Matilda was the only one in the village that didn't look emaciated. In fact, despite being the oldest in the community, she looked the best out of everyone.

Alice always wondered how the old woman managed to be well-fed while the rest of them sometimes went days without even a single crumb.

Agnes informed Alice that Matilda had connections to royal families in need of life servants at no cost, and in exchange, they fulfilled any supply list she provided them.

While Alice hated the thought of her child being a servant their entire life, death being the alternative option made it less terrible.

The next day, Alice followed the directions Agnes gave her and made the small stroll into the woods to Matilda's home, hoping Matilda would have an opportunity for her child once it was born. She knew no one would want it until it was old enough to be of use, but maybe the old woman had an idea of what to do in the meantime.

Alice felt amusement upon first seeing Matilda's home and thought it absurdly funny she was considering giving up her child to a little old woman who lived in a cottage in the shape of a boot. Going from the very bottom to the roof, there were many windows with odd, elongated outside drapes that reminded her of shoelaces. She nervously giggled to herself as she approached the door, building up the courage to knock.

Alice sat in the wicker rocking chair her father made years ago for her mother, the same one she sat in when Alice had been inside of her, thinking back on that day. Alice rubbed her belly and thought of her first impression of Matilda.

When the door opened that day, she expected to see the withered old woman she usually saw strolling in the village square. Though she was hunched slightly and had an aura of immense age seeping off her, she looked no older than Alice, which seemed impossible. The shock must have been evident on Alice's face, and she tried to disguise her confusion. When Matilda stepped out of the shadows and into the doorway, her face and body seemed to understand she needed to be older than she was, and in the sunlight, Matilda took on features that more fit the age she should have been. Alice convinced herself that the shadows in the home had only played tricks on her eyes.

Matilda had eagerly welcomed Alice inside. They spoke for what seemed like only a few minutes, but when Matilda escorted her back outside, the sunrise was setting, close to disappearing beneath the treeline. Before she wandered back home, Alice had turned back to the little old woman. Matilda told her she would arrive when it was time for the child to be born. Alice had wondered how Matilda would know. As if she could read the question on Alice's face, Matilda told her her intuition was stronger than most. Matilda told her she would take care of it all and Alice wouldn't have to worry about a single thing.

Now that the time was getting closer, Alice was starting to worry about everything, uncertainty creeping in. But she had only eaten once in the last two days, and a few neighbors in the village had died from starvation and sickness. She knew it was the only option she had.

After sitting and thinking about that first meeting for far too long, Alice noticed her back aching greater than normal. The acknowledgment of it caused the ache to grow, and she felt the urge to stand and stretch. Every bit of her was exhausted and she knew she should take a nap, resting her mind and body. She was restless, however, and knew the task would be easier said than done, but she decided to try, at least. She rose from the chair and instantly felt a pressure between her legs. A warm trickle of some unknown liquid creeped slowly down her inner thighs, dripping to the wooden flooring beneath her. She reached her hand under her knitted skirt and when she pulled it back out, blood covered her fingers. Her eyes grew wide and panic set in.

Her unborn child pushed its limbs against its confinement—Alice could see the movement on the surface of her stomach, the skin stretching even farther beyond what she thought it was capable of. That same pushing sensation exploded further down as if the child was trying to stand up inside of her, putting weight much heavier than it was onto her pelvic bone. A scream began in her chest as a piercing pain erupted throughout her abdomen, back, and vaginal area.

The scream fell short when a knock came at the door. Alice couldn't move, and her voice didn't work well enough for her to call out to whoever was standing outside.

As if knowing, the door swung open and someone rushed inside. Alice didn't have the chance to see who it was before another stabbing sensation overtook her. She bent forward, squeezing her middle. The scream that had been interrupted poured violently from her throat. She was quickly helped to her small bed, and as she lay on her back, she opened her eyes and saw Matilda staring back at her.

"It's time to get the child out." Matilda's voice was firm. "Do exactly as I say. Do you understand?"

Alice could only nod, then another intense cramp overwhelmed her, and she was screaming again, her abdominal muscles tightening. Alice's nod quickly turned into a violent head shake. Her entire upper body shook left to right as she muttered, "No, no, no, no."

"This will not be easy. You cannot be weak or you will lose your life and the life of this child!"

Those words struck equal amounts of fear and strength in her, and she clenched her jaw, allowing herself to settle into the experience her body was enduring. Matilda kept her face near the center of Alice's opening, giving occasional updates on the process. Alice could hear Matilda's voice but as if she was hearing it from ears foreign to her.

After what felt like days of immense agony but couldn't have been more than a few hours of contractions that kept getting closer and closer in timing, a pain unlike anything before took over.

"It's time! Push. Push now!"

Alice clenched her jaw even tighter, her teeth grinding together, and pushed. She could feel the pressure build and turn into an intense burning as her center stretched.

"That's it. Once more. Push!"

As quickly as the pain began, it ended when the being she had grown inside of her slipped from her body and into Matilda's waiting arms. The small cries that filled the air sent goosebumps up and down Alice's body, and her original decision to give her child away felt shaky again. She tried to sit up and see, but Matilda had wrapped the baby up and hidden it.

"Is it a boy or girl?" Alice asked. "Please, I'd like to know at least that."

Matilda didn't answer the question but said, "You must rest. I will take care of the child now."

"But ..." Before Alice could finish her sentence, Matilda severed the umbilical cord that connected them and pulled the placenta from her, causing her to wince uncomfortably, then tossed it all into a basket that Alice hadn't realized Matilda brought in with her.

"Rest. I will take care of the child," Matilda repeated, then cradled the infant in one arm, scooped up the basket with the other, and hurried out of the cottage before Alice could utter another word.

Two years later

Alice thought about her child every day since

the moment Matilda took them away from her. She wondered if they had been given a name, what their laugh sounded like, or even if they had the same dimple on their chin as she did.

One day, her curiosity got the best of her and she found herself walking down the same path she had the first time, years before. She told herself she would stay hidden within the privacy of the trees just in case Matilda still kept the child. Alice knew Matilda must still have them given their age—they were still too young to be of service to anyone. But Alice didn't know the details of everything once Matilda took control. Thinking about it made a guilty twinge rise in her gut. She scolded herself for not asking more questions but quickly reminded herself how limited her options had been. She made the best decision she could, she told herself, but somewhere deep inside, she didn't fully believe that.

Alice approached the end of the wood where the clearing leading to Matilda's boot-like cottage opened up. She stopped suddenly and covered her mouth with her hands in shock as her eyes laid upon a little girl she hadn't expected to see. The girl had light brown curls that bounced in rhythm with her playful running. Alice's heart ached at the sight of the child her body had grown and delivered into the world. Noticing a bandage on the girl's left hand, she wondered what had happened. She knew children were clumsy, so she hoped it was nothing more than a minor thing. She wanted to get closer, to see the child better, but she pushed that thought from her head.

Alice took a sudden step back when she saw Matilda walk out of the front door. The young girl stopped, and her joy was replaced by something else. Alice watched as the girl—her daughter, she corrected herself—timidly put her hurt hand behind her back. Alice quickly realized the child was showing fear.

"Edith, that's enough! Come!" Matilda moved to the side and pointed a finger into the cottage.

The little girl hesitated, looking down, her hand still behind her.

"Edith, now!" Matilda didn't yell, but her voice was firm, sending a chill down Alice's spine.

Something felt wrong, but Alice tried convincing herself that even though she hadn't been in the child's life since birth, it was nothing more than a motherly protectiveness coming over her. She told herself that Matilda wouldn't harm the child she was trying to give away despite her being nothing more than a servant. Yet she couldn't shake the feeling that things weren't what they seemed.

As the door closed behind them, Alice stood in the same place a moment longer before she turned to leave. She would return the following day, hoping to catch a glimpse of Edith again.

The next day, Alice crept to the same hidden place within the trees. Edith was nowhere to be seen, and Alice hoped the girl would eventually make her way outside. No sooner than the thought popped into her head, the boot-like cottage door opened and out came the energetic toddler.

Matilda was right behind her, her hands on her hips. "You may have only a few moments outside, Edith! Then we must head back downstairs. Do you understand?"

Matilda waited for a response, and when she didn't receive an immediate one, she scowled further. "Edith, answer me at once!"

Edith's excitement at being outside was wiped from her face as she turned to face the older woman. "Yes, ma'am. I understand." She sounded much older than she was, and something about that made Alice's chest ache miserably.

Alice watched Edith the entire time she played, until Matilda showed herself again and demanded that Edith head back in. Alice had been so enamored by Edith's joy, like the day before, that it wasn't until it had been taken from her again that she noticed the bandage on Edith's hand was different. It was a new bandage, but Alice also realized it covered more of her hand than it did the last time she saw it.

Edith cradled her arm against her chest and slowly made her way to the door, disappearing into the shadows of the cottage before Matilda followed her in and shut the door behind them both.

Something tugged at Alice's core, and she felt pulled in the direction of the cottage. A desperate need came over her suddenly—a need to go down to wherever Matilda took her daughter and bring her back up aboveground, to run her far, far away from that place. Other than the bandage on Edith's hand, Alice had no other reason to do so except the dread bubbling in her gut, but as she stood there in the confinement of the wood, the feeling grew. That single reason was a good enough reason for her.

She created a plan in her head to return the next day and confront Matilda. She wasn't naive. She knew that when the girl was to be traded as a servant, her life would never be her own again and she would never be completely safe. At the time, it was a better option than the alternative of burying her child in the ground before she could even learn to walk. Seeing her at that moment, an actual being and not just the idea of one, Alice realized she would do anything that needed to be done to guarantee the happiness and safety of young Edith.

Alice stood on the doorstep, her chest puffed up, ready for any confrontation with the old woman she might face. She was determined to leave with her daughter in hand. She refused any other outcome, and she would let it be known that the deal she made was no longer something she agreed to. She didn't care what she would have to do to break it.

Knocking only once, the door opened almost immediately. Matilda's glaring face appeared, and Alice's confidence wavered.

"What are you doing here?" Matilda demanded.

"I've come back for my child." Alice's voice began as a whisper then grew. "I've come back for Edith."

Hearing her say the girl's name, a shocked look came over Matilda. "Been sneaking around, have you?"

"I ..." Alice started to answer but didn't know what to say.

The old woman rolled her eyes and waved away whatever response Alice would try to give. "You desire to see your child. That's what any mother would want, I suppose. Come, come. Sit down at the table and have a cup of tea with me while we discuss everything. Don't you worry, I shall give you what you want, my dear."

Alice slowly entered the cottage, and as her eyes adjusted to the darkness inside, she realized it wasn't as dark as it seemed from the outside. She looked all around, taking in all she could. The foyer immediately led into the kitchen. To the left and right, entryways could be seen that led into other parts of the home.

Matilda cleared her throat, getting Alice's attention, and pointed to the kitchen table. "Sit. I will make us tea."

Alice walked to the handcrafted wooden table and sat in one of the matching chairs. As she made herself comfortable in it, she thought it was sturdier than it looked.

There were many noises being made while the old woman prepared the tea, her back thankfully to Alice, giving Alice a few more moments to breathe and prepare herself. After a while, Matilda finally turned, two tea cups in her bony hands.

Alice went to stand and help but was told to sit back down.

Matilda carried the cups to the table and placed one in front of Alice, holding on to the other for herself. "So," the old woman sat down in the chair opposite her, "you want the child back?"

"I want my daughter, yes," Alice answered. She brought the tea to her lips, blowing on it before sipping carefully.

"Then agreements do not matter to you?"

She put the cup down. "Of course they do, but you must understan–"

"Drink your tea, please." Matilda motioned toward the liquid still steaming in front of Alice.

Alice was taken aback by the sudden interruption. Instead of arguing and causing the woman to fight her on the issue, Alice raised the cup back up and took two very long, painful drinks of the hot beverage. If the temperature hadn't slightly burned her mouth, she would have noticed the filmy residue left over on her tongue and palate. Instead, she put it back down, only a small amount left, and tried speaking once again.

"I was saying ..." But she stopped when her head began to spin. "I'm sorry, I–" She looked at Matilda, and the woman appeared fuzzy. The image of her danced in Alice's vision despite Matilda not moving at all. "What's h-happening?"

She looked down at her near empty tea cup and panicked. She tried to maintain consciousness, but she was too weak against whatever Matilda had done. "You p-poisoned m-me?" Alice asked, her speech slurred.

"Don't be absurd. I've simply given you a powerful herb that is putting you to sleep. When you wake up, you shall see your daughter."

Alice was confused. "But why would y-you ..."

"This is the only way, I'm afraid."

That was the last thing Alice heard from Matilda's mouth before she passed out, her head falling forward and landing in the old woman's expectant hands.

Alice's head felt like it was going to burst when she finally woke up. Her chin lay on her chest, and she felt the tips of her toes scraping the floor. She lifted her gaze and saw she was suspended by her arms from the ceiling in the center of a room she had never been in before. A tightly bound rope was secured around each of her wrists, cutting into the skin painfully, holding her in place.

Across from her, on a table very similar to the one she previously sat at in the kitchen, Edith sat, staring at her.

"What an interesting thing it is to be a mother. I have never been given the chance. Of course, I have had many children in and out of my life, but sadly, with the life I've chosen, I've never been able to keep any for longer than a few years before what needs to be done is done." Matilda stepped out of the shadows, wringing a towel in her hands and tossing it across the room into a pile of what looked to be other towels.

"What are you talking about?" Alice asked. Her hands became more numb the longer she dangled.

"You stupid girl. You truly believed, like all of the others, that I just give these children away?"

Alice furrowed her brows, unsure of what she was being told. "You don't?"

Matilda chuckled. "Well, I do. But not in the way that you all think."

"What other way is there? I don't understand anything you're telling me. None of this makes sense! Let me go! Let Edith go!"

"I can't do that, my dear, not when you've given me the chance to finally be a mother after all these long years alone." Matilda walked up to Edith and ran her long, wrinkled fingers down the girl's chubby cheek.

Edith looked up at her with equal amounts of love and unease.

"You can't have her! I won't let you!" Alice screamed.

"Oh, no? But you already have."

Alice ignored the chuckling from the old woman and tried getting her daughter's attention. "Edith, look at me. I'm your mother—your true mother. You grew and came from my body."

Edith turned her gaze in Alice's direction. She stared for a moment, and when Alice was hopeful that the girl believed her, Edith frowned. "You're not my mother."

"I am. I swear to you I am." Alice's voice and eyes pleaded with the child to understand and believe, but no amount of effort made a difference.

"Are you finished?" Matilda asked mockingly.

"What are you going to do to me?" Alice almost hoped she wouldn't receive an answer.

"What I've done with every child that has ever been given to me. What I'm grateful I no longer need to do with Edith. You will be fed to the keeper of my soul, the one who gives me the ability to continue living even after all of you are gone from this dying world."

At that, in the floor beneath Alice's feet, a circle that she hadn't noticed before appeared. A bottomless pit into a vast emptiness opened up, and her body was consumed by a fierce heat. It was a painful warmth she could feel spreading throughout her body, cooking her. She felt herself slip through her restraints, and when she looked up, she realized it was because she was melting out of them. Her body was slowly liquifying from the blazing air shooting up at her. Before she dissolved even further, she took one last look at her daughter; pure amazement spread across the young girl's face. Alice remembered she had promised she would do anything it took to guarantee the happiness and safety of Edith, and if this was what it took to do that, she knew she wouldn't hesitate to do it again.

She wanted to tell Edith, despite never knowing her, that she loved her, but her mouth was broken. Within seconds, the rest of her body slipped from its bondages and she finished spilling into the pitch-black pit before it sealed again.

THE SHOEMAKER

Laura Bilodeau

As I stand here in line, joined by degenerates and criminals from all walks of life, I can't help but ask myself how I ended up here. Wives of scorned men, thieves, heretics, murderers—I am none of these things.

I am a man of God, a loyal husband to my wife, Joan, a doting father to Matilda and Alice, my beautiful daughters, a tireless shoemaker, and asset to my community. The things they've accused me of are not, in fact, anything I have done or ever would do.

And now, I'm in line to face my inevitable execution before my family and friends and those I've known my whole life. How can this be?

The air is heavy with dust and residual smog from yesterday's burnings.

Today, seven of us are set to have our executions carried out. I believe in my heart of hearts that King

Thurstan and his gaggle of geese find pleasure in our pain, thus why they choose the things they do to us as they do.

We've been holed up in a cell in a makeshift prison beneath his manor for three days without food or water. The women, becoming more frail by the day, are fatigued and unstable on their feet. The men, losing faith and mental fortitude, are becoming short with one another. If it wasn't for the metal shackles binding our ankles, leaving us a shameful few inches to move from the wall, they would've beaten each other to a bloody pulp by now, before the executioners even have their turns. We are forced to sit and wallow in a collection of our own filth, a mix of urine, feces, and, for some, even blood or vomit, unable to move from our places.

My fingers are rubbed raw from clawing at my ankles in an attempt at freedom, my knuckles blistering from laying my bare hands upon the stones surrounding us, my hips, shoulders, and seemingly every other part of my body littered with bruises from sleeping on the cold cobblestone floor.

I've begged and begged for someone to listen to me, to no avail.

King Thurstan has accused me directly himself, and at the top of the food chain, his words are worth their weight in gold.

He claims I'm being held accountable for the death of his younger sister, Beatrice.

She had been regularly coming into my workshop, and he knew that. Beatrice had wider feet than many of the women in the village, so I would custom fit her shoes. But when she went missing, King Thurstan passed that buck onto me.

What he doesn't know is that while journeying home two Mondays ago, I saw him raping her in the woods leading to my home, just beyond twilight.

He held her by her curly, golden hair with one hand, grinding her face into a rock he had her bent over, whipping her backside and legs with the other. What happened to the poor girl following that night I do not know, nor do I want to. I just know I may very well have been the last one, minus Thurstan, of course, to see her alive.

It wasn't until a week later that her body was found in those very woods. Beatrice was found propped upright against a large oak tree with a noose around her neck and her face hardly recognizable. Whether she hurt herself or she was coerced into doing so is a subjective mystery.

But it doesn't matter now; it's been pinned on me, William Chamberlain, the shoemaker. There is no hope for me; the end is near, and I'll be forced to take his secrets to the grave with me.

The shrill, piercing screams rip me from my trance, bringing me back to the living hell I'm about to endure.

I'm fifth in line, the pecking order randomized, but two people are taken at a time. Where we are is a large clearing atop a fearlessly steep hillside littered with jagged rocks and underbrush. We can't directly see the plateau unless we are the very first in line, as that is where the punishment takes place.

It is part of the cruelty that we do not see what is to come the day of our own execution, more so for those at the end of the line than anything. We are left to brew in our own fears and isolation. We have been forced to sit through dozens of other men and women's executions the past three days. It's just another form of the mental degradation they provide us.

Prior to our turn on the chopping block, we are brought out, chained to one another to sit in the front row, surrounded by our comrades and community members as the day's executions are carried out. I've seen times where the torture continues for days on end, and others where it is quick and simple. But one way or another, the pain is never a lacking element.

One of the first, and most bizarre, I saw was on one of the earliest days of my incarceration.

There was just one man in line that day. He was accused of raping and killing seven young boys in the village. First, he was stripped naked and bound by his hands and ankles to a sawhorse-type device. From what I can tell, Thurstan has a knack for binding and debilitating his victims.

The mothers of the seven lost boys took turns giving him a verbal lashing while rubbing honey all over his body, leaving no space uncharted, with a straw bristle brush.

Almost instantly, bugs formed feasting parties on his face and groin. Without accessible hands, the irritation must've been heinous; I can only imagine.

Thurstan came from behind the crowd with a donkey. To the crowd's entertainment, it began licking the man fervently.

At first, he was laughing uncontrollably, releasing his bladder numerous times. Beads of sweat and tears cascaded from his eyes and cheeks but were slowly turned from tears of laughter to tears of pure agony.

You see, donkeys have a tongue that is similar to barbed wire, but that didn't immediately affect the man as he had a barrier from the honey. Over time, as the donkey licked and splurged on his treat of a man, the barrier became less and less, and that barbed tongue was slowly but surely shredding the man's skin bit by tiny bit.

That's not what killed him though—it just aided in the untimely and merciless misery. What did him in was suffocating on his own saliva. Not being able to stop laughing or screaming to properly swallow, paired with being bound in a supine position, made clearing of his throat nearly impossible. It took the majority of the entire day for the man to perish before us all as the crowds whooped and hollered at his dismay.

How these people find such pleasure in these ordeals really disturbs me in my core, and knowing they will all show up in splendor to do the same for me is nothing short of disheartening and embarrassing.

Alas, the screams are quick, and the chanting of those gathered in the crowd has simmered.

My time must be nearing.

As expected, the next two are taken from the line, a man and a woman, both I met only once in my life but neither who deserve execution for their accused crimes.

The woman, Greta, is elderly and frail, the caretaker for her husband, William, who is also sickly and will now be alone to face his own slow and painful death.

I can't recall the name of the man, but his son had come into my shop with him once, before yuletide many years ago, and we struck up conversation while I shined their shoes for them.

Once Greta and the man are shuttled away from our line, I, along with a young man accused of serial arson, am ushered forward.

The sight before us is the most bleak and grim thing I can imagine. An oversized wooden barrel, similar to what whiskey is casked in, is positioned at the forefront of the hill's peak. Brackets are situated in eight places, and the man and Greta are being roughly secured to those brackets by their wrists and ankles, side by side, by two of Thurstan's largest goons.

The crowd, knowing what's to come next, begins whooping and hollering with excitement once again.

Fear erupts within me. Every pore on every surface of my body is leaking with sweat and tears. The quiver in my lip has numbed my jaw, and my teeth are sore from being clenched. My heart is shivering and rattling against the ribs encasing it. Catching my breath is a feat I'm consciously performing every second.

"Ladies and gentlemen! Here we have Greta, a woman who knows nothing about loyalty or honesty to her kind, spreading blasphemous lies about I, King Thurstan, in an attempt to dethrone me. And Alexander, a gluttonous thief. A derelict who has been robbing our bakers in cold blood. These two have been tried for their crimes and found guilty, with executionary sentences awarded to both of them. You all know what's next, so without further adieu, we bid you criminals farewell!"

Without missing a beat, the men who locked Greta and Alexander to the barrel shove the wooden device, sending it careening down the hill with zero regard for anything in its wake. Death and destruction are its only purpose.

The crowd roars with excitement, silencing the deafening screams of the two before me until the screams are no longer. A calm washes over the onlookers, and it is again quiet, filling the space with anticipation of who's next.

"I didn't do it, man. Look what they're going to do to us! I'm innocent! I've never done anything to anybody!"

The man beside me has fallen mute, my pleas bouncing off deaf ears. He doesn't even bat an eye at my desperation.

I *need* him to listen to me. I need *someone* to listen to me!

I thought my heart was beating fast before; I couldn't have fathomed it would be how it is now. Certainly, I'll die of a heart attack before I even get up there, at this rate. I can feel my pulse reverberating through each of my veins like a gong. It's the only sound filling my ears. And my neck feels stiff. Not a single bit of this is pleasant for me. It's not supposed to be, though.

Two of Thurstan's men, larger and more stoic than the last, Bartholomew and Alaric, convoy toward me and the criminal beside me. It is they who are elected to escort us to neverland.

My gut is telling me to scream and plead with the men, to fight with unfathomable desperation, and they may spare me, let me run and claim I got away somehow. My brain knows my reality is grim; these men are no better than any of the others. They're just sick, twisted products of Thurstan's deceitful games.

"DON'T TAKE ME! I DIDN'T DO ANYTHING! I'M INNOCENT. I BEG OF YOU, SIR, PLEASE! I have a family! Don't do this to me. I didn't do anything wrong. I'm telling the truth."

I clasp my hands and wave them toward the men like a vagrant in the streets begging for somebody's last few coins.

They look right through me, their eyes like glass,

empty and devoid of any emotion or sympathy.

The man assigned to collect me lowers his rust-colored brow and scoffs. "Don't waste my time, *peasant*. You are a *murderer*, and you will be treated like one! I'm hungry, and you are burning daylight. Now, move it! Lord Thurstan is waiting!"

I can't believe this is really happening to me. I'm being ushered to my untimely death for a crime I did NOT commit. I will never see Alice or Matilda grow up, find love, or have families of their own. I will never kiss my beautiful wife again, or smell her sweet, natural aroma. I will never lay nestled against her bosoms or feel her plump buttocks through her nightgown again. None of my achievements to date will matter anymore. The dreams I have for myself, my family, or my business will never come to fruition. Once this day is done, I will be no more.

But the townsfolk will return home to their cozy beds, with full bellies and hearts gleaming after today's festivities. Their proclivities to massacre are matched only by the resounding fear emanating from within me.

Secured at the ankles by heavy-duty chains, each step feels more like a mile. Beyond the mental torture, the weight of the devices is slowing me down dramatically. My sobs are growing heavier with each shuffle forward, ultimately causing me to trip over an exposed tree root in the soil. This only exacerbates both the immense physical and emotional pain I am in and pisses off Bartholomew.

"Get up, you mangled coxcomb. I told you, I don't have time for this."

"PLEASE! Sir, let me go. I'm innocent. I'm in pain. Let me go to my family."

Bartholomew gives me enough chances before one good whack from his meaty, bare-knuckled paw across my lower jaw silences me. He grabs onto the fleshy area on the back of my neck and drags me forward as the crowd comes into view.

The first face I see I recognized immediately. It is that of my beautiful wife, Joan. She appears disheveled and exhausted. Evidently, this has taken just as much a toll on her as it is on me. Her blue eyes don't shine in the light like they always have; they melt me, but with sadness instead of adoration. Her hair lays flat and unkempt with obvious snarls, her eyes baggy from crying. I feel so guilty seeing her like this, guilty for something I didn't even do. This is the worst torture a man could endure, I'm certain of it.

"Ladies and gentleman ..."

Thurstan begins again with his booming voice. An air of arrogance and bravado surrounds him, encapsulating me in disgust.

"Here, we have Godwin. Many of you know him as the man who set your home or your businesses ablaze, taking everything you've worked for, a serial arsonist who we will not tolerate amongst us.

"Next, we have *this* ruttish, rump-fed ratsbane. I've been waiting for his time before you all. He murdered my innocent little sister, Beatrice, in cold blood after she turned him down at his shop. Beatrice was *not* a whore. Let us not forget her memory and make him pay for taking her from me, and all of you."

Thurstan thrusts his daunting chin in our direction and lifts his chiseled arm. "Godwin, have you any last words?"

Moments go by, though the man beside me holds his mute vow. He hangs his head lower than before and slowly closes his eyes. Seeing him so emasculated is difficult and paradoxical. For a man who caused such a stir in the village, I expected him to be singing like a canary about all his griefs of the world around him and all the people who have ever done him wrong.

"So be it, then. Not another word from you, peasant."

It's now or never. I'm still in a world of pain from Bartholomew's blow to my jaw, but if he gives me any chance, I will speak my truth. I'm going to die either way, but my wife deserves to know.

While Alaric is locking the padlocks on Godwin, Bartholomew struggles to contain me.

I'm thrashing back and forth, likely making it worse for myself. It definitely doesn't feel pleasant with the prickled wood stabbing into my back and ribs.

Alaric grabs hold of one of my wrists with an impressive force, seeing as he is considerably smaller than Bartholomew. Clearly, he has had lots of practice doing this. He rams his knee into my groin, and my thrashing ceases, replaced with throaty gags and moans.

I'm secured to a barrel now, my body a shameful display before my community and loving family.

"And you, you bedswerving cumberworld? Any last words from thee?"

"IT WASN'T ME! It was Thurstan!" I barely manage to stutter out the words. I can feel every vein in my face and neck flexing as my face begins to burn red with anger. "It was Thurstan. I saw him myself, he was raping Beatrice against a boulder in the woods. He's framed me! Someone stop ..."

I didn't get to finish my plea.

Thurstan and his men scurry up and shove the barrel down the hillside.

Gravity is the centerfold of the torture here, a long, arduous process which batters us until our dying breath. Each revolution of the barrel is met with thorn bushes shredding our skin, revealing the tissues and bones beneath. Jagged rocks crack every bone that holds us whole, muddling our cartilage and our blood, creating a crimson gravy to coat the only meat left on our bones.

We go airborne more times than I can remember, causing me to black out and wake up in a panic at least three times. We finally make it to the bottom, the barrel still attached to us somehow. I don't know how I am so unlucky to have made it here alive, but I imagine I won't be leaving.

I don't believe Godwin survived much of the fall. He only made one single sound the entire way down, and that was before we hit the first rock to send us soaring through the air. Between that and the impact as we landed, he is definitely worse for wear. Listening closely, I can't hear any semblance of breathing coming from his side of the barrel.

I know every bone in my body is broken. I have gaps where there should be teeth, and what is left for teeth in my head are just small fragments. Only my left eye is able to open, and I use that term loosely—it's more of a sliver of skin I can manage to see through, but my vision is blurry, so it does me no good, anyway.

The breeze on my open wounds feels like a million razor blades, enhancing the agony I'm already in.

Around me, I can make out the sounds of one or two other unlucky survivors. I attempt to call out, to know I'm not completely alone down here, but no one answers.

I close my eye and try to relax as an unfamiliar calm and peace wash over me. I no longer feel pain, no longer feel remorse. I feel nothing but warmth and comfort. Is this what dying feels like? I focus on what I do know.

I am William Chamberlain, the shoemaker, and I will die an innocent man.

Marrowland

KK Monroe

Lest I forgo formality, I must write this in haste.
Forgive me the quickness, my shaking scrawl.
Alas, it must be done.

This parchment serves as my testament. I, one Duncan Godwin of the Benedictines, stand in The Glory of God as my witness to horrifying events. Lecherous *maleficium*. Satan's fornications. Unnatural manifestations of nature. Black arts and evil putrefaction of physical and spiritual form, this record serves as warning.

For the Church.
For Britannia.
For us all.
We must be ready.
Our immortal souls depend upon it.

Everywhere, death creeps upon the people. An encroaching darkness of moral and spiritual decay, the taint pollutes the water, crops, and air. Soil once abundantly fertile is seeped with the blood and death of warring men, a treacherous leach of virility. Presentiment of famine comes in due time, how can it not? The fragile fibers of our decency and character are felled by devious machinations of men who lust for power and seek dominion over all. We are lost. God will protect us, but only if we commit our eternal souls, reshape our will, and act in gracious servitude to His everlasting glory.

Much already has been lost to obscurity. Behold as evidence, nearly four centuries have passed since the Romans unhanded Brittania. Little to no records exist of the time that came after, to guide us. Vigils of history abandoned, we cannot know how dark the darkest days grew.

Emperor Honorius bid the people a final farewell with dire caution. *Fight bravely and defend your lives... you are on your own now.* See, I know this—how? From reading the record, though the letter itself vanished. As Honorius predicted, we have fought countless enemies for nearly four hundred years and continue to this day with little movement forward.

In the 6th century, Christian monk Gildas reflects, also in his writings, of what followed Rome's final unhanding. *After this, Britain is left deprived of all her soldiery and armed hands, of her cruel governors, and of the flower of her youth, who went with Maximus, but never again returned.* I know this, again, because the record prevails.

Yet, what precisely transpired in those darkest days remains unknown.

However unsavory, the written word, a chronicle of our past (and present), is all that stands in testament to the trials of men, withstanding the foulest weathers of Time. This is how we survive. I pray. By the pen. And a return to our highest order of righteous holiness, to thwart the brevity, the insidious fallibility of our enigmatic memory. We must record all that has come before. That is if we have any hope of one day emerging from these still-dark days; to rise up into the illuminating glow of golden angels and enter into a prosperous and blooming civilization. We must strive to escape this current ruinous, bloody existence.

This latter 8th century anarchy—we, that is all together in England, the Anglo-Saxons and Britons alike, must swear an oath to bind ourselves to the study of our past, reflect upon it, and act with moral fortitude!

Act to correct our errors.

Atone for grievous sins!

Repent, rebuild.

Pray!

Weed out insidious malfeasance.

I shudder to think what will happen if we don't.

Should these be my last words, regard them with utmost sanctity and import. Guard them with your life! Darker days await. Another presentiment of evil looms on a distant horizon, a time when this penning shall serve a greater purpose for mankind; wielded as divination, a manifesto, our spiritual weaponry, to extricate and eradicate malignant magic from our ranks.

The lad arrives at the priory—a consecrated, eremitical hermitage—and my present prison. An ominous specter, foreboding events, the lad appears from the dead stillness of night and sets upon the oak door, pounding. Fisted blows amplify against the priory's stone floors and walls. Heart-stopping bangs snatch me from fitful sleep. Understand, I dream not dreams.

But miasmic nightmares with unsheathed claws.

Visions of violence, famine, pestilence, utter barbarity; its blight spreads and infects, ravages villages, towns, castles, and inner kingdoms, polluting all.

Whilst to the north, Anglo-Saxons, Britons, an influx of invaders clash. The Britons persistent, their foothold slips against Beorhtric, the King of Wessex. Blood-chilling tales travel from the south. News sent by an unexpected missive from the abbey, a breach of my unwitting hermetic seal. The news frightens me. Telling of a new threat. Blood-lusting, frenzied savages cross perilous oceans from a snow land, heathen, devil-horned warriors who wear little else as armor, cast wooden sea dragons on the shores of the Isle of Portland.

What if Beorhtric's troops fail?

'Tis only a matter of time before the invaders arrive at my holy door. What, then, shall become of the priory, and myself, unarmed and avowed against violence?

Fear pricks my skin as I descend the stone stairs, hand trembling the candlelight. The hammer resounds, made from my own fist on this side of the door.

My blows silence the incessant pounding.

"What business do you have here? State what you seek."

A muffled response comes like a whistling through a reed, whiny and child-like.

I free the wooden lever and crack open the door, one foot braced against the lower eave. The stranger won't overtake me so easily.

"They call me Leofric and I've come to fetch ..." The lad visibly flinches. Locks of brown hair stick to the wetness on his forehead. Despite the chill, sweat rolls off him with the pungent odor of ripe onions, salt, and vinegar.

A strange malady afflicts the lad.

Rapidly blinking eyes, facial muscles contort and twitch equally, to the steady count of the intake and release of my three long breaths.

"Mum said not to say *fetch*, I forgot. I've come to ask, beg you, sir, to return with me. Let me come inside for a rest, please. It's cold. I've come a long way. I'm tired and quite hungry."

A snort from the yard and I stiffen, relaxing at the sight of a saddled nag grazing.

"You're a man of God, are you not? I've come to the right place, have I? Haven't strayed afar? Marrowland needs a man of God." The lad hesitates, then mumbles, "You seem dressed like one."

"'Tis the place you seek." I open the door. "Come, before the air gets inside."

"I'm so thirsty."

About to dip cupped hand into the stoup beside the window, "Wait," I halt him, my fingers dipping and sprinkling sanctified water across his startled face. Beads of holy water cling to the impenetrable grime on his skin. I make the sign of the cross.

An unfamiliar, Leofric's eyes grow incredulous when I bless him.

He is a peculiar visitor to have. From a pagan village like most, farmers depend upon the crop and hardy livestock, rely on cycles of nature, the waxing and waning of the moon, omens from Nature; a keen lot at reading awful auguries.

We sit at the table, the candle flickering between us. I hand him a mazer of water. Leofric sucks the liquid greedily, wiping every so often with the sleeve of his stained farmer's smock. The lad gasps for breath between hasty swallows.

"What brings you in this manner?" I implore.

The lad appears half my years in age, at least, trim and muscled from rigorous manual labor, like me. His brown eyes are shallow and shift with murky emotion.

When the candle's wick grows short, releasing a final puff of smoke, I retrieve another from the pantry, stopping to light it by the fire of the stone hearth.

"The Devil's come to The Marrows," Leofric whispers to me, lest the Devil hear his unholy name spoken. Out of habit, I genuflect, striking the beam beneath the bench, and a dull pain invades my calf. I form the sign of the cross again, speaking holy words to consecrate us both.

A stunned stillness overtakes the lad.

"Leofric, I await."

"What are you called?"

"Father Godwin."

My response puzzles the lad, for I am not his father in the sense he understands.

"Mister Godwin, I don't wish to speak of it, truly. Mum says I must, if you're to come. Are we safe here? Mum says I'll be safe here. Is it true?"

"'Tis a safe haven," I assure, fits of trepidation accosting my spirit. For I am not certain it is safe with the current state of affairs in Britannia. "Proceed."

The lad tells a story which freezes my blood. Horror and consternation fill my face, sucking the pasty parchment of my skin into the hollows of my cheeks. My disturbance at each lurid detail grows until ice cracks brittlely in my veins.

When finally he is done, the string of rosary beads slips reassuringly through my nimble fingers. The smooth surface of the beads comforts me. Clasping the cross to my chest, I beseech protection and strength, until our eyelids fall heavy with fatigue.

Soundlessly, I lead the lad to the empty cot, handing him a fresh mazer when he sits.

"Mister Godwin, are you here all alone?" he queries, and I nod with concession. "Aren't you frightened here by yourself in such a large, empty dwelling?"

The priory is not particularly large. Compared to others, it's considered quite small: four rooms on the upper floor, a cot, the one he's in. I imagine it must look like a castle to the simple farm boy.

"God is with me."

"I don't like being alone," Leofric mumbles drowsily.

"Now, sleep for the journey," I tell him, but he is already soundly so.

For the first time in ages, sleep comes for me swiftly. My head falls leaden to the straw laid across the monastic slab of stone. Sleep pitches me into irrational configurations yanked from an addled mind. The hallucinations of a man unconscious, poisoned by gluttonous inebriation; visions rise from oily, nightmarish putrefaction.

I dream of the witch. I dream only of the Witch of Marrowland.

The Witch's hawked, crooked nose beneath a cloaked hood. Black and bloody mouth yawing from within a sea of terror, the Witch emerges from obsidian-laced fog. Her form stretches, malleable as clay. Her feet dangle and float above the ground.

With the maleficent grace of Satan's minion, the Witch rides a swift current.

She sets down before me.

One pale forefinger uncurls. A daggered fingernail—long and razor-edged—the bladed quill, armed by a lancing tip, hovers before my eye. My legs twist and turn beneath the scratchy blanket, kicking out against empty air. The Witch cackles with the voices of a hundred demons rejoicing from the pits of Hell.

The needle lancing pierces my eyeball and plucks the fruited orb from its socket with a sickening, wet sound. I howl like an animal caught in a metal, toothy trap, writhing in agony. Hoarse bellows rise and fall, untethered.

Below, the lad stirs but does not wake.

My struggles are in vain for I am, assuredly, impotent against the dark arts.

The Witch's serpentine tongue darts and swirls, testing and tasting the bloody edges of my torn, pulsing socket. Lustfully, the devilish tongue laps and licks the ravaged flesh, plunging deep into the cavernous pit.

Bolts of pain jag through me. Anguished shrieks explode from my chest. Vile juices leak from her hungry mouth and run down my face, scalding open wounds.

"Eyes hold the sweetest jam." The witch cachinnates amidst my feeble whimpers.

The wicked, hideous creature tips her head back and slides the glistening orb into her gaping maw. She positions the organ gently between maligned teeth. With the tender press of sharp enamel, the eyeball's delicate skin bursts.

Raw, sticky egg whites dribble from her lips into the cleft of her sharp chin.

Abhorrent putrefaction—the Witch thoughtfully chews then swallows.

The witch is unrelenting. The hungry black orifice latches onto the throbbing wound firmly once more and does not relent. My agonizing sobs and screams fade to helpless moans. She slurps and titters bloody juice, bits of flesh between her teeth, licking her mottled lips jubilantly. With renewed intensity, the lips and mouth press more tightly than ever before, drawing and pulling fiercely.

The rest of the evildoing nightmare I cannot recall.

By Leofric's estimation, Marrowland is a two days' ride from the priory. The knock-kneed chestnut nag carries us both honestly and far before we, double-seated, dismount one by one and settle in for the night.

The lad proves capable and astute, building a small fire.

Embers kick from the flames as we warm our hands. Curiosity piqued, I say, "Tell me of the marrows. Do they grow and flourish in your village? What do they taste of?" I assume this a safe matter to discuss, the darkness of night pressed around us.

Intrigued by how the lad's region earned its name, I have only glimpsed the roughest depiction of the fabled cucurbit upon an aged scroll from some foreign land. Left to grow large on the trailing vine like a gourd, its skin dark green and thick, the flowered fruit remains myth. Nowhere else does this marrow appear or is it proven to exist in Britannia, so imagine my surprise when Leofric inferred it.

Visibly trembling against the damp coldness, Leofric stares into the fire. Our breaths form thin rings of mist which dissipate into the night air. "Grow, Mister Godwin? Taste? We don't *eat the marrow*." The solemn lad shudders and spits, sticking out his tongue amidst drool. "The marrow is bad. Evil."

"What is it then," I hunch to the fire, cheeks reddening, "if not a crop?"

Dismay fills young Leofric's face.

"A crop?" he stammers. "Nay. Can't say what it is, but it's not a crop. I'm not permitted near The Marrows. Best see for yourself once you get there. James can take you, but I won't go. Mum won't allow it. I naught wish to ever see or touch the marrow."

Leofric crosses his arms, falling silent.

When we at last doze, our backs pressed firmly against the stout hulls of two trees, visions of what the lad spoke rise from phantasmagoric pneuma and reshape as real and solid as any in this world.

Fires burn throughout the night. The lad stands on the edge of the clearing and stares at the carnage of the battlefield. Thick charcoal smoke billows and shrouds much of the slain troops. The smell of death is everywhere: in the bitter, sooty ash that coats the lad's tongue; in the blood-soaked soil that presses against the soles of his shoes; in the strewn viscera spilled by warring factions.

Hungry and hopeful, one of the village mongrels slips from a copse of trees, an obsidian, wolf-like beast with a strikingly long, sharp snout and piercing amber eyes. The beast lifts its nostrils and scents the air, lips curling in a snarl. Its hackles rise in jagged tufts of midnight fur. The mongrel emits a low, continuous growl and backs away, vanishing the way it came.

The lad's gaze draws to another—movement from within the clouds of thick smoke. A shape from the far side of the battlefield enters and walks through the grave of the dead. Around the specter, smoke parts to form a clear channel for passage.

The lad gasps.

"Sorcery!"

Behind the hooded figure, a cart drawn by horse is led in hand. The figure transects heaping mounds of human carcasses. The smoke clears further, discerning the figure is tall yet misshapen, knotted along the back with a prominent bulbous hump beneath the neck.

The specter crouches and wraps canvas around something unseen before lifting the parcel, not as large as a man, up in arms. As the figure turns, a corner of the covering slips, and a braided length of flaxen hair falls free.

Shaking, the lad gawks in disbelief. A young lass!

How has a lass come to be mixed with the fallen?

Before he can consider, the figure draws the horse and cart more quickly behind. The canvas-wrapped body lies lengthwise on the front seat like a sacred parcel. From the folds of a long, tattered black and green frock, a sharp blade is revealed.

Stopping to pry and hoist armory with unheralded strength, the sinister specter lifts and hacks various appendages from dead soldiers, cleaving and sawing, tugging until meat releases bone with snapping tendons, dry cracks of cartilage. The figure heaves and tosses the bounty of tattered limbs into the cart until it is nearly full.

The lad shakes with sick. Horror leaks from his eyes.

Posthaste, he turns and races off.

I watch the lad, Leofric, go.

I am alone here now, beholding with thine own eyes. On the scorched field amongst the defiled, soulless soldiers, flames of Hell burning purgatory, I bear witness.

At the edge of the distant wood, the Witch turns back. Ragged bloody- and mud-stained tatters of frock and hood dance with lascivious intent. Her hands unfurl, fingers like needle-pointed spines, the same from my nightmare, patter and pip.

The Witch reaches up to the heavens and plucks curses from the air.

Alighted crimson, those unholy eyes fix on me. Accursed! I shield myself, nearly tumbling in my panic. The Witch's gaze holds. Coal-hot sensations permeate me. I shall not fall. I shall not! Alas, I do, to the blood-infected earth. Suddenly, a looming pit opens beneath me and I am tumbling through, frail and defenseless as a wee babe.

"The Witch is coming, the Witch is coming," Satan's minions pitch from the tumultuous, tormenting darkness as I fall. "Behold the power of the Witch!"

I start awake to the sound of an owl hooting above me, my skin cold pocked with beads of fear. Twice now, I beheld the Witch of Marrowland.

Twice now, I crave to abandon this forsaken mission and escape back to my spiritual studies, the solidarity of the hermitary, which no longer seems a prison.

In the ruinous clearing, pyres stacked with countless bodies burn—a cyclonic incendiary of fire, smoke, and acrid soot. I press a cloth to my nose to quell the cloying, gagging detritus. Burning, the quickest means for villagers to dispose of the spoils of *victus*, is an unsavory task left to the people of the land.

Once done, a fresh page shall turn. But for the unsettling tale of a witch who hides amongst them. The tale of Leofric's encounter has spread throughout the village with the speed of flames igniting mounds of old, dusty hay.

James helms the wagon. We travel together, stopping at each wattle and daub dwelling we encounter. The leather satchel at my side holds precious vials of holy water and the rare *Codex Vaticanus*, which I guard with my life.

As we journey, villagers shift and eye one another with suspicion, whispering.

The people appear to welcome me—a stranger of a strange faith—well enough.

I knock and enter each home with stated clear intent. I seek evidence of malfeasance, Satan's lures: witch bottles, vessels with bodily excrement—blood, urine, hair; unnatural objects or occurrences—infestations of vermin, abominations of livestock, carvings, depraved artifacts, rattles of bones; of the flesh—buboes, fever, discolored phlegm, malignant pustules, rank growths of skin, unwed maidens with child; of the household and barns—practices or acts that go against God.

After each examination, I consecrate the polytheistic dwellings and families, which they allow despite their pagan ways.

The people are afraid and desperate for protection, regardless of the source.

My fingers grow rough from gripping the cross; the pages of the ancient holy, biblical scripture are worse for wear after each thumbing. I discover nothing during my scrutiny, much to my relief.

James clicks his tongue, slapping the reins twice against the steed's dappled rump. The wagon lurches forward, and my stomach drops with queasiness at the sudden motion. We rock and jitter, swaying precariously atop the uneven ground. The man has been appointed my guide and protector.

"Take me to The Marrows. I must see," I urge.

"Nay, I don't advise it."

True to empiricism, I bear the unfaltering need to dissect the matter properly for the written record. "Winnowing chaff from wheat is how we glean the bounty, is it not?"

James stares ahead, his farmer mind churning. Clopping hooves against rocks in the rutted dirt of the track, we veer off sharply. At the sudden change in balance, I shift wildly to the left, colliding with the man. To the woods we go, onto ruts hidden by crepitus grass, worn down at some juncture and partially regrown.

James halts the steed, reaching back for a long-handled sword; a thick-bladed dagger is already sheathed in one boot. "Villagers don't venture to The Marrows."

"Why is it so?"

"You'll see soon enough. Stay close. Don't nose around unless I tell you so."

Is the Witch hiding in The Marrows? Will the Witch strike when we least expect? The gloom of the forest renders my weary sight even dimmer.

We walk for a long time. The woods thicken, then open rather unexpectedly into a barren, dusty land where hardly anything grows except withered clumps of vegetation that favors rolling hay.

I am perplexed by the lack of vegetation, the absence of trees, the gloomy shadow. "Why is it cast here when there's no covering? Is this the place?"

"Nay, you'll know it. Make haste. We shan't remain here come dark."

Following behind James, my gaze rests on the sword slung across his back. He carries the weapon with deftness, a certain familiarity.

"You served the King, up in arms?" I query.

"Bloody hell, no king of mine." James screws up his face in disgust. He turns again and leads us away from the barren land into a gathering of broadleaf trees.

We journey beneath the arch of branches and intertwined foliage, the forest around us devoid of any sound. No birds chirping. No animal cries. No distant rustling or movements. There is only the sound of our feet against crisp, rusted leaves.

We step across fallen branches, twigs snapping loudly underfoot.

In the uncanny silence, the dry cracks startle me stiff.

The preternatural quietude of the woods unnerves me.

Unease sprouts with each shift of shadow, each twisted peel of bark, a part of the supernatural visage of the Witch in disguise. "Maybe it's not necessary." Sweat drips from the back of my neck. "Maybe we turn back, head for home."

"Aye, you feel it now." James leers at me not unkindly. Two missing teeth form a wide space between his upper teeth. The tip of his tongue pokes through the gap as if to test it. "The taint in The Marrow runs deep, runs through it all." His rough fingers scratch the reddish, wiry scruff on his face with a rasp. "That's why the village was moved plank by plank years ago."

"The entire village relocated?"

"Aye. Dwellings used to start just a few yards to the east of where we came in. Then, after a bad time, a sick yarn, *my gop won't speak it!* Villagers up and took their homes down. Moved the whole lot, resettled in the village you've come to know. They moved as far away as they could without abandoning the land itself. Dug fresh wells. Wouldn't use stones from the original wells since they're full of marrow rot."

I am mystified. "I beseech you, explain."

"Marrow leeches into the water first, then the soil, then *all that remains*. Shame is, the soil is good, aplenty, richly fertile. The seasons aren't too extreme. The land is ripened for growing and harvesting. Otherwise, the people would have abandoned it. Many did. Couldn't bear living near the woodland, knowing what it bleeds."

James slows and steps with care. "Place your feet with mine," he instructs.

I fall in stride behind him and step only into each impression left by his treads in the loamy soil.

Trees loosen and change in variety; trees with bleached bones and black scars and slashes on the trunks which resemble strange carvings rise. Scars run deep into their bark. A bilious mustard substance oozes from whorls in the pale trunks, leaking down the stems of the trees, where it gathers and pools around the knotty roots.

Bewildered, I stop.

Foul odors of gaseous human excrement and animal decomposition accost me. I rip the cloth from my pocket and place it over my mouth in a gag. At the base of the trees, ooze burbles and bursts with vague splashes, releasing vapors that hiss.

Folding and mounding, the ooze twists into ribbons

as thick around as sausages, radiating out from the epicenter of each tree. In all directions, viscous vines snake and cross until we find ourselves in a tangled web.

Filled with uncertainty and gut-churning disgust, the cloth flitters from my hand, landing at the divergence of two streams. I reach for it, and James barks, "Leave it be, Father! Lest you wish to perish the most gruesome of deaths."

I jerk back, hands shaking.

"Await."

James moves stealthily, overstepping the mustard veins, sword unsheathed by a freshly gloved hand.

Arching his back, he heaves the blade and cuts through a stout, low-hanging branch with all his might. One hand seizes the felled branch, pulling it toward him, positioned at arm's length.

The dagger emerges.

James strips bark from the branch, cutting off the bone-white sheathing, chipping at the black, ominous scars. The blade nimbly separates layers until the sharp tip reaches pale wood, which James cracks open with a hard snapping of wrists. Once the center of the wood is entirely exposed and smooth, he says, "This is what you seek."

James thrusts the cleaved wood in my direction.

Whilst mindful not to move from the spot, I peer at the offering.

"Go on, take a better look." James steps high and wide toward me, avoiding the traps at his feet. "See for yourself."

Reflexively, my hand slips inside the leather satchel and seizes the crucifix. Studying the cleaved branch, my eyes widen with understanding.

The heart of the wood is gritty, gray mottle, the choicest of food. The seat of animal vigor. Fatty, soft, and richly gelatinous, sweet succulence meant for covetous imbibing. On any other occasion, such as a celebratory feast of oxen bones, the lifeblood in bones melts into a man's tongue like freshly churned butter.

The discovery astounds and horrifies me. The seat of life should not exist in the hollows of the accursed, blanched trees but only reside within the bones of living, breathing creatures of God's design.

"Herein lies the marrow of Marrowland and its bloody namesake." Teeth clenched, James motions to the oozing coils which appear to expand and contract with breath. "At least, in part, this is the taint I speak of."

He hurls the branch as far as it will go, dusting his gloved hands with hard slaps.

When I at last depart the village, evident relief lightens in the faces of the villagers who have gathered in procession to bid me farewell.

Astride a fine white steed, the wartime mount abandoned after the recent battle, the villagers bequeathed it to me as a parting gift. I ride out feeling taller and smaller than I ever have before.

Leofric is not glimpsed amongst them.

Melancholy blossoms like a dark flower of regret in my chest. I have failed to unmask the Witch for the frightened lad. The grueling search proved futile. It yielded no answers or clues into what Leofric had witnessed.

No lass had been found amiss. No trail had led me to Satan's lair.

No evidence of an unwed with child by the Devil's seed had been uncovered.

Wartime stress reconfigures a man's constitution. Perhaps what Leofric saw was a mere figment of his youthful, war-torn imagination?

I ride from the village, glad to be rid of the unsavory cause.

Riding for many hours, weary and drowsy, I yearn to stop but do not want to sleep outside alone. As if conjured, a light appears in the distance.

A torch set in a window.

Here, I stop, dismount, and knock upon the door.

A pale-faced maiden opens the door and invites me inside. "Sit for a spell." She is agreeable and pleasant in countenance, provides respite from my worry, a much-needed reprieve from the arduous journey. "Care for a peck?"

I agree quickly.

Before me is set glossy slivers of meat, stewed potatoes, a hunk of thick-crusted bread from the burning hearth. The plate is a feast.

Ravenous, I eat hurriedly.

The peculiar yet not unsavory tender slices wrap around my tongue. "What is this? 'Tis most unexpected," I murmur, finding the meat odd yet satisfying.

I chew and swallow, taking another bite.

"I'll fetch a pail of goat's milk from the barn to warm our bellies." The maiden hesitates just outside the door. She turns back and gives warning. "Whatever you do, don't look in the back room." The entry shuts firmly behind her.

My hackles rise. Outside, the wind pitches high with shrillness, rattling the threadbare door. Cold gusts enter through cracks between thin planks, chilling me despite the roaring fire.

Behind me, a door creaks open.

Grasping the metal torch, I rise, unable to contain myself. Far from the village, the village reaches me still.

With tremulous trepidation, I creep toward the back room. The maiden's warning beguiling, I perch on the eve of the doorway, thrust light into the darkness, and poke inside. The instant stench of death foils me, fills me with perfusions of fear.

Dim light wavers across a mountainous jumble of gruesome bones contained by a large wooden trough. The trembling glow uncovers bite marks, distinct scrapings of teeth. The bones are stripped clean but for meaty tufts clinging beneath bulbous, cartilaginous joints. It is the cleaved limbs of the slain soldiers.

I draw a few steps closer despite my will to run, for there is something else which draws my eyes to it.

At the center of each bone is a whittled hole of uniform concavity—the exact size and shape of the Witch's black, marrow-sucking mouth.

Memory of the terrible nightmare at the onset of my journey shocks me. I have another, even more terrible, realization. "No," I gasp with revulsion, and the slivers of meat I gobbled down with supper rise with a sickly gurgle.

Vomitus projects from my mouth, spewing across the floor.

My heel strikes an object, a poppet, a handful of trinkets.

The trinkets scatter, rattling.

No child lives here!

I flee the forsaken place, screaming with all my lungs.

Scrambling upon the steed, I kick it to a full gallop, and we thunder toward home.

The priory provides me solace. Time passes, and with it, the nightmares diminish. Grueling labor keeps me fit. The only company I keep is the chickens, goats, and steed. The livestock fared better than I feared, grazing the fields and drinking from the traversing streams in the hills during my absence.

One morning, a curious white hare hops from the woods to watch me toil in the gardens. I welcome the docile creature's steady attention and companionship. It has returned every day since.

Harvesting and seeding keep unbidden thoughts away, mostly.

Days of autumn shorten. Nights arrive more quickly.

During the evening, a hot sticky paranoia, a cloying suspicion, afflicts me. I find myself jumping at every shadow, at the slightest noise, until I deem myself jittery and ill at ease and generally unwell in mind and spirit.

I tend my spiritual garden with renewed fervor.

At long last, a missive arrives by courier from the abbey—the long-awaited reply to the journal I've kept, my telling of Marrowland, my fastidious account of the lurid details of those dreadful days, the Witch, the harrowing discovery in the woods there, for the historic record.

Eager, I open the letter, ready to answer the abbott's call to action.

Father Godwin,

Upon reading of your experience, I am stunned by your news and most disturbed by your present condition. I shall send Father Constance, posthaste, to rejoin you—for two is better than one in times like these! I fear solitude weakens your constitution. The company of brethren, I believe, is the remedy. In the meantime, may God be with you in the darkness.

Abbott Cyrius Bartholemew

After finishing supper—a thickened bean soup, goat's cheese, and hearth-baked bread, a knock comes at the door. I open it, expecting Brother Constance, and the white hare from the garden hops across the threshold. Its pink nose and long whiskers twitch. Its gentle button eyes gleam.

The hare's eyes blaze red with the raging infernos of Hellfire. A blurry trickery of shamanism, the creature shapeshifts before my eyes, growing tall.

The Witch of Marrowland is at my door!

Aghast by her blasphemous metamorphosis, I shriek and flail, stuttering back.

A flourish of bloody, tattered rags, the Witch thrusts upon me. Her arms stretch and snake to grip me in a vise. Wrapped from my neck down to my feet, I am bound. When the Witch moves, the invisible iron shackles remain.

Spellbound!

The Witch's black mouth leaks glossy ribbons of blood and other vile fluids. Rank offal accosts my nostrils. Spiny nails clasp to my face.

At first, tender and loving, the Witch embraces me like a lover, draws me near.

Her bloody orifice distends into a gaping black maw. Inside, I glimpse an abyss, an impenetrable blackness which sucks and rips fleshy threads of my corporeal form from my bones, spiraling out amid floating gore. My screams of agony are unraveled.

Oily blackness sinks me deeper.

Knotty, deformed knuckles ridge my face. My head is pressed between both hands; the iron clasp pushes together in a torturous head-crushing device. Cracks and snaps. Bones break. A searing, soul-crushing pain.

Keening, animalistic wails explode from the ugly mash of my face. It is I, I undone. I do not recognize the stranger.

The Witch proves a most formidable adversary. She is wickedly strong, imbued by Satan's lust, unrelenting in depravity and brutality; I cease to struggle.

For I am powerless.

Sour digestive soup burbles in my throat, the same vociferous babbling of the brook that feeds the gardens, which I carved with my own hands.

The slow crush extrudes one eyeball, shifts pressure, mercilessly springs the second, vanquishing me to icy darkness. Each bloody, vitreous orb is left to dangle by its stinging coil. She pops the organs free and into her mouth, swallowing them down.

The Witch smashes my head like a rotten gourd, scattering bits about.

My spirit screams horribly, for my mouth is gone.

The wicked serpentine tongue swirls, lapping and licking fleshy splits. Her black mouth slurps, titters and feasts, leaks caustic saliva—coarse salt thrown on hundreds of raw wounds. Rotten teeth nibble, they nip, rip. Vigorously, the vile, devious abomination bores through the chamber of my skull, latching to the opening like a babe on a tit. The Witch draws and pulls forcefully, suckling, *suckling*.

Until nothing remains of my marrow or my eternal soul.

Abbott Cyrius,
I have come to the priory as you instructed. Upon my arrival, I find it empty. There's no sign of Father Godwin. In the fortnight and five days since my arrival, he has not returned. I shall await him while overseeing matters of the priory as is my holy duty—tending to the livestock and gardens, upholding its fine working state in his absence, since there is no other. The harvest proves bountiful. The livestock are hearty and fruitful in production of eggs and milk. Plenty for me to live on—with dry goods in the cellar. A noble steed resides in the barn. Not one of ours as far as I can tell. I will tend to it. Exercise it in the fields to keep condition until the snow arrives. Outside, a portion of the gardens require tilling and seeding. My toils are great, yet I am not alone. A brilliant-white hare keeps me company while I work. I believe the curious creature is a sign of prosperity, sent by God to welcome me to my new home.
In Holy Grace,
Brother Constance

SCREAMS FROM THE DARK AGES

Heather Ann Larson

The dank halls of the dungeon level were dark, foreboding. The few candles lit along the way illuminated very little, providing nothing more than a dim glow, making visible only a small area beyond their flame. The only sound was a low melody emanating from the harp in the library. The music was haunting and enchanting, and it drew her in.

She ran her fingers along the rough brick of the walls. The dirt floor was cold and refreshing on her bare feet. Although the small pebbles poked into her as she walked, she did not feel pain, so calloused were her feet. Something such as her had no need for shoes, no need for warm clothing—not when alone in a castle full of empty memories and ghosts.

As she neared the library and its tranquil music, a small mouse scurried across the floor in front of her. Instinct took hold; she lunged for the rodent. The mouse was quick, but she was far faster. Centuries of experience, and the bite of a forsaken one, had given her the best reflexes, speed, and agility ever known. She had the poor thing in hand before it got halfway to the hole in the wall it had been aiming for.

She started with the head, severing it at the shoulders with her razor-sharp teeth. She was so hungry; it had been a long time since she had fresh blood. Humans and animals alike knew to stay away from Castle Draydon. The rumors of nightwalkers inhabiting the castle were true, and all were smart enough not to test whether the vampyrs had left or if they remained. Even the nocturnal animals hadn't remained, at least not the ones that knew better. The little mouse was a stroke of luck, or it was dim. Either way, it was dead.

The lady continued down the hall. Her love was calling her; the music of the harp crescendoed as she entered the library. Ruby-red lips and fierce black eyes turned to greet her as she entered the room. She smiled as Katherine stood, turned to her, and embraced her. Lady Eleanor shared her meager meal, then her supple body, with her love.

Baron Reginald Stonehaven reined his horse to a stop at the castle's entry gates. He had left ahead of his family to get the lay of the land and to make a round through the castle before they arrived. He wanted everything ready so they could unload the moment the rest of the party arrived. It had been a long three weeks, and he was ready to sleep in his own bed and feast at his own table. He could see there was a lot of work to be done before that would happen.

His right-hand man, Lucien Thorne, came to a stop beside him. "Looks like the damned thing has never been lived in, it's so run down," he commented. He looked to Reginald, who shook his head. "You sure this was a good move, Reginald?"

Reginald shook his head, wondering the same thing as Lucien. Was it a good move? He bought the castle and land, deed free and clear, for a price too good to be true. That usually meant things really were too good to be true. But they also needed to leave Lancaster in a hurry, as the Stonehaven name had been smeared by Reginald's brother. In fact, Leopold's actions were so scandalous that Reginald's family had been attacked in the square in retaliation. Reginald forbade his wife, son, and two daughters from leaving their home. He put the word out he was looking for new lodgings; a letter about Castle Draydon, outside of Penrith, came back rather quickly. The cost was right, and he had no other options at that point. It was either take the offer or risk being beaten just for going to the market.

Looking at the place, he could see why it came in at such a low sum. Most castles appeared a bit run down; Castle Draydon looked derelict and forgotten. Built in the middle of a hillfort, it stood tall and menacing over the surrounding land. The moat was dry and cracked. The outside of the stone perimeter wall was crumbling. The drawbridge appeared at least functional, but Reginald needed to test it before he would dare allow his family on it.

The men gently spurred their horses, allowing them

a slow pace toward the lift. "All this decay and deterioration, yet the front gate seems strong and well cared for," Reginald said. "Maybe this means the entire place isn't as bad as this outer wall." There were a few places on the drawbridge that would need reinforced, but that should be easily managed with a few planks.

Lucien had his doubts. He had heard whisperings of Castle Draydon, had shared what he knew with Reginald. He didn't take it kindly when Reginald scoffed at him, when Reginald told him to pull up his breeches and get on with packing, that such things didn't exist. But Lucien had seen things, had battled things not natural to this world. His family was well-known for being a line of powerful witches and wizards. He felt an ominous sense of doom around the whole mission they were about to embark upon.

He almost didn't come, had decided to leave Reginald's employ before the family left, but he felt a duty to them in the end and decided to make the journey. Lucien's family had worked with the Stonehavens for two generations prior; Lucien wasn't about to be the one to break that bond. And he felt he needed to protect them as far as his abilities would allow, which wasn't much—his mother had been far more powerful than he. He just hoped what he knew would be enough.

Still, seeing the castle in its condition upon their arrival, the whisperings clawed their way back into his mind. It was coming on sunset, and he didn't like the feeling he was getting from the structure. It gave off an aura of blackness, of death. He wasn't sure he wanted to go beyond the drawbridge.

Lucien was drawn out of his reverie when Reginald dismounted and made his way to the portcullis entrance. As there was no way to close it from the outside, it had remained open for many years.

"This damned thing better close. The whole winch and chain are rusted. This will need replacing first thing," Reginald told Lucien. "Start taking notes now; we will need to get men and supplies as soon as possible." Reginald shook his head again. "Maybe the inside ..." He trailed off, hoping beyond hope that too much work wasn't needed to make the place at least livable. He loved his family, and it would break his soul if this place was so dilapidated that fixing it would be impossible.

She heard them miles before they arrived, but she wasn't certain they were coming to her castle until they were a few miles out. It had been *years* since a human dared step foot in Castle Draydon. She was giddy with excitement, something she hadn't felt in a very long time. She practically skipped to the dungeon library to tell Katherine the news, assuming she was there. While she didn't have a lot of information, she knew the humans were coming to the castle, and she knew it was two men on horseback.

She did, in fact, find Katherine in the library, a room she seldom left those days. Katherine loved to lounge in that room, to sit at the harp or inhale the scent of old parchment, a smell that intoxicated her. Lady Eleanor found the room dull and boring, but Katherine thrived there.

Lady Eleanor thrilled in the hunt, and it had been many a year since she had been able to properly hunt her prey. With the presence of these males and their horses, she knew she and Katherine would feast grandly, which would give them renewed strength and vitality. The few meager animals they had feasted on in recent years sustained them, but they didn't truly give them life. That was something that had to come from a human. The beautiful beasts they were riding would also supply them with a significant meal, one they could keep alive and take from over a long period of time.

The ladies of the manor made their way to the tallest tower and watched the guests as they assessed the perimeter of the place. They could tell the gents were unimpressed with what they found. There was nothing they could do about the bailey, but the men would expect that to look similar to the rest of the hillfort's perimeter anyway. But they could improve the interior of the place somewhat.

Lady Eleanor and Katherine were a blur as they went through the entrance hall, dining hall, and kitchen, attempting to rid the rooms of the obvious absence of hot-blooded life over the last hundred years. They had unnatural speed and agility, granting them the means to get the dust, dirt, cobwebs, and crumbled pieces of castle cleaned up before the men were at the portcullis. The kitchen was reassembled to a presentable state.

Then they went upstairs and took two rooms, the room belonging to the master of the castle and the servant's room next door, giving the bedrooms a look that said company was expected. They could continue with the other rooms after the men settled for the night.

They would let the duo get comfortable that first night. For that solitary night, the men would get the rest they needed. The ladies would give them just enough time to drop any worries they had. After that, it was anyone's game.

The men became more downhearted as they entered the bailey and saw the further neglect of the place. Reginald only hoped the stables were in good enough shape to hold the horses for the next few nights, at least until he could get them cleaned up and reinforced if necessary. His wishes for that were granted, as the stables were in better shape than anything they had come across on the grounds to that point. The stalls, surprisingly, looked mucked, and there seemed to be fresh hay present. Perplexed, the men put the horses in, gave them a bit of a rubdown, and went back outside to inspect the well. They took their traveling bags with them.

The well was also in relatively good shape. It had been covered, and the crank was housed well, meaning there was minimal rust. The bucket appeared in decent shape. Lucien drew water for the horses; it was clean and smelled sweeter than any water the men had ever smelled before. The horses seemed to agree with the assessment and drank heartily.

The two walked across the bailey to the front doors. The door appeared to have not been barred properly, and it swung open as they approached, the hinges creaking loudly, eerily, a long *reeeeeee* as the doorway widened inch by painful inch. They looked at each other, then back at the doors. Lucien thought he saw a shadow cross the threshold, but he concluded it must have been a trick of the light as a second glance yielded nothing present. He turned to ask Reginald if he saw anything, but the man was already striding inside, having set his bags down hastily just outside the entrance, his focus set on a gilded mirror hanging just inside the great hall.

"By the gods, this is an exact replica of the mirror my grandmother had hanging in her great hall," he said. He was shaken—that mirror had been commissioned by the greatest mirror maker of the time. He knew there was no duplicate. "How in all the world could this mirror have ended up here? To my knowledge, that mirror still hangs in the hall of Stonehaven Castle to this day." He was visibly trembling, his eyes wide as saucers, and Lucien became concerned.

"We must go sit, Reginald, let this shock pass. Surely this mirror isn't the exact same as your grandmother's. There must be something different, no matter how small the detail." Lucien tried to calm his friend and boss, but his words weren't getting through. It was as though Reginald was in a trance he couldn't be brought out of. Lucien couldn't understand the sentiment anyway; the mirror was cracked, the gold was flaking, and it had the overall aura of a cheap trinket.

Lucien managed to get Reginald seated at the long table in the great hall, thankful there were still a few old chairs and the banquet table to sit him at. He ran back out to the well and drew up water for the poor man. He also stopped by his horse and grabbed a jug of fermented cider, knowing Reginald was going to need something to get him back on track.

Going as fast as he could without spilling the water bucket, Lucien reentered the castle. Just as he passed into the room, he thought he saw the shadow of someone walking just down the hall to the left. It prickled his senses, put him on alert. He stopped in his tracks, peering into the darkening hall. "Is anybody there?" he asked. He was absolutely certain a person had walked into a room down that way. He shook his head to clear it; he didn't have time for shadows. He continued into the great hall.

He found Reginald walking the length of the room, running his hand along the wall and muttering to himself. Reginald's head was on a swivel, trying to take in the contents of the room as quickly as he could.

Reginald couldn't believe the things he was seeing. They were exactly the same as his grandparents' castle. *How can this be? What in the bloody hell is going on here?* he asked himself. He hadn't been to Stonehaven Castle since his wedding day twenty-five years ago, but he had been there every day from when his parents died just after his thirteenth birthday until the day he took Sibyl to be his wife. He knew every tapestry, painting, and relic in detail. He had been a curious boy and had explored that place thoroughly—he knew every stitch, stroke, and melding from a hammer with intimacy.

So how did those things get to Castle Draydon? It was impossible. He turned to Lucien, who had cleared his throat to get Reginald's attention. The look on Reginald's face was utter bewilderment.

"Lucien, what the devil do you think is going on here? There is no possible way these things can be the same," he said, stumbling again as the heaviness of the place oppressed him.

Lucien still didn't understand. The place, whilst clean, was in tatters. The wall hangings were threadbare, the paintings were sun-bleached to a dull hue, and the refectory table was chipped down its length. It was almost as if the men were seeing two different rooms. He was stymied. He decided they had traveled too hard over the last few days and needed rest. Things would turn around in the morning.

Reginald must have read his mind, as he turned to

Lucien and said, "Maybe we just need sleep, my good man. My mind feels adrift, foggy. I can't hardly focus on a single thought." He rounded the table and headed toward the stairs, which were off the entrance to the great hall. "The bedrooms are surely upstairs. Let's see if they're at least clean enough to kip for one night. We can get things more prepared on the morrow."

Lucien was grateful Reginald was finally thinking straight. His brain might be foggy, but he had voiced what Lucien had been about to say. He followed Reginald up the stairs, feeling weary and beaten.

There were five bedrooms; Reginald had been given a verbal tour of the place when he took the deed. He knew the master's room was the second door in, the first room being the servant's quarters. He was told the rooms were adjoined by a small door that locked from the side of the master's room. He had the key for that door, along with a key to all the other bedrooms, in his possession. He had, however, left it in his bag outside the front of the castle. He prayed the bedroom doors were unlocked.

Lucien tried his door first and nodded to Reginald as the door opened and he went into the room. He couldn't believe his eyes. In comparison to the great hall, the servant's room was tidy, spotless, and welcoming. The bed looked to be dressed and ready to accept him for the night. There was nary a speck of dust in the place. Even the chamber pot was clean, free of rust, polished to a bright shine. The difference between there and downstairs was astonishing. How had it been so well preserved?

When Reginald opened the door to his room, his jaw dropped. An enormous four-poster bed abutted one wall; it was covered in a lavish fur. Light curtains were drawn, and a canopy hung suspended from above. A large chest of drawers stood on the opposite wall from the bed. A chest lay at the foot of the bed, and a lush rug covered nearly the entire room. *Sibyl is going to think she died and went to Heaven*, Reginald thought. *She's been talking about these fancy beds for years now, and here she'll have one of her very own. She won't know what to do with herself.*

The men met back in the hallway several minutes later, travel weary and ready to end their day. They trudged back to the entrance to gather their bags, discussing the state of their rooms. They agreed the previous deed holders must have readied things for the Stonehavens upon transfer of ownership. After ensuring the front doors were barred tightly, they made their way back upstairs and bade each other good night as they went into their separate rooms.

Reginald didn't bother to dig out the key to unlock the door between the rooms. With only the two of them there, and having seen nobody for miles and miles, he wasn't concerned about needing Lucien during the night. Even their inability to draw the front gate closed didn't cause him concern. He expected no unwanted visitors and no conundrums. Come morning, they would explore the rest of the place and prepare the rooms for his family, who were due to arrive two days hence.

Lucien woke feeling rested but disturbed. He had dark dreams through the night. The wizard part of him knew it was a bad omen; his dreams had contained the teeth of feral cats, dripping blood, hearts thumping in increasingly slower beats. He saw funeral shrouds and a procession of mourners, though the faces were all blurred. The background remained foggy and dismal the entire night. Throughout the dreams, no matter what was happening, he heard the music of a harp, its tune slow, haunting; it felt ominous. Although the morning brought bright sunshine and birdsong, Lucien knew dark events were on the horizon.

Reginald also felt restored from a night of uninterrupted sleep on an incredibly comfortable bed. But he too harbored feelings of restlessness and doom. He thought this absurd. The morning dawned clear and beautiful. There was a gentle breeze bringing with it the scent of wild chamomile and heather. He could hear the birds chirping outside his window, proclaiming all was right in the world. He knew they had a lot of work ahead of them that day, but he wanted a few more moments of solitude and comfort before it all officially started.

The two met at the large table in the great hall twenty minutes later. They decided to start their day in the kitchen as they needed to eat anyway. Sharing a look of concern, they headed that direction. Both men had low expectations of what they were bound to find.

Surprisingly, the kitchen was in good order. There was minimal dust and dirt, and the dishes were in usable shape. The wood stove was empty and clean, and the cooking top appeared up to the challenge. There was even a stack of wood nearby, which they placed into the stove and lit to heat the room. Lucien went to retrieve their food bag, and the two dined on dried meat, dark bread, and a bit of ale. With so much to do, they knew lunch would likely be supper, so they figured they better eat whilst they could.

The tour of the estate went quickly, as they found all the bedrooms in the same state they found their own the previous evening. Seeing as how the kitchen only needed a good scrub and a broom, he left that to the maids upon their arrival. They also left the library and the dungeon level for later. With little to do inside the castle, they headed outdoors.

Reginald decided they would focus on the gate first, followed by the garden. They didn't have the chain and winch to replace the rusted ones, but they could fortify its sturdiness with pieces of wood they found in the stables. He made mental notes about the length and type of chain and winch they would need as they worked. He decided the gate itself didn't need much work. Upon closer inspection, the worst of the damage was to the wall, which he had no intention of attempting to fix, and to the moat, but only because it was dry. A healthy rain would fill it up.

The work on the drawbridge took more time than the two initially anticipated it would, and it was midafternoon by time they were finished. Lucien went to find a spot for Sibyl's garden—the two would plant vegetables and several plants used for medicinal purposes. He had observed what he thought would be a perfect spot yesterday as they were riding up to the stables, but he wanted to stand in the spot, get a reading on it to see if he felt a vitality that would yield good crops.

As he crossed the bailey, he glanced up to a window on the second floor, likely one of the bedrooms, although it wouldn't be his or Reginald's because their rooms lay on the opposite side. He thought he saw a figure standing in the room, but when he blinked and looked a second time, there was nothing there. But he could feel a negative energy coming from that direction. His dreams came rushing back to him, and he felt a chill rush down his spine, making the hairs on his neck stand on end and his skin feel like something prickled it. He had had this feeling before; nothing good had come of it.

He advanced toward the plot of ground where he planned to put the garden, but his head felt foggy and detached, like he wasn't there. The bleak feeling from his nightmare stayed with him, he couldn't shake it, and he walked right past the intended plot and into a cemetery that lay just beyond. *What the devil?* he thought. *How did we miss this yesterday? It's so near the stables, I can't believe we didn't see it.* Indeed, the size of the graveyard was so large he was stunned they hadn't found it last evening. There were approximately twenty headstones or markers where he presumed bodies were buried. With a number that large, he assumed an entire family must have died out there. But it had a shadow to it like it was trying to stay hidden, and a feeling of dread and torture emanated from it. Even in the daylight it had a dim quality. He needed to find Reginald and tell him.

While Lucien was happening upon the hidden cemetery, Reginald was on a mission to ensure the garderobe was in acceptable condition for his family and to make sure there was a chamber pot in each bedroom. It wasn't a job he was looking forward to, but he knew it was an important one to address. He would, however, leave the cleaning of the items to the maid staff. He also needed to see if there was still a usable tub; he knew Sibyl would want to bathe the children and herself as soon as they arrived. Seeing as how it was quite cool in the evenings, he also needed to find some rocks to heat for the water.

Unable to explain it, he suddenly felt forlorn, downtrodden. He put his hand against the wall outside the bathroom, the weight of this feeling crushing him; he almost fell to his knees but managed to stay standing. He shook his head, trying to clear the cobwebs. He just missed his family—he hadn't seen them since he left ahead of them three weeks past—and the feeling overcame him in that moment. That was all it was. He resolved to pull it together and get on with his work. He would see them tomorrow.

He had just entered the lavatory when Lucien came in, short of breath from having walked at a near jog. He could tell by the strained look on the man's face it was important.

"Boss, I found a cemetery on the property. It's just past the place we talked about for the garden. I don't like it, Reginald. It's giving off an aura of pain and despair." Lucien hoped Reginald understood the gravity of what he was being told. What was coming off that boneyard was a warning, and he needed Reginald to understand the gravity of the situation.

Reginald wanted to scoff at Lucien, to tell Lucien he was going mad, but he was also starting to feel uncomfortable in the estate. The feelings he just experienced, the fact this castle felt like a replica of his grandparents' castle, and the restless feeling he had upon awakening that morning were all beginning to take their toll. He could sense something wasn't quite right about Castle Draydon, yet there was nothing he could do about it. He held the deed, had spent a lot of coin on the purchase, and they were stuck with it. For better or worse, they would have to figure out what exactly was going on in that place and deal with it forthwith.

He knew Lucien was more knowledgeable about the subject of gloom and doom than he was, so he deferred to the man. "What do we do, Lucien? We can't go back, for Sibyl and the rest will arrive on the morrow. I own this castle and this land. We have nowhere else to go." He was hopeful Lucien had a solution already brewing.

The men walked back to the great hall, where Lucien

sat with a book his mother had given him many years ago. He needed time to look through it, to see what his family knew about what he thought they may be dealing with. He asked Reginald to bring him some strong cider ale to help him think; what he really wanted was for Reginald to leave him be for a few moments. He needed to channel his energy and focus on the task at hand, and the raw fear pouring off Reginald was clogging his mental clarity. Lucien was scared too, but what was emanating from Reginald was nearly palpable. It was interfering with Lucien's concentration.

While Reginald was in the kitchen getting the cider, Lucien closed his eyes and let his mind wander where it would. Images flashed through his head at a rapid pace: a beautiful maiden with flowing jet-black hair and vivid green eyes; a man that seemed to be a stranger, cast in shadow, approaching the castle, riding a colossal charcoal-grey stallion; his visage coming into view as the rising sun rounded the side of the castle, his skin as pale as parchment; a sense of immense terror and a struggle, feelings of helplessness as the maiden's family was away; and finally, the man with a stake through his heart and two crimson lines of blood running down the woman's neck.

He snapped out of his trance, her fury raging through his veins. His heart was pounding wildly, her anger boiling right under the surface. He jumped to his feet. The need for violence pulsed through him—he was ready to destroy the next living thing that came into his sight. He also experienced an intense hunger, a gnawing in his very soul for the life energy running through his own veins. Another image, a family slaughtered, the poor young thing standing over them crying although no tears came, blood on her hands and face, a shovel and the young woman covered in dirt as she stood beside the graves. But then . . .

One final image flashed through his mind, and with it came the most overwhelming feeling yet. He felt love, the kind that holds no boundaries and unites two souls together for the eternity of eternity. He glimpsed an exquisite form with golden curls down to its waist and lips the color of the brightest red apple. He longed for her, his heart feeling like it would explode from his chest with how much he needed to be with her. He saw locks of shining straw-colored coils intertwined with lengths of coal-black tresses.

Without warning, the feelings left him.

He stumbled, falling to his knees. The weight of their situation crashed into him like a pile of logs. He knew they were doomed; he had felt their hunger, their need to satiate their thirst with the blood of a human. It had been so very long for them, and he knew there would be no escaping their desire.

It then dawned on him there were two of them. He had been so overwhelmed with the feelings from the images and the swiftness of their departure that he hadn't put it together immediately. Two blood drinkers, nightwalkers of lore, resided in the castle. One more feeling raced through him; despair. He and Reginald were going to die, and there was nothing they would be able to do to stop it from happening.

His thoughts went to Reginald's family. They must be warned before they entered the gate, or they too would be bound to the same fate. How could Lucien possibly convince Reginald of what he had seen? Would they be able to warn Sibyl and the children in time?

He racked his brain, trying to remember what his mother had done last time the threat of these beasts was nigh. It came back to him slowly, the memory hazy but almost at his fingertips. *A red flag. She put up a red flag*, he remembered. Would the arriving party understand the significance of that warning? It had been years since such a threat loomed, and he was worried the significance of it would be far buried in their memories.

Lucien's head cleared when he heard Reginald hollering from the kitchen entryway. He jumped to his feet and ran to his friend, finding him pinwheeling, bewildered and looking like he was lost, his eyes roaming the great hall.

"Lucien, what has happened here? The tapestries and hangings, they're all changed. They look old, destroyed. The table, my god, the table looks like someone took an ax to it. What devilry has hold of this place?" Reginald was at a loss. He had never believed in things beyond the physical world, the things Lucien told him about. He was utterly confounded and wandered the great hall, a stupefied look on his face.

Looking his friend in the eyes, Lucien said, "The glamor has worn off, my friend. I believe I know what we're dealing with here, and I must warn you—we have a fight on our hands. We very well may not make it out of here alive." It broke Lucien's heart to tell Reginald those things, but he felt the man must know the truth. They needed to prepare.

Holding Lucien's gaze, Reginald whispered, "Wh-what do you mean, you know what we're dealing with? What glamor? What the bloody hell is going on here?"

Suddenly, a susurrus of whispering fabric danced and floated through the room. The men looked at each other, eyes wide, faces completely terrified. There was something there with them. Reginald was thinking of the tales of the place, wondering if mayhap they were true after all. Lucien, knowing what they were about to come face to face with, felt his stomach drop. He wasn't ready.

The men turned, in sync, toward the front of the great hall.

A woman stood there, or the shadow of one. Her back was to the men, but they could define it as female nonetheless. The shadow was tall, lithe. It seemed to be wearing a dress with flowing skirts that blew in front of her, although no breeze was present. Her hair, beautiful and flowing even though it was a silhouette, reached below her shapely buttocks, fanning across her back and over one shoulder. This phantasm was the embodiment of beauty and lust.

Lucien took a step forward, then another, hypnotized by the appearance of the specter. *I am right*, he thought. *The castle is home to nightwalkers. Are there only the two? Even at that, we hardly stand a chance*. He was terrified, and the primal part of his brain that warned him of pending danger tolled like a church bell on Sunday morning.

Like Lucien, Reginald was terrified, and he was frozen to the spot. His family was on their way, due to arrive tomorrow midday. What would his wife think of a ghost in her new home? The children would refuse to stay, he was certain of that. *What am I thinking? There is no such thing as ghosts*, he chided himself. *I have lost my bloody mind*. He regained his ability to move and was backpedaling, running into a chair and thumping firmly into the seat. His backward direction continued, and the chair toppled over. Reginald's head slammed into the stone floor, and everything went black.

The ghost seemed nonplussed by all the commotion, like she couldn't hear or didn't care. Lucien was thankful for her nonchalance and rushed to help Reginald up. When he realized Reginald was unconscious, he panicked. He didn't know what to do. He didn't want to leave the man passed out and vulnerable on the floor, but he had to risk fetching a cold rag and some cider.

Deciding the supplies he needed to wake Reginald up were more important, as the apparition hadn't moved since they first saw it, he ran into the kitchen. He grabbed a stray rag, which he wet in the bucket of water they had gathered earlier in the day, and the bottle of cider they drank from at breakfast. He also grabbed a blanket to place under Reginald's head. He didn't remember why in the world a blanket would be there, but he didn't care at that moment.

When he reentered the great hall, he gasped and stopped dead in his tracks. The thing was kneeling over Reginald—and his suspicions were confirmed. Lucien could see the woman's face clearly, could see the skin of her clawed hands outstretched, tracing the lines of Reginald's neck. She was as pale as the flour his mother used for making bread. "You're a vampyr," he hissed. He had seen one other vampyr in his life, and he was lucky he was alive to tell the tale.

Her head snapped up when she heard his words. She gave him a wide, seductive smile, her pointed fangs dipping just below her top lip. Her talons gently raked down Reginald's chest, stopping just above his heart. She cocked her head as if challenging Lucien to make a move.

Reginald's body quivered as the sharp nail of her forefinger pierced his skin through his jerkin and shirt. His eyes popped open in surprise; he was unsure where he was, how he got there, or why there was a beautiful woman bent over him. Then he realized she was slicing into him, and he looked down at the knife. Except there was no knife, only razor-sharp fingernails as long as a wild cat's and twice as sharp. He looked to her face and noticed her lack of complexion, noticed the waxen features of her skin, how it appeared as thin as a flake off a pastry.

He looked to find Lucien as he tried to crab crawl away from her. The pain from the talon puncturing his skin stopped him from moving more than an inch or two. He found Lucien and saw the absolute terror on the man's face. Reginald knew he was damned at that point. He had heard Lucien's story, but he hadn't believed it at the time. He knew what was likely to happen over the next several moments.

He looked back to the woman, considering whether conversation would help. Would she even speak the same tongue as he? He couldn't be sure, but he had to try. He knew his very life was on the line, and his instinct to survive was in full gear.

"Ma'am, I'm ever so sorry if we've disturbed your place of residence," Reginald began. Always the nobleman, he was well spoken despite his immense fear. "I have just purchased this castle, and I was unaware there was already someone in ownership of the property. If you please, my companion and I will promptly be on our way to find different lodgings for the time being."

Lady Eleanor laughed a deep, throaty laugh. The audacity of this human, this man, to presume she would simply step aside and let him leave after she hadn't dined properly in a very, very long time was comical to her. She intended to have her victim, and she always got what she wanted, at least since the time of her turning, that was.

Taking a step toward the two, Lucien brandished a wooden cross. It was a simple thing, just two pieces of wood nailed perpendicular to each other, with a smaller length on the top than the bottom, but it was blessed by the bishop. He knew the cross itself would be ineffective; the old wives' tales were untrue and dangerous to those who held stock in them. However, the one he had was wrapped in a fine silver filament, barely thicker than a piece of hair, which would have a great effect on the monster. Although a human would be unable to see the thin strand, he was aware the vampyr could see it. The silver would burn her skin wherever it touched, and the nightwalker wouldn't be able to heal where it came into contact with the talisman.

The vile thing recoiled at the sight of the instrument. It hissed and retreated, moving faster than Reginald had ever seen anything move. She sat on all fours, on the balls of her feet with one leg slightly raised, giving her the appearance of a panther he had seen in his daughter's picture book. She continued to bare her fangs, lips pulled back in a hideous snarl, as she slunk out of view, disappearing into a darkened recess in the far wall.

The men didn't need to speak to each other to know what the plan was. They were leaving right that moment. They weren't going to waste the opportunity to escape. Lucien knew for certain that if they stayed, they would both die. He didn't believe their deaths would be the quick, painless, merciful kind of deaths, either. He knew that monster would savor every moment of torturing them she possibly could.

They took off at a run toward the front entrance, Lucien remaining behind Reginald, maintaining his sense of duty. His family was bound, and he would honor that loyalty to the very end, no matter how bitter it may be.

They were mere meters away from their escape when another creature of equal beauty and grace dropped from above to block their way. Her wavy hair was as golden as the sun, her lips as ruby as the deepest red rose, and her skin was the color of a fish's underbelly. She had the finesse of a deer, immediately jumping toward them upon her landing in the doorway. She was centimeters from them, her eyes brilliantly wild and her teeth fully exposed. She was ready to eat, and she wasn't going to hold back as Lady Eleanor had.

A quiet whisper on the floor behind them told the men they were blocked in. A megrim entered both their minds, making them feel the lowest they had ever felt. The melancholy piercing their souls reduced them to feeling worthless, and they looked at each other with tears streaming down their faces. They knew it was their end.

Each of the women locked eyes with a different male, and a calm fell over the men. They became hypnotized, which, in turn, anesthetized their pain and fear. No longer afraid, their tears dried and their hearts calmed. This pleased the ladies as the taste of terror, in opposition to popular myth, tainted the taste of the blood. They used their hypnotic power to soothe their prey and to mollify them into submission. The more cooperative the victim, the more delectable the meal.

Taking the men by the hands, the women led them underground, to a place deeper than the men knew existed. Lady Eleanor and Katherine danced and giggled along the way, feeling like school girls about to have their first kiss with a secret love. They were starving, and the prospect of the meal within their grasp made them giddy.

Reginald and Lucien maintained their vacant stares, their minds poisoned beyond the ability to think or reason any longer. They were flies trapped in a spider's web. There would be no escape and no mercy, but they were far past the capacity to have such thoughts, anyway.

The ladies brought the men to their dining room, a small room with a simple eight-person table and elegant chairs they had moved from the great hall when it was in its glory. Lady Eleanor insisted they use their manners and eat as ladies of their class should eat. They would enjoy their meal with sophistication and grace. They buckled the men to the table with leather straps they had attached many years ago. As Lady Eleanor stood above Lucien and Katherine stood above Reginald, they released the hold over the men's minds.

The two looked around the room with wild fear in their eyes, struggling against the restraints holding them in place. Reginald's lack of belief didn't preclude the fact he was about to be destroyed by the very thing he previously touted as something that didn't exist. Lucien, however, knew exactly what was in store for them. Both men thought about Reginald's family and what they would arrive to tomorrow.

Knowing Reginald and Lucien weren't the only humans the women would be receiving in the castle, they agreed to fully satiate their need with the men. They would drink to their fill instead of rationing them out like they originally discussed. Because children mend quickly, and the children were coming.

The last sound from the men was their high-pitched screams as the vampyrs exposed their fangs and moved in, caressing the necks of their victims with their crimson lips before they partook.

THERE'S A RUMOR OF WITCHES HERE

Jae Mazer

...Leonidas said around his mouthful of food.

Leaf wondered if she should regret wooing this man.

"Witches, you say?" Leaf said. "Sounds like foolishness to me."

"Except it's not," Leonidas said as he stabbed his lamb with the tines of his fork, his passion for the subject of witches and the collapse of society taking hold. "Stories of hexes from the east, sexual relations with the Devil, curses, potions, poisons."

"Nonsense," Leaf chuffed into her glass of mead.

"I'm surprised you don't subscribe to belief of spiritual decay," Leonidas said, using his utensil to motion to the gold cross that rested at the nape of Leaf's neck.

Leaf traced her collarbone, coming to rest on the

precious metal, the tips of her precisely manicured fingers gliding across the gleaming totem.

"I believe in what's real," Leaf said. "Facts. God's love."

"If one believes in God, they must also believe in the Devil and his servants."

"Foolishness," Leaf repeated.

She breathed deeply, heaving out her chest, drawing Leonidas's attention away from his brain. It was not her first foray into the world of men. She knew how to set their attention astray.

"Anyways," Leonidas said, "I am glad to be here, hunting the Devil's concubines and co-conspirators."

"And why is that?" Leaf asked.

"Because I get to enjoy the pleasure of your company."

A tingle of heat kissed Leaf's cheeks as she dared hold Leonidas's gaze for a moment longer than was proper for a single maiden in a public place. She already teased the reputation of harlot by being out and about unaccompanied by a father or brother, priest or politician. There was none in her life, of course, which made it impossible to be anything but alone and isolated, unless she wanted to tiptoe the precipice of indecency by cavorting around solo.

No matter, though. The world had been in disarray for quite a spell. Leaf had felt the effects even decades after the fall of the Roman Empire and as far as her cottage on the outskirts of York. York still teemed with culture, though, which was why she ventured to the market to see what men came sniffing for excitement. Like this bloke, who had blown in on winds out of Constantinople.

"And why do you suppose witches have chosen this place to reside?" Leaf asked, dodging Leonidas's flirtations.

"Tales on the ocean and in the sand," he said.

"Murmured rumors in the ports about the disease here. Or lack thereof."

Leaf cocked her head and raised a neatly plucked brow.

"Surely, you know," he said, "though maybe you wouldn't. Not unless you've traveled afar."

"Know what?"

"The reaper has his grip on most of Europe," he said. "The Black Death lives large and loud, rotting everything in its wake."

"As it has for quite a spell now," Leaf pointed out.

"But here," he said, "death here is light and low. Few and far between."

"Oh, I wouldn't say that," she said. "There are many who have perished here."

"Not like elsewhere," he said, leaning in as if he was divulging taboo information. "There's not nearly enough graves for the number of dead piling up in other locales. Mass graves spill over, so the church is trying to burn the bodies, but the piles grow faster than flames can consume. Death toll rises like the rancid smoke, but here, here ..."

Leonidas paused to drink of his mead, the sweet thickness lingering on his mustache, glowing in the flame from the candelabra in the center of the table. He was a beautiful man, Leaf thought. A shag of chestnut curls bounced on his brow as he spoke with vigor, and his eyes were deep and dark as pitch. His beauty was why she had drawn his attention at the market earlier that day, dropping her handkerchief and causing him to misstep with the sway of her hip.

"Well, I, for one, have no problem if death has overlooked my tiny swath of the isle," Leaf said.

"If I can find the cause, though—or the cure, as it were—it could slow or end the decimation across the lands."

Such a kind man. And smart too. Both detective and doctor, traveled and wise. Dispatched all the way here, to this place that death neglected, to this alehouse where candlelight accentuated Leonidas's black eyes, high cheeks, and sharp jaw. The sight and sound of him, the beauty, summoned a swell and heat at the open of Leaf's thighs. She parted her knees beneath the table to allow the heat to disperse, and she willed her essence to waft and find Leonidas's nose.

"Well, a toast then," Leaf said, lifting her chalice of mead, "to finding the secret to death and life."

"To creation and destruction," Leonidas toasted, and their goblets clunked a thud through the noise of the alehouse.

They drank, they dined, they scooted closer until the outsides of their legs were pressed into one another. Leaf fanned herself with a fan made of bone and heirloom lace, a small hint of the beauty she possessed. She wished she could have freely worn her silks out in public, but she needed to blend in as a commoner and as a single woman on the prowl. Commoners and peasants wore wools, abrasive to the skin with little room for air or comfort, and her shift and kirtle were no exception. Her outfit was tied tightly to her throat and covered every exposure of her flesh. Leaf longed to tear away the fabric and toss it into the wood stove burning in the center of the ale house to allow the sweat soaking her milky skin to breathe and dry in the heat of the flame.

Thoughts of being naked in the center of the alehouse, with Leonidas's eyes upon her, caused her nether regions to moisten further. She shifted in her seat, her hand finding Leonidas's knee, wondering about the girth and length that rested hidden just above the touch of her hand.

Leonidas stammered. "We should, um ... Shall we call it a night?"

"We shall," Leaf purred, and poured the rest of her mead down her throat as she maintained eye contact with a sweating, squirming Leonidas.

They walked out of the sauna of the alehouse into a drizzly night, sheets of moisture like gossamer glowing around the torches that lit the row of doorways of the lane. Leaf cocooned herself into her cloak to shield herself from the cold, and as anticipated, Leonidas took this as a cue to drape his arm over her and pull her close. They walked past a handful of doorways lit by torches, until the doorways and torches ran out and the road split and turned in opposite directions. Leonidas took Leaf by the shoulders and placed his palm on her cheek.

"Your place?" he breathed, but didn't give her a chance to answer before his breath was in her mouth, his lips pressed on hers.

Their hands fumbled at layers of fabric, unable to feel curves and nooks through the heavy fabric. An ache radiated through Leaf as she craved for Leonidas, and his frantic pawing suggested he felt the same.

But ...

"It cannot be my home," she said, panting into him as his hands fondled the fold of fabric overtop her breasts.

He kissed her hard and deep before he spoke again, pressing his tongue on hers, enticing a gag.

"Why?" he asked.

"My ... I live alone. It would be improper."

"I want to be improper," Leonidas said.

Leaf groaned into his mouth. She wanted him to be improper too. She wanted him to ravage her, to experience pleasure amidst all the sickness and pain that had plagued Europe over the past few years.

"Your place," she said.

Hands everywhere, seeking skin, craving release.

"Can't," he said. "I came with other detectives, a nursemaid, a scribe."

Of course he did. He traveled from faraway lands to discover the solution to the plague that threatened the future. It was more than a one-man job.

Could she? Could she bring him home? So what if he found out. So what if he knew, if it meant euphoria and pleasure, only if for one night.

"No," she said, and pushed Leonidas away. "We cannot, then."

Devastation painted his face.

"For now," she clarified. "I will come up with somewhere."

His expression softened. She worried she wouldn't see him again to follow through with the tension, but he came up with an idea.

"I shall meet you at half two in The Purple District," he said.

It took control of every muscle in her body not to wince, grimace, to scream in his face as rage and anxiety gurgled in her veins.

"Yes," she said through gritted teeth. "The Purple District. Sounds splendid."

Leonidas stripped her of her glove and pressed his wet lips on her knuckles.

"My heart aches for our next meeting," he said. He stepped to the side, offering her the crook of his arm. "I shall walk you home."

"No need," she said. "I'm close. And no one of danger is out and about these days, what with the sickness and all."

He hesitated but conceded, offering her a slight bow as he backed away. She answered with a deep curtsy before turning on her heels and sauntering down the lane, feeling his eyes on her backside the whole time, until she rounded the corner and disappeared into the night.

The heavy door closed with a whoosh, closing out the silence of the night. Inside Leaf's cottage, the fire crackled the beat and cantor of a haunting lilt, the screams of the embers a chorus of sopranos. Beyond that, silence. Leaf's heart was a stone in her throat as she listened for movement, for voices, for scratching. But there was nothing but the symphony of the fire.

Leaf pulled off her boots to quiet her steps, but her clothes whispered as she crept through the flickering dark. Her cottage was only one room—a kitchen on one side with a small oak barrel that served as a table, a sitting room designed around a stone fireplace in the wall, and a single bed tucked into an alcove along the back wall. There was nowhere for anyone to hide, to spy upon her, but still she felt eyes following her movements, felt the air disturbed by long, knobby fingers reaching for her.

Witches, Leonidas had said.

Leaf shivered, the movement rustling her shift. She held the fabric to keep it from speaking and went to the fire, where her hanging pot was simmering, and grabbed the ladle to scoop some water for tea. The minute her fingers wrapped around the wooden handle, she stifled a gasp. It was wet, warm, gritty. The ladle slipped from her fingers, falling into the pot, and splashed scorching water on her cheek. Leaf recoiled, her hand finding the burn on her cheek, spreading the gritty moisture over her face.

Leaf calmed her breathing in an attempt to cease her heart from thundering against her ribs. She went to her bed and sat and, with her dry hand, picked up the hand mirror resting on the bedside table.

It was impossible to tell how bad the burn was. The mirror was tarnished and yellowed with age, and the only light in the cottage came from the pulsing embers of the fireplace. But besides that, the spot on Leaf's cheek where the water had sizzled her flesh was streaked with a dark smear. Oily black was fingerpainted down the side of her face from the gore on the ladle. Leaf imagined it was wet soot, the byproduct of a belching, dying fire, but she knew better. Even in the yellow reflection she could see the black had a crimson tint, and she could smell the coppery tang of blood smeared close to her nose.

"You should not be in here," Leaf said.

A raspy laugh wheezed from behind Leaf as weight rested itself on the bed.

"I do not want you here," Leaf said through trembling lips.

"Nor I you, sister," the voice growled.

Hot breath warmed Leaf's cheek as a thick, pocked tongue wriggled its way into her ear. Leaf shook her head and made to stand, but meaty claws held her in place. A hand dense with warts and bite marks wrapped around Leaf's bare throat as another hand slithered its way beneath her cloak and wrapped around her waist, jagged nails piercing the wool and poking into the flesh of her belly.

"Release me," Leaf demanded.

The hands did not release her, nor did they venture farther.

"Unhand me!" Leaf shrieked.

The hands held tight as Leaf writhed and contorted, tearing the fabric of her clothing as she fought to get away. Leaf managed to stand, and the hands began clawing, ripping away Leaf's clothing as Leaf clawed back, her fingers searching for purchase on her assailant's face.

"Be gone!" Leaf screamed.

"Be gone!" the voice mimicked in a phlegm-coated baritone.

After much flailing and tearing and struggling, Leaf broke free of the hands' grasp. The voice rumbled a low laughter that spawned deep in a jiggling belly. Face to face, Leaf took in the voice of her unwanted companion.

"What have you done?" Leaf asked, despite knowing the answer.

Before her was a woman, gnarled and naked, long breasts resting atop her thick thighs as she stood at a crooked angle. Patches of hair sprouted from her mostly-bald head like a birch broom in the fits, and oozing pocks marred most of her wrinkled flesh. But Leaf was used to all that. What was new was the gleam of crimson over the woman's mouth, cheeks, and chin, and the chunks of fat, gore, and shreds of meat dripping from her rotted maw all over her bare chest.

"Tails, what have you done?"

Tails belched, and the stench of rotting meat and turned cream wafted from her mouth to Leaf's.

"What have *you* done, sister?" Tails asked.

"Nothing this night," Leaf said with a pout.

"Lies," Tails said.

"It's the God's honest truth," Leaf said, crossing her heart.

"Let me see," Tails hissed.

Leaf hated her sister pert near as much as Tails

hated her. But she wouldn't be called a liar. She had wanted to have done something, but she couldn't have brought Leonidas back here, not with his nose sniffing for witches. Not with Tails residing in the cellar out back.

"Fine," Leaf said. "Have a look."

Leaf undid her ties and laces and allowed her torn clothes to fall to the cottage floor in a heap. The heat from the fire warded away any gooseflesh that might have risen and kept her nipples soft and flat. She removed the emerald pins from her hair, freeing her lush auburn mane, the thick curls spilling down her body and resting on her buttocks and abdomen. Tails sniffled the air, and she stepped close to Leaf.

"I smell no seed," Tails said.

"Fuck no," Leaf muttered. "Ew."

Tails commenced her inspection, examining every bit of Leaf's body, exploring with her fingers, lifting Leaf's breasts to look beneath, and parting Leaf's gash to examine the folds of her labia.

"Freckle there, mole here," Tails said, like listing an inventory. "And yer left titty—she yet sags a tad lower than the right."

Tails thrust three fingers up inside her sister, scraping the walls of her vagina with jagged, necrotic fingers.

"Ouch!" Leaf yelped as Tails rooted around inside her.

Tails withdrew her fingers, licking them and pondering the taste.

"You speak the truth this night," Tails said. "The same imperfections remain. Your bits be loose still, and sour with yeast."

Leaf glowered.

"And what of you?" Leaf asked, stabbing a finger through the air at Tails's bloody face.

Tails's face contorted, slitting near in two as she broke

into a smile, revealing sharp teeth and black gums that oozed infection. Between her teeth were clumps of gristle and fur hanging like tendons in her mouth.

"Their numbers swell," Tails said. "They scuttle in the night. I hear them in my skull."

"The ships," Leaf said, more to herself than her sister.

"Ships?" Tails said, cocking her head like a spaniel.

"I met a man," Leaf said, jutting her chin in defiance. "A beautiful man. Came off a ship hailing from Constantinople."

Tails's eyes widened with horror.

"No," Tails hissed.

"Yes," Leaf confirmed. "A detective. A physician here with a crew to investigate a rumor of witches."

"You leave them alone," Tails hissed.

"And you stay away," Leaf spat back. "It's none of your concern."

Flab and bulbous muscle rippled through Tails's body as she stood tall, straightening and swelling until she towered over her sister. She stepped close enough that her long breasts pressed against Leaf's perky firmness, then she spoke directly into her sister's mouth.

"It is ALL of my concern," Tails growled, her voice a bitonal duet of demons. "You bring ruin upon this place."

"You seek anarchy, debauchery," Leaf said. "I am purity."

"You are a disease," Tails said.

"I am beauty," Leaf said.

"You are ugliness," Tails said.

Leaf slapped her sister, sending a wad of mucous and teeth flying across the room. Tails touched her mouth, swiping away the fresh blood and pus released by the new split, and glowered at Leaf.

"There is balance," Tails said. "*We* are balance. But I will soon tip the scale, dear sister, and you will plummet."

"Be gone, crone," Leaf said. "I tire of your vileness."

Leaf turned her back on her sister and crawled under the blankets, the smooth silk gliding over her bare skin like water. Her body remained tense until she heard the whoosh of the door opening and closing, marking Tails's departure to her nightly escapades.

"Happy hunting, dear sister," Leaf murmured as her eyes fluttered into dreams.

The night was wet. Tails loved wet. She relished the hot moisture between the folds of flesh draped over her crooked skeleton.

Ship.
Constantinople.
The scratching inside her bones.

The journey to the docks was long, made longer by Tails's lumbering gait, one leg quite a bit shorter than the other, her many stones of weight dangling from her frame. The drizzle spewing down on the English countryside didn't help. Tails had wrapped her feet in leather to protect from root and stone, but the squelching suck of the mud slowed her walk to a slog.

But on she ploughed, determined to conduct her business under the shroud of the night sky with nary a star to light her doings, thanks to the pregnant clouds.

The smell of wood and salt reached her nose, the waste of men and the leavings of critters.

Perhaps she was too late. Perhaps they had dispersed already and she would have to hunt the town, risking exposure.

As she approached the vessel, which was bobbing lazily at dock, she heard them. Tearing, scratching, squeaking.

"Good," Tails murmured.

Tails licked her lips, her dry tongue dragging across the open sores that festered there.

The gangway door was closed and latched. That was excellent. That meant although a few would have found their way out, the majority would remain, feasting on leftover meats and root vegetables that had spoiled on the journey.

Tails dared not open that door. They would release into the night, rolling over her like a wave. A rope ladder dangled over the ledge, knocking against the side of the ship with a thud like a heartbeat. Tails groaned as she hefted her weight to hoist herself upon that ladder. Up and up she struggled, her bare breasts dragging across the wood, splinters piercing her nipples. The exertion was immense, and with every heave and pull, her bowels released their pressure, dribbling down the insides of her legs and splashing into the drink below.

Finally, she breached the top, rolled over the edge, and flopped onto the deck. She allowed herself one, two, three breaths before she rocked and rolled herself to her knees and crawled for the steps leading beneath deck.

They scuttled and screamed as Tails slid into the lower compartments.

They ran and hid, clawing each other as they tried to find hidey holes in crates, beneath planks, in piles of soiled clothing.

Tails would find every single one.

With impossible quickness, Tails snatched the first rat as he tried to burrow into a sailor's urine-saturated braies. She held the rat up to her face, and even in the dark, her feline eyes could see the white larvae wriggling at the base of each and every one of his coarse hairs.

Plague fleas. Passengers from afar, hitching rides on these poor, innocent rats.

"I'm sorry, friend," Tails said to the rat. "It be not your fault, but you deliver death, nonetheless."

A knock and crack rang through the white noise of the panicking rats as Tails's jaw unhinged, opening a chute that descended straight down her gullet and into her guts. She deposited the rat, and the poor rodent mewled and screamed and clawed his way down her throat as her muscles pushed him down. The boiling acid in her stomach made quick work of him, dissolving his fur and melting the flesh from his bones in an instant.

She would have to be quick. Night was stale, and dawn would arrive too soon. And with dawn, eyes would be able to see her, the monster, the ugliness she had become as she absorbed it from their world.

Tails grabbed another rat, then another, dropping screaming balls of meat and fur down her chute. Her belly filled and distended, and she squatted on the floor, bearing down to defecate the tiny, clean bones once her acid was done with the meat. The pile of bone excrement grew as the rat population dwindled, until there was nothing but the sound of Tails's own belching and flatulence filling the plague-free ship.

"This one is lovely," Leonidas said as he admired the painting before him.

Leaf grimaced. She knew when he suggested bringing her to The Purple District she would have a rough time hiding her displeasure.

The Purple District was known for its beauty. A hidden catacombs in the underbelly of York, The Purple District was named as such for its fanciful, bold art and innovative mediums and supplies, including the coveted purples only the royals usually possessed. The deep purples were achieved by harvesting the fluids of snails, a rare and difficult practice, hence why the clothing of monarchs, patriarchs, and spiritual leaders was often dyed in that hue. Proof of superiority and power.

Here, the rabble rousers kept art alive by creation and exhibition—paintings, sculptures, fine music, poetry. Live readings and performances echoed through the tunnels, reverberating off the beautiful canvases and artful creations slathered all over the walls and pillars.

"And they say creativity is on the decline," Leonidas chuffed. "I'd say quite the opposite, as you see here. When you try to repress a thing, that thing grows muscles and limbs and a life of its own."

"It's gratuitous," Leaf scolded.

"It's life," Leonidas countered. "Art is knowledge and beauty."

"I don't prefer it," Leaf huffed.

That caught Leonidas's attention. He tore his eyes away from the attack of colors on the canvas in front of him to stare at her. She didn't look away, willing herself to be strong as he appeared to hone right through her retinas and into her soul.

"My apologies," he said after a few moments of silence. "I thought this would please you."

"It does not," Leaf said.

She was uncomfortable in her skin around all this art. Everything itched, and saliva pooled beneath her tongue. Her belly issued a demon's growl, threatening to set her hunger free. And Leonidas was watching her, examining her as if he knew the thoughts that resided in her brain and heart.

"Allow me to show you one last thing before we depart," he said.

"We cannot just leave?" she whined, and stomped the heel of her boot.

"Indulge me," he said, and cupped her cheek in his hand.

Those eyes. Ethereal and wanting. He was beyond beautiful. She craved to have him alone, to expose herself entirely and have his eyes explore every dimple and crevice on her body.

"I suppose," she said.

Leonidas hovered over her face, his lips brushing hers before he took her hand and led her down the corridor to an alcove and a low wooden door. A guard was poised outside, and he looked both her and Leonidas up and down with scrutiny as they approached.

"What is this?" she asked.

"Rumors of art so exquisite it is to be kept airtight and hidden from torch light. A single candle illuminates this exhibit, nothing more. And only two people at a time may enter."

"You and your rumors," Leaf said, poking Leonidas playfully in the ribs.

She felt anything but playful, though. She felt trapped like the plague rats she knew had stowed away on that ship. She wanted to screech and claw her way out of The Purple District and escape to a tavern, an alehouse, out to the muddy streets where she would be a bright and bold rose among muted weeds. Here, she felt as grotesque and bland as her tainted sister.

"Make this quick, please," she uttered.

Leonidas nodded at the guard, and the young man opened the door and stepped aside to grant them entry. Leaf's boots clip-clopped into the room, and her eyes took their time adjusting to the dark. The air displaced by the door shutting and barring them in caused the single candle to throw shadows flying around the room like banshees. Leonidas fetched the candleholder, lifting it high to illuminate the walls.

It was like someone had punched her in the stomach. Leaf's breath was ripped from her by the beauty displayed before her, gleaming like the fires of Hades himself.

"Egyptian artisans were the first to recognize the durability and malleability of gold," Leonidas explained. "Gold-leaf forging was popular in the East. It's been gaining favor among the artists here ever since the fall of Rome and the dispersion of peoples from the East."

Gold glinted in Leaf's eyes. Scenes crafted with the precious metal, gold on painted canvas, depicted the shining skin of gods and goddesses lounging, playing stringed instruments, eating various exotic fruits. One creation in particular—a dark-haired woman forged in gold playing a rebec crafted of the same—mesmerized Leaf. Tears swelled in her eyes and a lump formed in her throat as she beheld the most beautiful piece of art she had ever seen.

Leonidas stroked the curve of her neck with his fingers.

"I knew you'd like it," he whispered in her ear.

Leaf's eyes did not leave the woman and her rebec as Leonidas's fingers lifted her skirts and toyed with the clasp on her stockings before finding the frill of her bloomers. His fingers glided into her, his thumb pressing precisely where it needed to for her body to surge with pleasure. As she ground her hips into his hand, her pleasure careening toward unbearable release, she never took her eyes away from the beauty of the gold woman and her instrument.

"Take me in your mouth," Leonidas purred as he withdrew his dripping hand from her clothing.

"Yes," she said as she licked off his fingers. "But not here. We've lingered too long. We're liable to get caught."

Leonidas bought her timid, embarrassed-girl act. He shot a glance at the door and nodded in agreement. He shifted the bulge in his pants, seemingly easing the discomfort of its eager escape, then took her hand.

"May I have a moment?" she said. "Before we go."

"Of course," he said.

He stood there. She waited.

"Alone, please," she said.

"Oh, um, okay," he stammered.

Leonidas gave her a look she couldn't read before stepping outside to stand with the guard. Once the door was firmly closed behind him, Leaf brought her attention back to the golden woman and her glittering instrument.

So beautiful. The kind of deep beauty that Leaf coveted. The source of the name she had granted herself upon her creation. Gold Leaf.

Leaf's lips and tongue explored the gold. Then her teeth strengthened, thickened, sharpened. There was tearing, chewing, swallowing. Strips of metal sliced the inside of her throat to ribbons as she consumed the entire painting, each swallow eliciting an orgasm so powerful that everything around her ceased to exist.

Tails watched as her sister floated through the door of their cottage, humming "Dies Irae." So entranced by whatever consumption gave her such pleasure, she failed to notice Tails soaking in a basin by the fire.

"Quite pleased with yourself, I see," Tails said.

Leaf shot her sister a look.

"What in the gods have you got done here?" Leaf said. "Why drag that huge thing inside? You're making a mess."

And what a mess she had made. Water splashed on the floor, along with a thick slurry of sage, long pepper, treacle, nutmeg, ginger, and rue—a witch's brew for the treatment of the plague. Tails used it to slow her deformation and deterioration.

"Had to bathe." Tails shrugged. "Didn't want to wait for dark to do it outside."

"'Tis dark out," Leaf said.

"Wasn't when I started."

Leaf rolled her eyes, but her sister would not bother her that night. Not after such a splendid day. Leaf ignored the hag festering in her fireside tub as she stripped out of her clothing, tossing it to the corner of the room to be washed out in the river later.

"*Kunta*," Tails gasped, her Norse seeping out in vulgarity.

"I am no cunt," Leaf said. "But mine sure is satisfied."

Leaf walked into the light of the fire and did a full pirouette.

"You're glowing," Tails noted with no short amount of snark.

And she was. Tails searched her sister for moles, mars,

wrinkles. There were none where there were some before. And her hair was longer, tumbling all the way to her knees, and a deeper red, almost the hue of fresh blood. Her breasts were fuller, nipples erect despite the moist heat of the cottage. And a spiderweb of viscous, clear fluid hung from her sex, dribbling lower with every spin.

Tails was about to scold her sister, to crawl from that basin and slap the stupid woman until her head spun off, but her rage was stalled by a knock at the door.

The sisters froze.

"Leaf?" a voice beckoned from beyond the oak.

"No!" Leaf whispered.

Tails could not suppress her grin. Speaking in Leaf's tongue, a haunting mimicry, Tails beckoned the lad in. "Do come in!"

The door swung open, and in strode a man who was wide and thick with muscle and stank of lust. His eyes were beautiful and wise, a gaze that could intoxicate even the most celibate.

No wonder she covets him, Tails thought.

Tails sank beneath the surface of the water, hoping the cloudy filth would hide her from prying eyes.

Leaf was horrified.

"You can't be here," she said.

Leaf tried her damndest to not glance over at the basin. Leonidas could not discover Tails. There was no telling what he might do. Her sister looked every bit a witch, and a man on a quest such as Leonidas's was apt to dispatch of such a creature with haste, lest she curse or kill.

"And why not?" Leonidas said. "You live on your own, yes? And ..."

He lost himself. His eyes wandered over her naked body, his face flushing red as embers.

"I just ... I ..." he sputtered.

It would be easy to get rid of him. To give him what he wanted, what all men wanted. He would take it, and then he could leave, and she and Tails would be safe.

"Well, it's just, if someone found out I was here alone with a man," Leaf said, twirling her fingers through a stray lock.

"No one will know," he said, practically pleading as she backed up until she was as far away from the basin by the fire as she could. Her bare buttocks bumped against the barrel serving as a table, and she hopped on top and crossed her legs.

"Oh, I don't know," she said, biting her lip and batting her lashes.

Leonidas came to her, and as he approached, she uncrossed her legs and let her knees fall to the side. He was on her in an instant, his hands groping her as she fumbled with the ties on his tunic and trousers. His attention elsewhere, she was able to steal a glance over at the basin and saw that her sister was submerged, still and silent. Tails required no air so would make no bubbles. Not unless she wanted to. And in the interest of self-preservation, Tails should want Leonidas out of there as quickly as possible.

Though Tails had been the one to beckon him in ...

Leonidas was not unclothed, but his cock had been freed from the confines of his trousers. Leaf groaned and allowed her head to fall back as he pushed himself inside her, his girth a near-painful pressure and stretch. But she was still soaked from her pleasure with the gold leaf at The Purple District, and he easily fell into a rhythm, tilting the barrel so it knocked on the floor as he thrust in and pulled out, increasing in tempo and violence as he grew ever firmer inside her.

"Witches," he panted as he pounded into her. "I came hunting witches and found ecstasy."

He sucked her nipple into his mouth and slowed his rhythm. Leaf grabbed him, prompting him to speed up, to finish so he would leave, but he slowed to a snail's pace.

"What's wrong?" Leaf asked.

"Rumors," he murmured.

"Of witches," she said.

"Of witches," he confirmed, that passion in his eyes reigniting. "Of life and death, good and evil."

His tempo increased, and he grabbed Leaf's hips, slamming into her hard enough she feared he might split her in two.

"Creation and destruction," he breathed.

Leaf felt him tense, and panic gripped her.

"No!" she shouted.

"I'm going to—"

But she wouldn't let him. She kicked back, toppling the barrel and slamming into the ground before he could finish inside her. He watched her as she scrambled backward, his hand on his shaft, jerking furiously and grunting until his seed spilled over the floor in dull plops.

"I am sorry," she said. "I just ... I cannot be with child. Not with the Black Death around and no family to help care for me and the babe."

"Of course not," he said.

Leaf did not like the smirk on his face. Didn't like the way he gave his dick a shake before stuffing it back in his trousers. Didn't like the way he looked at his puddle of semen, then over at her, exposed and splayed on the floor.

"Or is it that you didn't want that inside you?" he said, pointing at his puddle. "Because it's rank. It's sour. It's slimy. A yellowed mess of salty, foul nastiness."

He took a few steps toward her, then bent down and ran his finger through the semen. When he approached her, he held his wet finger to her face.

"Or," he said, "is it because this is ugly?"

Vomit rose in Leaf's gorge.

He knows, she thought. *Oh fuck, he knows, he knows.*

"Rumors," he said, standing and walking away from her. "Rumors of a village that had been spared by the plague ravaging the lands. Rumors of art and creativity thriving in a time when elsewhere it appeared to be on the decline."

"What are you on about?" Leaf said. "I'd like you to leave now."

"You know what other rumors reached my ears?" he said as he poured himself a chalice of mead from a bottle on the wall. "Rumors come to me 'cross Nordic tongues. Tales of dichotomy, of Witch Pairs existing in precarious balance but fighting to topple one another. One driven by eradicating all that's awful and ugly and one driven by beauty."

Leaf's eyes shot to the basin, at the stillness there. Then to the door. Should she escape? But if she did and he happened upon Tails, Leaf's life would still be in danger.

"Driven by beauty, but not to create it or admire it," he said, stepping close again.

Leaf leapt to her feet, to face this man, and stood her ground.

"One witch craves to destroy all the beauty," he says. "To consume it and therefore wield and exude it all on her own. These witches become more beautiful with every piece of art and creativity they devour and destroy, therefore dulling their surroundings and bolstering their radiance."

"This is madness," Leaf said.

"That's what you did, isn't it?" Leonidas said. "That's where the art went, the gold leaf woman. I went back to the gallery after we parted, back to an empty space where that beauty had once been."

Leaf took a step away, toward the door. Leonidas grabbed her by the wrist, and she snarled.

"Don't think I didn't notice the blood on your teeth, witch," he growled at her. "The gold cut your gums, did it? Shredded your throat?"

Leonidas drew a blade from his belt. Leaf was quick and had her talons on his throat in an instant, but a gleam on the hilt of the blade caught her attention. She dared to look down. And Leonidas paused to let her.

The hilt of his weapon was encrusted with all manner of jewels the size and clarity of which she had never seen. Rubies, emeralds, diamonds. A rainbow of stones that glistened of wealth and stardust and absolute natural beauty. Leaf's teeth shifted in her mouth, new rows cutting through until she had row after row of teeth sharp and strong enough to consume exquisite silks, precious metals, and priceless gems.

No longer in control of her urges, Leaf dropped to her knees and opened wide, preparing to take in that hilt like Leonidas had asked her to swallow his cock. But before she could wrap her lips around those gems, Leonidas crumpled on top of her.

"Hey!" she screamed, and wriggled out from beneath his weight.

Tails was standing there, bath water dripping on the floor, hand bloody, Leonidas's still-beating heart clenched in her claws.

"Thank you, sister," Leaf said.

Leaf made quick work of the blade, chewing through both gems and metal, shattering her teeth in the process. No matter. She would grow new ones, as she always had.

"Monster," Tails growled.

"I am not the one who eats rats." Leaf laughed, spraying bloody gem shards into the air. "I am not the one who is fat and ugly and smells like hot sewage. I am not the one who grows more foul with every diseased maggot and flea and rodent I stuff into my distended guts."

Leaf looked down at Leonidas's body and the hole punched in his back where Tails broke through skin and bone to seize his heart. He was such a beautiful man. That hair, that thick cock, those eyes ...

Leaf rolled Leonidas over and slithered through his blood until she sat astride him, lowering herself onto his engorged phallus.

"I slow the sickness by eating the rats," Tails said. "I can save. I can heal."

"At the price of being the ugliest cunt in the land," Leaf said with a shake of her head and a thrust of her hips. "Not worth it. I'd rather be a flourishing rose in a dead landscape. Gold in a pile of ash and ruin."

Leaf cupped Leonidas's cheek in her hand and rode his dead meat. Her nails were glistening with gilded sparkle, her skin even more flawless than it had been a moment ago. She looked into Leonidas's vacant gaze, and though those eyes were staring into a distant nowhere, they were still as beautiful as they were when he was alive.

Leaf slid a nail beneath Leonidas's eyelid, dragging it in a circle until she had severed all the nerves, veins, and tendons, freeing the eye from its socket. With tendrils of gore hanging from the eyeball, Leaf lifted it to her face, licked the beautiful black iris, then placed the eyeball deep in her mouth, between her molars. A bit of pressure and the eyeball squirted down her throat, gushing like semen had from Leonidas only minutes before. Her orgasm hit her swift and strong.

"I don't only consume death and plague," Tails said from behind her. "Death and plague are not the only ugly things."

"Mhmmm," Leaf mumbled as she popped the second eyeball in her mouth.

"You know what is even uglier than the plague and the death it causes? Uglier than open sores, swelling in the groin, sick pouring from every orifice?"

Leaf was busy savouring Leonidas's eyeballs and bloated cock inside her when her sister knelt next to her, pressed her breasts into Leaf's back, and rested her head upon Leaf's shoulder. Leaf stopped swishing the eyeball fluid around her mouth and swallowed hard.

"You wouldn't," she said.

Tails did not answer.

"I die, you die," Leaf said.

Tails reached around and embraced her sister, one hand upon her face and another upon her breast.

"You are the ugliest disease of them all," Tails said.

Shock and panic prevented Leaf from moving out of her sister's embrace, from avoiding the teeth that clamped down on her windpipe and ripped out her throat. With a swift strike from her powerful elbow, Tails snapped Leaf's spine with the sound of a whip crack, rendering her immobile. Tails tossed her sister's body away from Leonidas's violated corpse and laid her out on her back.

Tails took her time.

She ate all of Leaf, starting at her toenails, working her way up, and devouring every bit of her with slow, calculated bites. She plucked out and ate every hair on her sister's body, sucked every bone clean, until Leaf was nothing more than a flesh face on a skeleton.

"No!" Leaf wailed. "I was beauty. Beauty!"

Tails smiled. Her sister knew the difference now. She knew the truth. The last thing Tails consumed was Leaf's face, eyes, and brain so Leaf could watch Tails turn into the most horrific creature to have ever existed. Too many limbs, multiple genitals rotting with all manner of disease, balls of maggots and worms replacing the layers of fat just below Tails's now-translucent skin. The horrors were endless, but Leaf did not get to see the extent before Tails swallowed her last bite, ending them both.

The cottage still stands, though claimed by nature. Vines, flowers, and mushrooms coat every surface, along with boils, blood, and pockets of infection. Ugliness and beauty, creation and destruction.

And in the middle of the room reclaimed by loam and grass and flora, a tangled mess of bones remains, embraced for all of life and death.

PUBLISHER'S NOTE

Thank you for reading Screams From The Dark Ages. This anthology wouldn't exist without you, the reader.

If you enjoyed this book, please consider leaving a review on Amazon, GoodReads, or your favorite social media platform.

Please visit our website for more information about our releases and signed copies of our books.

www.brokenbrainbooks.com

Other Anthologies by Broken Brain Books
Screams From The Ocean Floor
Screams From Beyond The Veil
Screams From Outer Space
Books of Horror Indie Brawl Anthology

Also available
Usher of the Fallen by LM Kaplin
Rorschach by Aaron Lebold
Mine by LM Kaplin
Fang Fiction by LM Kaplin
Ruby's Cube by Lyla Diamond

ABOUT THE AUTHORS

Christina Henry
Christina Henry is a horror and dark fantasy author whose works include GOOD GIRLS DON'T DIE, HORSEMAN, NEAR THE BONE, THE GHOST TREE, LOOKING GLASS, THE GIRL IN RED, THE MERMAID, LOST BOY, RED QUEEN, ALICE, and the seven book urban fantasy BLACK WINGS series.

Her short stories have been featured in the anthologies CURSED, TWICE CURSED, GIVING THE DEVIL HIS DUE and KICKING IT.

She enjoys running long distances, reading anything she can get her hands on and watching movies with samurai, zombies and/or subtitles in her spare time. She lives in Chicago with her husband and son.

You can visit her on the web at
www.christinahenry.net

Laura Bilodeau
Laura, author of Defeating the Moose, Dr. Grinsaw and others is a CT based author who has done pretty much nothing meaningful in the last 28 years she's spent on

this floating rock

Elizabeth J. Brown
Elizabeth J. Brown was born in Kent, England. This probably explains her obsession with tea and cake. She currently writes the Brimstone Chorus series - dark fantasy horror featuring demons, witches and a whole host of things that go bump in the night.

Her debut novel, The Laughing Policeman, takes place in 1980s England and features detectives, dark supernatural forces and dry humour.

When she isn't in front of her laptop or spending time with her family, Elizabeth is usually absorbed in a book, film or anything that involves the strange, fantastical or supernatural.

Get your FREE Brimstone Chorus starter story at elizabethjbrown.com

Elizabeth Devecchi
Elizabeth Devecchi spent her formative years in Rhode Island before setting out to gather degrees and experiences. She writes in a variety of genres and styles, but horror holds a special place in her heart.

Wicked House Publishing released Elizabeth's debut horror novel, A WHISPER IN THE DARK, in October 2024. Upcoming releases will include: short horror story "Open House," to appear in a Running Wild Press anthology in 2025; and thriller/suspense novel, A TWIST OF THE LENS, to be published by Wicked House Publishing in mid-2025.

Elizabeth is a member of the Horror Writer's Association, Rocky Mountain Fiction Writers, and Italian American Writers Association. She currently resides in Colorado with her family, which includes an ever-changing menagerie of pets and "guest creatures."

Savannah R. Fischer

Savannah R. Fischer is the permanently exhausted pigeon in charge of two well-loved chaos gremlins. When not with her family, she can usually be found in her cave, wrapped in an oversized blanket and dreaming of spinach puffs. She wants to show her gremlins that they can do hard things, even when it's scary, like pulling the wrong lever and ending up in a pit of alligators. No llamas were harmed in the making of her works of horror.

Asia Brito Guerrero

Asia Brito Guerrero is a writer who has written spooky stories all her life. Most of her tales are created from personal experience mixed together with a deranged imagination and ideas sparked from a lot of sleepless nights. She currently lives in Phoenix, Arizona with her husband where they're raising their two feral children together. She can usually be found on her couch with her laptop nearby, drinking too much iced coffee, and eating tacos for breakfast, lunch, and dinner.

Kimberly Nicole

Kimberly Nicole lives in the USA, deep in the south. She grew up in the 90's as an Army brat and had the privilege of traveling to many different states and countries. She loves her baby boy, all animals, the color red, and all things horror. She uses fear as a form of pain relief to combat CRPS, fibromyalgia, and other personal demons. It has been a lifelong dream of hers to write and publish a book one day and she finally decided to reach for that dream at the crisp age of 34. She hopes you enjoy spending time with her words. <3

Heather Ann Larson

Heather Ann Larson is an experienced indie editor and author of several anthology stories.

She is the editor of this anthology as well as its predecessors, Screams From The Ocean Floor and Screams From Beyond The Veil as well as The Books of Horror Indie Brawl Anthology. She has also edited novels by authors Justin Boote, Sean McDonough, Timothy King, D.W. Hitz, LM Kaplin, and more.

In her spare time, she... Who are we kidding? There is no spare time!!!

MJ Mars

MJ Mars is a geek, ghoul, and horror enthusiast living in Lancaster, UK. Her debut novel, The Suffering, was published by Wicked House in 2023. When she isn't writing, you'll find MJ playing pool, trying to skateboard (badly), or listening to rock music. She owes every success to her mis-spent youth.

Short story collection, We've Already Gone Too Far out now! Coming in 2025: The Fovea Experiments, a second novel to be published by Wicked House. MJ is currently working on a sequel to The Suffering.

Jae Mazer

Jae Mazer is a Canadian who was born in Victoria, British Columbia, then grew up in the prairies of Northern Alberta. After spending the majority of her life battling sasquatches in the Great White North, she migrated south to Texas to have a go at the armadillos. She is a connoisseur and creator of gothic horror, splatterfolk, splatter westerns, and folk horror. She's degreed, has won awards, been in anthologies, owns a couple of breweries, has chameleon hair and lots of skin ink, and enjoys mustard and alcohol.

ABOUT THE AUTHORS

KK Monroe

K.K. Monroe grew up terrified of what lived in her overhead bedroom vent...and the rest is history. By day, a clinician; by night, she writes or stares blankly at a wall, lost to the nebulous void—honestly, we don't know where she goes. It's pretty creepy. First born American to parents raised under an oppressive communist regime, life as a kid didn't involve censorship of books or movies.This literary freedom allowed the young reader to fall deeply in love with The King, Jack London, Michael Crichton, Sidney Sheldon, and so many more. K.K. lane-hops genres in both her reading and writing interests. Horror is her first love. She's obsessed with Slavic mythos and the dark Balkan folklore of her heritage with several exciting projects underway. In the meantime, check out this author's debut, a vintage cosmic horror collection, THINGS FROM THE DARK on Amazon.

Jeani Rector

While most people go to Disneyland while in Southern California, Jeani Rector went to the Fangoria Weekend of Horror there instead. She grew up watching the Bob Wilkins Creature Feature on television and lived in a house that had the walls covered with framed Universal Monsters posters. It is all in good fun and actually, most people who know Jeani personally are of the opinion that she is a very normal person. She just writes abnormal stories.

She is the founder and editor of The Horror Zine, and has had her stories featured in magazines such as Aphelion, Schlock!, Strange Weird and Wonderful, Black Petals, Bewildering Stories, and many others.

Lisa Vasquez
THE MOTHER OF MONSTERS

Lisa Vasquez creates vivid, twisted horror with the precision of a scalpel. Each calculated word cuts into the reader's psyche with fleshed out characters. Her writing style has been compared to the works of Mary Shelley, Baz Luhrman, and Grand Guignol by John Palisano the Bram Stoker-winning author of Nerves and hailed as, "A writer of nightmarish vision and a new poetic voice in today's horror genre," by Peter Molnar, author of The Clockwork Lazarus."

The editor-in-chief of Memento Mori Ink Magazine, Lisa has led her team to Amazon's Best Seller list with its debut, August 2024, issue and repeated the win for the Winter 2025 follow-up. She is not only an advocate for mental health, Women in Horror (Vixens of Horror series), LGBTQ+ awareness, and the Indie dark fiction community as a whole, she is frequently commended for her mentorship programs, and has designed covers for some of the most recognizable authors of horror and splatter punk.

When she's not nursing a cup of beans or leaves and flipping people off, Lisa can be found hunched in front of a glowing, magic box bringing new monsters to life.

She is deathly allergic to bullshit.

Christy Aldridge

Christy Aldridge writes horror. She's heavily influenced by writers such as Stephen King and Clive Barker, and her semi psychotic family. She dwells in a small town in the sticks of Alabama with her assortment of dogs, cats, goat, and snake.

Ali Jane Sweet
Ali Jane Sweet lives in Nova Scotia, Canada where she spends most of her time staring at the ocean (or wishing she was by the ocean), thinking up dark tales which she rarely writes down. If she does happen to write them down, she rarely finishes them.

She has two other short stories published, one in the spring edition of the Fear Forge anthology and the other in Dancing Through the Shadows, a charity anthology. She also wrote a chapter in the collaborative novel, Netipotcalypse.

She is enrolled in an editing course and plans to go full-time as an editor after she graduates. Her cat, Peaches is her biggest fan (but only if there is tuna involved).